To Margaret,

Enjoy the read &
best wishes to you.
Sincerely,
Amasa Mast
7/9/10

Also by Anasa Maat

A Little Bit Of Honey

'Til Death Do Us Part

Anasa Maat

Kill...or be Killed

AN AMERICAN TRAGEDY

Book layout Design:
Martin Maishman

Printed in Canada

Nutany Publishing Company
Newark, New Jersey 07102
Tel. 973.242.1229

ACKNOWLEDGEMENTS

Not having had a personal experience with war, writing this book presented some real challenges for me. I am grateful to the Vietnam veterans that I interviewed and who were willing to give so generously of their time to share some of their experiences and knowledge with me.

I am especially thankful to Mr. Emerson Crooks for helping me to gain insight into the readjustment Vietnam veterans were faced with upon their return home through his own personal experiences; and to Mr. J. Richard Watkins, author of *No Regrets*, for taking the time to provide me with details about Vietnam that I needed in order to give the book the authenticity I was looking for. I, also, thank my husband, Hadren W. Simmons. Although he never served time in Vietnam, Hadren is a veteran of the Vietnam era and provided me with much useful information about military life.

The video and audio recordings of "Winter Soldiers," by those courageous young men who testified in Detroit, Michigan, on January 31, 1971 about the atrocities of the Vietnam War, were an invaluable source of information. Those veterans are to be commended for having had the courage to speak out about war crimes committed in Vietnam that would otherwise never have been told.

I am also grateful to my editors, Diane Raintree and Claudine Curry, for their timely editing of this book. Special thanks go to Martin Maishman, my designer, who is so easy to work with. Edna Bailey Woody, thank you for volunteering your proofreading skills.

DEDICATION

This book is dedicated to Johnny Jackson, one of the nicest guys I ever met, and a Vietnam veteran. The tragic end to Johnny's life inspired me to write this book.

Johnny, you are thought of often and truly missed.

CHAPTER

1

*H*is screams were piercing like the shrill of a whistle, and loud enough to wake the dead. They rang out into the night like the roar of a lion in the quiet, still jungle. They bounced off the white walls, and made loose glass in chipped and crumbling window frames rattle. The screams could be heard up and down the corridors and through closed doors, ringing out in stairwells two floors above and two floors below. Pills in little bottles sitting behind locked cabinets shook from the fierceness of the sound. The loud screams, though disturbing for most, had become routine for many awakened by them and for hospital staff on night duty.

The screams were a signal that Specialist Four Roberts, the handsome, young patient in room 320, needed another injection. Once he received the shot, it would be a matter of minutes before he calmed down. The difference was like night and day. Before the injection he was screaming and flailing about, wildly, considering the arm and leg restraints that were used to keep him from acting out the night terrors he experienced on a regular basis.

The restraints had been put in place the same night that David Roberts had arrived at the hospital, after he had awakened out of a deep sleep, leaped out of bed and tried to strangle another patient. Following that episode, he was placed in a private room and shackled to his bed at night. David Roberts, called simply Roberts by his friends and comrades, was a troubled man. The least of his troubles were the bullets that had shattered his shoulder and ripped through his right thigh while on duty in Vietnam.

Whatever was troubling Roberts and causing such terror seemed to disappear less than ten minutes after the night-duty nurse administered the injection. First his eyes stopped rolling in his head, and then his hands and feet stopped flailing. The sweat that was pouring from his forehead ceased.

Wiping his head with a towel with one hand, while holding his restrained wrist with the other hand, Dorothy Campbell, the night nurse assigned to Roberts, detected a drop in his pulse, signaling that he was responding to the injection. Finally, Roberts closed his eyes for a few seconds and then fluttered them open. A smile came across his handsome, brown face, revealing even white teeth. He had a warm glint in his large dark eyes.

"Hi, beautiful," he said, looking at her with wide, thoughtful eyes.

"Hi." She smiled back at him, untying the wrist restraints.

"Want to finish our chess game?" He reached for the chessboard, each piece still in place from the previous night, sitting on the nightstand beside his hospital bed.

"Okay, if you're ready for another butt kicking, I'm ready to deliver." Dorothy removed the restraints from his ankles.

The chess game was as much a part of the nightly routine as the screams, administration of the injection, and removal of the restraints. Each night, Roberts and Nurse Campbell would get to make three or four moves before the medication really kicked in, sending Roberts into a sound, restful sleep that usually lasted until the next shift of nurses were due to arrive.

This routine had been going on for three weeks now, ever since Roberts, his shoulder and upper leg bandaged where the bullets had been removed, had been brought into Angel of Mercy Hospital on a stretcher. He had been flown from a field hospital on a base camp in the combat zone, where some of the best trauma surgeons were stationed, to Hawaii on a military medical plane and then taken via military ambulance from the airport to the hospital. The staff at Angel of Mercy Hospital had the responsibility of nursing wounded soldiers like Roberts back to health.

All of the doctors, nurses, and orderlies that were assigned to Angel of Mercy Hospital were American military personnel serving in various branches of the armed forces. The building itself was almost fifty years old; it had first been used as a military hospital during the Korean War. The concrete structure appeared sound and sturdy, although plaster was crumbling in a number of places. Even with recently installed fluorescent bulbs, the building lacked sufficient overhead lighting, depending a great deal on the abundant Hawaiian sunlight that poured through the windows.

Wounded soldiers generally stayed in the facility a minimum of three weeks and no longer than six weeks. After the second week, the fate of the injured was generally determined. Most returned to active duty, even back to their same units. Some were sent home either for further treatment or to join the ranks of civilians after having earned an honorable medical discharge. David Roberts' fate had not yet been decided.

"So, how am I doing?" he asked Nurse Campbell, flashing a boyish grin.

"You're going to lose this game regardless of what you do." She gave him a serious look of triumph.

"That's not what I meant. Am I getting better? Have you heard anything about what's going to happen with me?" He studied the chessboard, contemplating his next move.

"Not a thing. What would you like to happen?" She studied his face, wondering what he was thinking. This was the first time that he had asked about his treatment or his future. She knew that his three-year tour of duty was almost over.

"I want to go home. I've had about enough of this man's army." Roberts moved his knight, further advancing into her territory on the chessboard.

"Good move. It helps me out a lot." She moved her queen to capture the piece. "I know what you mean. I've had enough of this war, too. I'm sick and tired of nursing men back to health just to send them back out into the Vietnam jungles. I'm ready to go home, too," she said before giving him a smug look of confidence.

"Where's your home?" He gave her a look that said you shouldn't have done that, as he quickly moved his rook to capture her queen. "Let's see how well you 'kick butt' without a queen." He flashed another one of those sexy smiles.

"Damn! You set me up for that didn't you?" She ignored the sexy smile and gingerly moved a pawn onto a safe spot. "I'm from Oxford, Ohio. Didn't I tell you that before?"

"I remember that you're a country girl, but I forgot what part of the country. Forgive a wounded soldier for forgetting a detail, okay?" He shrugged his shoulders, still smiling.

"You're forgiven. If you ever see Oxford, you will never forget it. It's so beautiful, with pretty green hills and wild flowers growing everywhere. I've been to a lot of places since joining the army, but nowhere as pretty as Oxford. You should visit once you get out of the service."

"Maybe I will, one day. First I've got to get out of the Army, though. Will you ask the doctors for me?" His voice pleaded with her. "Ask them how much longer I'll have to stay here. See if you can find out where I'll be going from here." His look was serious again, one of anxiety.

"You can ask them yourself. You've made good progress since you first got here. Your wounds have healed up wonderfully. The bullet that you took in the chest barely missed your heart, thank God, and the injury to the leg has healed like new. You won't even have a limp after a couple more weeks of physical therapy. If it weren't for the emotional issues, I'm sure they would send you back to active duty." Nurse Campbell studied Robert's face for a reaction as he studied the chessboard.

"I don't trust these doctors," Roberts said without looking up from the chessboard. "I don't want to go back to active duty. I don't want to go back to Vietnam. I'm sick of the killing. They'll be honest with you if you ask. You're sort of like a colleague or something. Me, I'm just a killing machine." He moved his queen before giving Nurse Campbell another of those glimmering smiles.

"Okay, I'll ask." She gave him a look that let him know she was on to that move.

"What did you mean about the emotional issues?" Roberts diverted his attention to the chessboard again, but not before she saw the troubled look on his face.

"The apparent loss of memory and the night terrors you've been experiencing," she said before focusing her attention on the chessboard. "You've been having them almost every night since you arrived here." She looked up at him with a worried expression on her face. "They don't seem to be getting any better. They can't release you from the hospital as long as you require nighttime restraints." She went back to studying the chessboard.

"I won't need any nighttime restraints once I get home. Once I get back to Newark, everything will be all right." Roberts settled back on his bed and started to doze off as soon as his head hit the pillow.

CHAPTER

2

The military hospital in Hawaii consisted of six white buildings arranged in a semi-circle along the edge of twenty-five acres of beautifully landscaped grounds. The administration building sat in the middle. On her way to the tall building, Nurse Campbell passed a beautiful flower garden. She inhaled the sweet fragrance emanating from the flowers as she hurried along the flagstone path.

Hawaiian gardens were simply gorgeous, unlike any she'd ever seen before. The lawns were always perfectly mowed, the hedges impeccably trimmed, and the tropical flowers were the most colorful she'd ever seen. She wanted to bend down and get a big whiff, but she didn't have time for smelling flowers. She hoped she wasn't too late. She wanted to catch Dr. Pushkin before he left the grounds for the day. She'd promised the patient in room 320 that she would have some information regarding his discharge when she reported for her 7PM to 7AM shift that evening.

Dorothy Campbell was a good nurse. Nursing was something she had wanted to do since she was nine years old. Her dream of becoming a nurse had taken root when her father gave her a nursing kit for a birthday gift. She had gone around taking temperatures and pulses and using her toy stethoscope to listen to the heartbeat of each member of her family for weeks. Her dad had dubbed her Nurse Campbell, and it had stuck in her mind all through school. She'd worked hard to make it a reality.

Dr. Pushkin's office was located on the sixth floor of the eight-story building. As she exited the elevator, Nurse Campbell looked left and then right for suite 628. She spotted the arrow indicating that Dr. Pushkin's office was located to the right. She moved slowly down the corridor in that direction. She wanted to give herself some time to form her questions. She didn't want Dr. Pushkin to get the impression that she had taken a personal interest in a patient. Such behavior was frowned upon in the Army Medical Corps.

As she approached the office, the door opened, and Dr. Pushkin started walking hurriedly towards her. Dorothy stopped and waited for him to reach her. "I was just coming to see you." She kept pace with him, moving in the direction of the elevator from which she had just emerged.

"What is it?" He glanced at her. "Nurse Campbell, right?" He spoke English with a slight European accent.

"Yes, Dr. Pushkin. I promised the patient in room 320, Mr. Roberts, that I would ask you about his discharge. Do you have any information that I can share with him?" She was grateful that they had reached the elevators. Dr. Pushkin was a tall man with very long legs. Dorothy had to practically run to keep up with him.

"Isn't he the one with post traumatic stress syndrome and night terrors?" Dr. Pushkin hit the elevator button repeatedly as though that would bring it up faster.

"Yes, he's the one. His wounds have healed sufficiently, and he appears anxious to leave the hospital and get on with his life." Dorothy followed Dr. Pushkin into the empty elevator.

"I've spoken to the resident psychiatrist about Mr. Roberts, and we both agree that returning to active duty is out of the question for the patient. Until we can find a medication that will control his night terrors, he will remain here. No discharge until the proper medication is determined, Ms. Campbell. We just started him on a new one; let's see how it works." Dr. Pushkin stepped out of the elevator and started taking long strides toward the parking lot.

Nurse Campbell followed him, struggling to keep pace with him.

"Will you be in to see the patient tomorrow, Doctor?" She wanted the patient to get this information directly from the doctor himself.

"In case you are not aware, Nurse Campbell, there is a war going on, and I have new patients arriving at Angel of Mercy every day that require my urgent attention." He was a little sarcastic. "You pass the information on to the patient. From what I hear, you are quite capable. The resident psychiatrist will make the final determination regarding Mr. Roberts' release." Dr. Pushkin stuck a key into his car door, opened the door and stepped into the vehicle without saying another word. He drove off, leaving Nurse Campbell staring at the back of his car.

THE FOURTH FLOOR of "B" building was quiet when Nurse Campbell came through the door from the stairwell. She'd made a habit of walking up the stairs just to get in a little extra exercise each day. Nurse Campbell was conscious of her weight. She still weighed 122 pounds, the same as when she graduated from nursing school two years ago. Her sparkling white uniform perfectly fit her five-feet-six-inch frame. The starched white cap crowned a head of bouncy auburn curls. She'd had a difficult time finding a hairdresser in Hawaii that knew how to care for Black hair. Finally, she had settled for an army nurse's mother who had been a hairdresser.

"I'm glad you're early tonight," the head nurse greeted her. "It's been a rough day, and I'm ready to get out of here." She gave Nurse Campbell a look that showed exactly how she felt.

"What happened?" Nurse Campbell asked, removing her sweater and placing it under the counter of the nurses' station. She looked into the small mirror they kept behind the counter and straightened her cap before focusing her attention on the head nurse.

Looking a little annoyed that Nurse Campbell hadn't given her immediate attention, the head nurse said, "Mr. Roberts fell asleep after lunch and had an episode of night terror during the day. We weren't prepared for it; no restraints, you know. It took three nurses, the resident physician and two orderlies to get him under control. That new medicine isn't working yet, and it makes him drowsy. Now he's falling asleep during the day, which creates problems. He can be dangerous, you know."

"How is he?" Dorothy's concern was obvious. "Was anyone hurt?"

"No. Not this time. But we can't keep him here in restraints all day and all night. The man is too intelligent to cope with that. He's perfectly normal when he's awake, even charming, but I guess you know that already." She raised her eyebrows at Nurse Campbell.

Ignoring the look, Nurse Campbell asked, "Is he sleeping now?"

"No. He's fully awake. He's waiting up for you." There was that look again.

It was a little after nine when Nurse Campbell finally got to room 320. She had completed all of her rounds before going in to see Mr. Roberts. She always saved him for last so she could give him whatever time she had left before the patients' lights were turned off for the night.

"Hi, beautiful," he greeted her as soon as she entered the room.

"Hi, yourself," she said, moving to fluff up the pillows on his bed.

"I was worried that you wouldn't get to me. Did you get a chance to talk to Dr. Pushkin? When am I getting out of this place? Do we have time to move a couple of the chess pieces?" He was full of questions for her.

"Wow." Nurse Campbell put her hands up to stop him from

bombarding her with any more questions. "I can only handle one question at a time. Yes, I spoke with Dr. Pushkin. He wants to wait and find a medication that will control the night terrors. By the way, I heard that there was an episode earlier today." She stopped speaking and looked at him.

He avoided making eye contact with her. "I don't want to talk about that now. What else did Pushkin say?" Roberts appeared embarrassed; he spoke softly and kept his head down as he spoke.

"He didn't have much else to say, only that the resident psychiatrist will make the determination when you will be released, and that you will not be going back to active duty." She smiled, hoping that it was good news that she had delivered.

They both looked up when another nurse dispensing medications entered the room. "Hello, Mr. Roberts," the nurse sang out cheerfully. "Time to take your meds." She handed him a tiny cup with his nighttime medications and another cup for water.

Nurse Campbell took the second cup and filled it with water from a pitcher on the table. She waited while her patient put the pills into his mouth and took a couple of sips of the water. Then she pulled out the chessboard, set it on his bed and pulled up a chair beside the bed. "Are you ready to take me on again?" she chuckled.

While her patient studied his next move, Nurse Campbell studied him. He was a good-looking man, tall, with short jet-black hair, tightly curled, framing a boyish face. He was clean-shaven with a flawless, creamy chocolate complexion and sparkling dark eyes.

When he looked up and saw her staring at him, his face broke into a big smile, revealing perfect teeth, white and shiny.

"Are you checking me out?" He gave her a flirtatious look.

"I was just wondering about you." She tried to refocus on the chess game.

"What are you wondering about?"

"I'm wondering what's going to happen to you when you leave here. Where will you go and what will you do?"

"I'm going home when I leave here, back to good old Newark, New Jersey. Newark isn't the greatest place in America anymore, not since the riot, but any place is better than Vietnam." He looked serious.

"What about the nightmares? How will you handle them? Don't you think you should talk to someone about them before you go home?" She looked down at the chessboard.

"I really just want to forget them. I want to forget everything that happened in 'Nam. I want to put this last year behind me and start out fresh. I've done my time. I served my country for three years. Now I just want to go home. All I know for sure is that 'war is hell.'" Less than three minutes later, he was fast asleep.

Nurse Campbell picked up the chessboard, being careful to keep the pieces in place, and put it on the night table until the next time. Gently she put the restraints on her patient. As she walked out of the room, her thoughts were on Mr. Roberts. *How is he going to put this behind him?*

CHAPTER

3

*T*he sun was streaming through the curtain-less windows of room 320 at 7AM. The quiet was deafening. Roberts lay on his bed motionless, still in the restraints placed on him the night before. For the second morning in a row, he awoke feeling refreshed, and full of energy, not tired and lethargic as he had felt the first three weeks he had spent in the military hospital.

Lying in the single hospital bed with starched white sheets, Roberts thought about the questions that Nurse Campbell had put to him three nights ago. How would he handle it if the nightmares were to continue once he got home? Although he had no recollection of them, he knew they must be awful if what the hospital staff and the other patients were saying to him was true. They had no reason to lie to him. Then, too, he always felt extremely fatigued when he woke up the morning after an episode. *Would talking to someone help?* he asked himself.

Roberts knew that the restraints were not only for his own safety, but also for the well being of the other patients and the protection of the hospital staff. Did he want to endanger other people once he got home, his family perhaps? No! He had to think about his mother, father, and sister. He didn't want to do anything that would hurt them. Maybe he should talk to Nurse Campbell to get her take on the situation. She came across as being very understanding and patient. *Hell, she's pretty, too, even beautiful.* He smiled at the thought of her.

Roberts attempted to lift his hand to scratch his nose. The restraints stopped him. *I can't live like this forever,* he thought. *I can't go home in this condition. Nurse Campbell is right. I've got to talk to someone about this.*

It was 7:30AM when the morning nurse finally entered the room and removed the restraints. Roberts got out of bed and sat in the armchair near the window. Looking out over the hospital grounds, his thoughts returned to Nurse Campbell. He was convinced that she would not understand about the war, the things he had witnessed, the things he had done. *Only another combat soldier who has experienced the same thing would understand,* he concluded. Roberts remembered the words his sergeant had repeated over and over again during his basic training. "Kill or be killed."

How many times during the year and a half that he had spent in combat did he have to resort to that very simple rule? How many times had he been afraid that he was going to die unless he killed first? Not only in the war, but long before that he had learned that in order to stay alive, sometimes, someone else had to die. He'd learned it on the streets of Newark. *Maybe it's a good thing that I have forgotten so much of the war,* he thought.

After his morning bath, he ate a hearty breakfast of eggs, toast, orange juice, and sausage. He took his morning medication and began to read his mail, a letter from his mother.

Dearest Son,

I hope this letter finds you well, at least better. We have been so worried about you, David, ever since we got the call that you had been injured. We have all been praying for you. Please write to let us know that you are all right. Your sister is engaged, although they have not yet set a wedding date. She is praying that you will be sent home soon; she wants you at her wedding. Dad has not been well lately. I feel that a lot of his illness is due to worry about you. Sometimes I feel so guilty that I encouraged you to go into the army. Daddy never wanted you to go. Remember? Things in Newark have not gotten any better. Since the riots, all the businesses are leaving the city. Jobs are hard to find. The streets are more dangerous than ever before. So many people are packing up and leaving the city. Daddy says we are not going anywhere. We will stay and help to rebuild our city. We can hardly wait until you get home. We all love you so much. Take care of yourself, Son.

Love, Mom

Roberts read the letter three times before folding it and putting it back in the envelope. He put the envelope in the drawer of his night table with the others. He thought about writing a letter to his mother. He didn't want her to feel guilty. It was his decision to enlist. The only reason she encouraged him was to get him off the streets of Newark. He thought about the events leading up to his decision to enlist in the army.

NEWARK, THE LARGEST city in the state of New Jersey was relatively stable in the mid-1960's, before the rebellion. Whites governed the city and owned and operated most of the businesses. The mayor and eight of the nine members of the city council were White. Young Black men like David Roberts had little opportunity to earn a decent living once they graduated from high school. Most of the government jobs went to the ruling majority. David thought about his high school days when he had the chore of paying the household bills for his mother.

Once or twice a month, he would trek downtown from "Our Lady on the Hill," the nickname for Central High School, and walk south on Broad Street to City Hall where he would pay the water bill. Then he would walk back another mile or so north on Broad Street to Public Service Electric and Gas Company to pay the electric bill. Finally he would walk another quarter of a mile further north, past Trinity Cathedral, to Bell Telephone Company to pay the phone bill. Rarely would he encounter a Black face when he visited these companies. The employees at the banks, City Hall, the department stores, the insurance companies, even the post office were White. He remembered wondering what he would do after high school.

The closer graduation came, the more Roberts had pondered his limited choices. Getting through high school had not been easy. So many times he had been on the verge of dropping out of school. There had been so many distractions. The biggest distraction had been the streets. Night after night his buddies would call for him.

"Hey, Roberts, you want to hang?" Greg, Jeff, or Big Man would ask him whenever he answered the telephone.

"No, man, I have homework," would be his usual response.

"Come on, man, you're missing out. We need you."

The "we need you" usually convinced him. Roberts was considered tough. He wrestled all through high school and was known to be good with the gloves as well. He and his boys often hung out at the gym and he'd earned a reputation for being a champion. His buddies knew he was good to have around, as protection for them.

Hanging out, though, had its drawbacks. Roberts really didn't like to think about the times they ran into real trouble in the streets. He and his boys ran together, but they never looked for trouble. Trouble would often find them, though. They were never armed. They stayed away from knives and guns, but often others they encountered had a knife or a gun. Roberts and his boys enjoyed rapping to girls, listening to music, dancing, drinking a little beer and occasionally smoking a little weed.

Trouble came when they went to the wrong party, rapped to

someone else's girl, or danced with the wrong girl. Sometimes trouble came when you copped a five-dollar bag from the wrong guy. Roberts remembered one such night when Greg, his best friend since grammar school, called wanting him to hang.

"Naw, man, I've got homework."

"Come on, man, I need you," Greg had pleaded.

"What's up?"

"Meet me on South Orange Avenue and Bergen Street and I'll tell you about it. Fifteen minutes, okay?"

Fifteen minutes later Roberts and Greg were heading up to Hayes Homes Housing Projects, looking for some guy named Crow.

"I'm telling you, man, this dude beat me out of five bucks. Look at this shit!" Greg had handed Roberts a small plastic bag that looked like it contained marijuana.

"Looks okay to me. How do you know it's not?" Roberts had put the bag up to his nose, sniffing it. "It smells a little different, but familiar."

"It should smell familiar. What does the smell remind you of, man?" Greg had shaken his head slowly up and down as though trying to jog Roberts' memory.

"It smells like pizza." Roberts said, Greg's nodding triggering his memory.

"You're damn right it smells like pizza." Greg put the bag back into his pocket. "It's oregano."

"O' what?" Roberts had no idea what he was talking about.

"Oregano, fool! It's a spice they use on pizza. My mother has this same shit in her cupboard. If I wanted oregano, I could have gotten it from my mother's cupboard, I didn't need to put out five dollars for this."

"So what you gonna do when you find this guy, ask for your money back?"

"Hell no! I'm going to jack him up and take my five dollars back, plus anything else he might have on him. He'll know better than to pull that shit on me again." Greg tried to look tough.

Looking tough and being tough are two different things. Roberts knew that Greg wasn't tough. All through grade school, everyone knew that Greg had a loud bark and no bite. He'd been beaten up so often by the time they entered fifth grade that everybody in the neighborhood knew that he was all mouth. Having Roberts for a best friend gave him courage. He could talk tough, but if his words weren't enough, Roberts would be his back up.

They'd found Crow that night. Lucky for them, he was alone when they encountered him hanging out on the same corner Greg had found him when he'd made the five-dollar purchase. Crow was just completing a sale. He glanced over at Greg and Roberts as they approached him, showing no sign of fear.

"You back already, man. I told you that's some good stuff didn't I?" Crow smiled, keeping his eyes on Roberts. "I see you brought me another customer. How much do you want, five or ten? You should get ten since you see how fast your friend smoked the five up."

"I didn't come to buy shit." Greg showed Crow his tough look. "Let's go somewhere and talk, man. Right now before I have to jack you up right here on the street."

"What's the problem?" Crow looked a little surprised.

"Let's go," Greg said again.

"Okay, okay. Let's go into my office." He gave them a weak smile and led them into one of the buildings of the housing project.

Roberts had looked around at their surroundings. Crow's office was the laundry room in the basement of the building. The room was unoccupied; aside from the turning of a dryer loaded with clothing, there wasn't another sound in the room except for Crow's heavy breathing. The look on his face coupled with the heavy breathing was a sure indicator of fear.

"What's up?" He shrugged his shoulders, looking from Roberts to Greg.

"What's up with this shit you sold me?" Greg grabbed Crow by the collar, practically lifting him off his feet.

"Man, I sold you the best shit selling on the street. What's your problem?" he asked again.

"Smell this shit, man. Smoke it yourself. Just give me back my money."

Roberts had watched as Crow brought the bag to his nose. "This is not what I sold you, man. What are trying to pull? This is crap. Get the hell out of here."

Greg grabbed Crow by the collar again. "Give me my money

back, man, before I have to kill you down in this laundry room."

"You ain't getting nothing from me, man." Crow tried to pull away from Greg.

Greg raised his fist and punched Crow in the face knocking him to the floor. He reached down to pull him up and was surprised by a left hook Crow threw to his jaw.

Greg went down and Crow jumped on top of him, pummeling him with his fists. "Get him, Roberts! Get him, Roberts!" Greg yelled. Roberts came behind Crow and pulled him off Greg. He held Crow in a bear hug, allowing Greg to wobble to his feet.

"Give me my five dollars back," Greg screamed at Crow.

"Okay, okay," Crow said, struggling to free himself from the bear hug Roberts had locked around him. "Let me go, man."

Roberts flung Crow across the room. "Give my friend back his money, or I'll put you back in the hold."

Crow reached in his pocket and pulled out a wad of money. He peeled off a bill and approached Roberts with his left hand extended. Greg, still wobbly, and looking like he was about to puke, was holding onto the laundry room table. Just as Crow reached Roberts, his right hand came up with a shiny object that he plunged forward with. Roberts turned to his left, sparing himself from being stabbed in the chest, but catching the blade of a knife in his right shoulder.

Crow pulled the blade out and brought it up again, trying to be more accurate with his placement this time. Roberts reached for the blade causing it to go through his left palm. He screamed in pain. Crow backed away for a second to regroup, still holding the switchblade. He glanced at the door as though he was considering running out of the laundry room. They heard a crash, and both Crow and Roberts looked toward Greg who had broken a soda bottle on the wall and was approaching Roberts. Crow looked at the door again. During that brief moment, Greg pressed the neck of the broken bottle into Roberts' good hand. Without hesitation Roberts moved toward Crow. He plunged the jagged glass into Crow's chest. He did it again. Crow tried to bring the knife up again.

"Kill him," Greg shouted. "Kill him before he kills you, fool."

Roberts plunged the broken bottle into Crow's chest again. Crow dropped the knife. Roberts stood over Crow as he looked up at him, his eyes begging for mercy. Roberts threw the broken bottle across the laundry room. It hit a concrete wall and shattered into a million bits of glass. Greg dropped down over Crow's body relieving him of the wad of bills and all the marijuana he could find. Blood was pouring from Crow's wounds. As they fled into the night, Roberts and Greg almost knocked over a woman coming into the laundry room to retrieve her clothes from the dryer.

"Man, I need to go to a hospital," were Roberts' first words to Greg as they made their way across Bergen Street. With his hand dripping blood and throbbing something awful, they walked to the emergency room at Martland Medical Center. Roberts' wounds were treated, but not before the police were called and he had to give a statement. They told the police that they were jumped as they waited for a bus to go home from the gym. He and Greg had agreed on a story that they thought would be the best course of action. That was just the beginning of a series of events that led Roberts to consider joining the military after graduating from high school.

CHAPTER

4

"Mr. Roberts. Mr. Roberts, wake up." Roberts opened his eyes slowly. He attempted to raise his arm, but discovered that he had the restraints on. *I must have dozed off, he concluded.* He looked up into the face of Dr. Mallard, the resident psychiatrist. "Did I have another nightmare?" He gestured toward the restraints.

"No, Mr. Roberts, you did not have another nightmare. From what I am told you have been free of night terrors for two days now. Perhaps it's time that we get you prepared to go home. If you remain free of night terrors, I think you can leave here in another week or so."

Roberts smiled. He was going home, back to Newark, New Jersey. He took out the letter from his mother and reread it. Then he reached into the drawer of the night table and took out a pen and a sheet of paper. He wanted to let his parents know that he would be coming home soon, and he wanted to relieve his mother of any guilt she might have been feeling about his enlistment. It had been his decision alone to enlist in the army. To make sure that he was doing the right thing, he had waited a whole year after graduating from high school to visit the recruitment office. Roberts thought about the events that had led him to make that final decision.

THREE WEEKS AFTER he, Jeffrey, Greg, and Big Man had graduated from high school, they were still experiencing difficulty finding jobs. Each day Roberts had the same routine. Out of the house by 8:30, he headed downtown to banks, insurance companies, the telephone company, the airport, the utilities company, every place he could think of, filling out job applications. After spending the morning looking for work, Roberts would head home, pick up his gym bag and head out to meet his friends.

The four friends had an arrangement to meet around two in the afternoon at the Friendly Fuld Neighborhood House on Morton Street where they would shoot a few hoops and talk about the events of the day. It was a little past two o'clock on July 12, 1967, when Roberts walked onto the basketball court. Jeff and Big Man were already running the court, playing a game of one-on-one. They waved him over when they saw him.

"You have any luck today?" Big Man had asked, tossing the ball to Roberts.

"Whatcha think, man?" Roberts had said as he dribbled down the court. "A high school diploma is useless nowadays. You need a college degree to get a job at an insurance company or even a bank. A high school diploma might get you a job on a garbage truck or flipping burgers at White Castle."

"You mean for a colored man," Jeff had said. "Man, I've been to every bank in this city, the post office, City Hall, everywhere you can think of and believe me there are no Black faces except for one or two janitors. I'll bet they had to have a high school diploma to get those jobs. Bank tellers and postal workers need more than just a high school diploma; they also need a White face." He'd looked disgusted. "I'll be damned if I'm going to spend my life flipping burgers at White Castle." He aimed and shot for the basket, missing it by a fraction of an inch.

"So what you gonna do, man, enroll in a college? Where you gonna get the money? Besides I don't know of any college that will take someone who graduated with a 1.9 GPA." Roberts and Big Man had both laughed at Jeff's expense.

"Laugh all you want, man," Jeff said reaching up and snatching the ball that Big Man was passing to Roberts. "I don't see where your good grades helped you out, Roberts. We're both in the same boat. No job and no money." He took a long shot down the court and made it.

Roberts grabbed the ball as it bounced off the floor, stepped out of bounds quickly, and passed the ball to Jeff. Jeff was dribbling when Greg had come bursting through the door, all excited about something.

"What's up, man," Roberts said as he headed in Greg's direction.

"Big trouble," was all he said. "Big trouble," he repeated breathlessly.

"What trouble?" Roberts said when he reached Greg.

"Yeah, man. Where have you been?" Jeff had followed.

"Big shit is starting up at the 5th precinct. Some White cops beat up a Black cab driver and people are mad. Shit is about to happen. Let's get up there." Roberts, Greg, Jeff, and Big Man had headed out the door.

WHEN ROBERTS GOT home that evening his shirt was bloody. He had tried to make it to his bedroom to change before his mother saw it, but his bedroom was right off the kitchen and that's just where she had been. Mrs. Roberts looked up from the sink, where she was washing potatoes for dinner, as soon as her son entered the kitchen. She'd heard him come in the door and was relieved. She'd heard the news flashes on WNJR radio talking about the violence that was erupting in Newark. She'd prayed that her family would get home safely.

"Thank God, you're home." Roberts remembered his mother saying. She'd started toward him to give him a hug, and then stopped in her tracks when she saw the blood. Not only was his shirt bloody, but he held a bloody rag up to his head. "What happened to you?" she had screamed. She had tried to examine his head as he tried to pull away.

"People were throwing cans and bottles at the precinct and I accidentally got hit with a bottle. I'm all right, Mom." He had tried to assure her.

"Let me see." She had taken away the rag and gasped. It was a large gash. "You're going to the hospital; you need stitches to close this," she'd said.

Roberts remembered his dad and Deneen, his younger sister by two years, coming into the kitchen at that time and convincing his mother that it was too dangerous to go outside. Police cars were all over the place, and things were really heating up they reported. Mrs. Roberts had cleaned and dressed the wound herself. She had done a good job, too. He barely had a scar from it. But throughout the dressing, Roberts had to listen to his parents discuss his future.

"There's no future in this city for a young Black man," his mother had said. "These kids stay in school and work hard to make something of themselves and what do they get when they get out. Look around this city. Tell me, where do you see Black men working? Not as bus drivers, not as postmen, not as clerks in city hall, no Black politicians, no bank tellers, nowhere except in the service areas. Nothing has changed since my parents came up from the south in 1920." She was exasperated.

"Maybe we should have sent him to college, or at least a trade school," Mr. Roberts had said.

"With what," Mrs. Roberts had screeched in anger. Where will we get the money? The money we make barely pays the bills around here. Even with a college education, it's hard for a Black man to get a job. Look at my sister's son. He spent all of that time going to college to get his CPA certificate, and now he can't get a job working for any large company, let alone with one of the accounting firms right here in Newark, the city of his birth."

"But, Mom, Cousin Wilbur is self-employed. He does just fine." Deneen had said.

"He works for himself because he has to," Mrs. Roberts had said. "No large company or accounting firm will hire him. The only business he attracts is from Black businesses, few as there are, and Blacks needing their taxes done from January to April 15. Most of these people can't afford to pay him the going rate for CPA services so he has to lower his prices for them. Yeah, he does fine all right, fine for a Black man." She'd hissed her frustration with the system.

"Maybe I should just enlist in the Army," Roberts had said, just as his mother finished bandaging his wound. "When I went to sign up for the draft last month, they told us about all of the opportunities in the service. I can get free education and even be able to send some money home for you to save." He looked from his mother to his father. His father had been the first to speak.

"That's the craziest thing that you ever said," Mr. Roberts had said. "Don't you know that there is a war going on? I was in World War II and I know for a fact, boy, that war is pure hell. They send you overseas to a place that you have never heard of and expect you to kill for them. They tell you it is for your country, the same country that won't give you a job, won't pay you a decent wage if they do give you a job, a country that doesn't give a damn about a Black man." Mr. Roberts had thrown up his hands in disgust.

"Then why did you join the Army, Dad? Why did you enlist to go and fight a war in Europe?" Roberts had searched his father's face for answers.

"I didn't have a choice," Mr. Roberts had said after a few seconds of absolute silence. "I didn't have a choice," he repeated himself.

"You don't have many choices either as I see it," Mrs. Roberts had said to her son. "The streets of Newark are becoming as dangerous as any war. At least if you go into the Army, you can come out with a skill and get a decent job when you get home. We can save some of your money for you so you'll have a nest egg when you get home. It may just give you the break you need." She looked at her husband, hoping to convince him.

"So many young Black men are getting drafted now," Deneen had said, shaking her head. "I just worry about the shape they will be in when they come home."

"If they come home," Mr. Roberts had said, not at all convinced.

"I'll come home, Dad," Roberts had said, looking at his father. "I promise you I will come home." He had hoped he sounded convincing.

Roberts had made up his mind. If he didn't find a job by the end of the summer, he was going to enlist. Why wait to be drafted? The recruiter he had met when he had gone to register had mentioned the

33

extra benefits enlistees received.

It was the pep talk that the recruiter had given him, the events of the Newark rebellion, and the lack of opportunities available to young Black men in the city that convinced Roberts to enlist in the military, not his mother. He would let her know that.

Dear Mom,

I just got word from the doctor that I will be leaving the hospital soon to come home.

My injuries have healed, and I'm feeling better every day. Please don't blame yourself for my decision to enlist. It was my choice and, at the time, it seemed like a good choice. I wish I could change it now, but it is too late. A lot of terrible things happened in Vietnam, but I am going to try to put it all behind me and get on with my life. Tell Deneen that I will definitely be home in time for the wedding. I still can't believe that my little sister is getting married before me. Let her know that I wish her the best. Tell her and Dad that I send my love and look forward to coming home.

Sincerely,
Your son, David

CHAPTER

5

The next few days were the happiest that Roberts could ever remember spending, despite the fact that he was a patient in a hospital hundreds of miles from home. He had convinced Nurse Campbell to delay giving him the nighttime medication until after she'd been in his room for an hour; he fell asleep too quickly after taking the medication. She had resisted at first, claiming that it would not be fair to her other patients.

"We're not supposed to show favoritism toward any patient," she'd argued.

"But aren't you supposed to make sure that the patients are happy and content?"

"Yes, but I have other things I should be doing besides playing chess with a patient," she persisted.

"Well, just do those things before you come to see me." He gave her his most charming smile. "Besides, don't you get a break? Can't you arrange to take your break in my room?"

"You're one of the few patients in this hospital that has a private room. I hope you know that?" Her smile convinced him that she was relenting.

"Well, some good has come out of my night terrors," he laughed softly, causing her to laugh with him.

"I'll see what I can do." She turned to leave. "Remember you get your medication no later than 10PM and lights out." She smiled again before leaving the room.

Nurse Campbell made it her business to be in room 320 each evening by 9PM and stay until the lights went out. She and Roberts played chess, joked about the hospital staff, and shared stories about their lives.

"I'm just a small time girl from Oxford, Ohio," she told him one night. "I've heard a lot of stories about you sophisticated men from New York and New Jersey. You enjoy taking risks and living dangerously. I'm not like that at all. I like things that are secure and solid." She looked up from the chessboard only to discover that he was concentrating more on her than the game.

"What do you consider solid and secure?" He tried to look serious.

"My daddy is solid and secure. He comes home every night at six; we have dinner together as a family; he always gives my mother his wages to pay the bills; and he fixes things around the house. My sister and I could always depend on him and my mom to take care of us while we were growing up. My mother never worried that my father was out doing things that would threaten our stability as a family."

"I come from that same kind of stability. I enjoyed having both my parents around for me, and I intend to do the same thing for the family I plan to have one day." Roberts smiled at her.

"Practically everyone I know in Oxford comes from an intact family. Divorce is frowned upon," Nurse Campbell said, not looking up, but focusing her attention on the chessboard.

"It's not like that in Newark. Single mothers raised most of my friends. My family was definitely not your typical Newark family. Trust me, I know how important it is to raise kids with both parents in the home. I grew up with that advantage, and I definitely want to pass it on to my own children one day."

"So, what are we talking about here." Nurse Campbell looked up from the chessboard. "Aren't we getting a little ahead of ourselves?" She looked a little alarmed.

"We're just getting to know each other. That's all. By the way, I think this is checkmate." Roberts smiled at the dismay on her face.

Two nights later, Nurse Campbell came into his room at the usual time, but this time she had a wheelchair with her.

"Your chariot awaits you," she announced.

"Where are we going?"

"Since you're checking out soon, I thought you might like a tour of our facility before you leave. Come on, get in. You just might meet some other patients that you know."

Reluctantly, Roberts put on his robe and sat in the chair. He wasn't sure he wanted to see any of his comrades in a broken state. He'd been in the hospital in Hawaii for four weeks, and he'd been almost completely confined to his room except when he went out for an x-ray or some other test. He'd seen some of the guys waiting in the hall for their turn to be tested, and it tore him up to see that some had missing limbs, scarred faces, and broken spirits.

During the first week that he had been hospitalized, he barely had remembered anything except the pain. He had been drugged so much that he scarcely recalled the surgery or the events leading up to his being injured in the first place. He remembered waking up a couple of times in the same room with two other soldiers who were moaning as loud as he was. Then, as his memory started to return, the night terrors began. After the first episode, they had moved him into a private room and started using the restraints.

Nurse Campbell wheeled him out of the room and down a long corridor with closed doors on each side. He didn't hear any moaning, for which he was grateful. They turned a corner, and there was the nurse's station. Three nurses looked up as they approached and smiled at him.

"Mr. Roberts, it's wonderful seeing you up and about. I hear you'll be leaving us soon." A tall red-haired nurse came up to him and touched his shoulder. "I'm so glad you're better," she said, then smiled before turning and walking down the corridor.

"We're going to miss you around here, Mr. Roberts. You certainly helped to liven up our nights around here," a short Asian nurse laughed.

"Good Luck to you, Mr. Roberts," the third nurse said. She was older than the others were, somewhat obese with curly white hair.

"Thanks," Roberts said. "You've all been so good to me here. I really appreciate all that you've done. I'll never forget you." Roberts waved as Nurse Campbell turned the wheelchair around.

"I'm taking my patient on a little tour," she said to her colleagues as she pushed the wheelchair in the direction of the elevator.

They got off the elevator on the ground floor and entered an atrium where half-a-dozen or so men were sitting around talking or reading magazines. No sooner had they entered the room than someone yelled out, "Roberts, I didn't know you were here." A tall, young blond man walked towards them. Roberts recognized him right away. They had served together in the 26th infantry.

"Frank, what are you doing here?" Roberts grinned at the young man.

"Same thing as you I suppose, recovering from my injuries, but I'll be going home in a few days; minus a couple of body parts, but still very much alive." He stuck his hand out initially, but then withdrew it quickly and reached down to give Roberts a hug.

Roberts returned the hug and then said, "Same here. I just got the word that I'll be going home shortly, too." Roberts continued to smile at Frank. He was so happy to see someone he knew. He wondered what body parts Frank was missing, but he didn't ask. He couldn't tell by looking at him. "Have you seen anyone else from "F-Troop?" Roberts laughed at himself for using the nickname that his troop had given themselves.

"No, thank God. I wouldn't want to wish what happened to us on anyone else. When are you leaving?"

"Soon I hope. I have medical clearance, but I'm waiting for my orders to come down. What about you?"

"Same here. What room are you in? I'll come and visit before I check out if it's okay with you."

"That'll be great. See you soon," Roberts said as Nurse Campbell started pushing the chair again.

A COUPLE OF DAYS later Roberts was surprised when Nurse Campbell showed up in his room early one afternoon on her day off. She looked beautiful dressed in a yellow sundress that made her light brown skin look radiant. She wore matching yellow sandals that revealed a recent pedicure. Her hair was loose, cap free, with curls bouncing. She had on pale pink lipstick that matched the color of her nail polish.

"God just answered my prayers and sent me my angel of mercy," Roberts said from his chair by the window. "To what do I owe the pleasure of this visit? I wasn't expecting to see you today, and I was wondering how I would get through the night." His smile was as radiant as hers.

"Dr. Mallard has given you permission to walk the grounds. You'll be leaving here in a couple of days, and he wants you to get a little exercise so you'll be fit to travel. I volunteered to take you out for a walk in the garden."

"You mean no wheelchair?"

"Not unless you feel you need one. Do you feel up to it?"

"Are you kidding? I'm feeling as fit as a king at the mere thought of walking in the garden with you. Can I get dressed in real clothes?"

"Do you have any? You were admitted in a hospital gown, directly from the army field hospital in Vietnam."

"Yes. I got a package from Uncle Sam yesterday with my orders and my traveling gear. I'll be dressed in ten minutes."

"I'll wait at the nurse's station for you." She turned to leave and then said as an afterthought, "Unless you need help getting dressed." She gave him a shy smile.

"Hmmm," he said as if he were contemplating her offer. "I think I can manage." He smiled at her.

When Roberts emerged from his room fully dressed, Nurse Campbell was stunned. To the best of her recollection this was the first time that she had seen him standing, fully erect. He looked so handsome. He stood at least six feet tall, and he was slim with a trim waist and long legs.

He was wearing his khaki dress uniform with a little cap. As he approached the nurses' station, Nurse Campbell could feel herself getting warm. The sight of him dressed in his uniform aroused her.

The walk in the garden was perfect. Nurse Campbell took him to see her favorite flowerbed with the huge purple flowers. This time she took the time to bend over and smell them. "Umm, they smell delicious," she said giving them a big whiff.

"So do you," he said, bending over to smell her neck, causing her to straighten up abruptly, knocking him off balance. "I'm sorry," she said reaching for his arm to steady him.

"I'm not." He reached and put his arm around her waist and drew her closer, smelling her hair now.

"Mr. Roberts, you've got to behave yourself," she giggled. "We're still on hospital grounds."

"But you're off duty."

"Yes, but you're still my patient, and I don't want people to get the wrong idea and start gossiping." She disentangled herself from his arm and put the proper amount of distance between them.

"Okay, I understand. But listen, how about a real date before I leave Hawaii? I will be officially discharged from the hospital tomorrow morning, and I'll be flying out of here day after tomorrow. Can you get tomorrow night off so I can take you out to dinner?" His eyes pleaded with her.

"I'll try," she said. "I'll try real hard." She looked into his pleading eyes and assured him that she would.

THE NEXT NIGHT, Roberts left the hospital on his own for the first time in over five weeks. He had over four hundred dollars in his pants pocket, accumulated from his meager wages, less the allotment he'd authorized to be sent home to his mother. He'd spent the last hour grooming himself for his first real date in over three years.

He had never been a ladies' man, partly due to his shyness with girls during his early adolescence, and then, too, because he had spent his last two years in high school going steady with his first real sweetheart, Rachel West. It had been a good relationship for the most part, but then she had broken his heart and left him two weeks before the high school prom because the captain of the football team had invited her to be his prom date.

Not bad, not bad at all, Roberts concluded as he checked himself out in the mirror. He looked good in his dress uniform. He put on his hat and smiled at his reflection before heading out the door. The three nurses sitting at the station whistled at him as he made his way to the elevator.

"Are you going home tonight, Mr. Roberts?" the short Asian nurse asked. She eyed him from head to toe.

"No, tomorrow morning," he said, pushing the elevator button. He hoped they wouldn't ask him where he was going all dressed up.

"You look like you got a hot date tonight," the older, obese nurse commented.

"I'm meeting a friend for dinner," Roberts said, grateful that the elevator door opened to receive him.

Nurse Campbell was waiting for him when the cab pulled up to the restaurant where she had suggested they meet. She looked gorgeous in a stunning red suit with a short skirt and high heel shoes showing off long shapely legs. He gave her a low whistle to which she smiled, blushing. Without saying a word, he placed his right hand on the lower part of her back and escorted her into the restaurant.

The restaurant was elegant with white tablecloths, sterling silver flatware, and shimmering crystal glasses. The centerpiece at their table was a beautiful silver candelabrum with an attached crystal vase containing beautiful purple flowers almost identical to the ones that Nurse Campbell had been admiring since she had arrived in Hawaii. After the waiter seated them, they looked around at their surroundings. The restaurant was packed, and Roberts noticed that they were the only Black couple there. He looked at Nurse Campbell and concluded that she was the prettiest woman in the restaurant.

"Would you like a glass of wine before dinner?" he asked.

"Sure. I'm not on duty. Will you have one, too?"

"Okay," he said just as the waiter came to take their drink order.

After the waiter left, Roberts reached across the table and took her hand. "This is the best thing that has happened to me in a long, long time." He squeezed her hand a little tighter.

"Me, too," she said.

"Do you think we'll ever see each other again after tonight?" He gave her a hopeful look.

"If we really want to, we will."

"I really want to see you again, Nurse Campbell."

"Please, call me Dorothy. You're not my patient anymore." She smiled at him as they locked eyes across the table.

"I really want to see you again, Dorothy," he said and then smiled.

"Then you will," she said, still holding his gaze.

Chapter

6

A n Army vehicle was at the hospital promptly at 6AM the next morning. Roberts was ready to go; he had been looking out the window since 5:30AM in anticipation. He raced outside when the vehicle pulled up, threw his duffel bag in, and climbed in with the other three soldiers already seated. A minute later, they were heading to the airport to get flights to their respective hometowns.

Frank Verducci was one of the passengers. He had come up to room 320 to see Roberts shortly after they'd met in the atrium, but Roberts had fallen asleep on him. The visit had been soon after his afternoon dose of medication. Frank didn't waste time reminding Roberts about the incident.

"Good to see you awake," he joked as soon as they were settled in the vehicle.

"It's good to be awake." Roberts laughed with Frank.

"Man, it's good to be alive!" a long-legged Black soldier said. "I'm Ferguson." He extended his hand first to Roberts and then to Frank and the third soldier.

"Hi, Ferguson," the three of them said in unison.

"Boy, the Army has trained us well," Frank said to the laughter of the three men before introducing himself to the others.

After all the introductions were made, Roberts repeated Ferguson's comment. "You're right, Man, it is good to be alive."

"I hate to think about those who didn't make it. I almost feel guilty that I'm still alive, and they're not." Ferguson shook his head in disbelief. "It's like we are the chosen ones."

"I feel the same way," Frank said. "I know you must be feeling bad, Roberts, losing your buddy the way you did."

"What buddy?" Roberts head shot up from the headrest.

"Your friend, Greg. Don't you remember?"

Roberts was silent for a few seconds before he responded. "Of course, I remember." He went back into his silent mode. *Greg is dead?* he asked himself. *No, I don't remember.*

From Hawaii, Roberts flew into California where he had a two-hour layover before boarding another commercial airliner that would take him home. The plane ride to Newark, NJ, would be a long flight over five hours. Roberts had boarded the plane at 11AM. As soon as he was seated, he took his morning medication, he didn't want any episodes of night terror while he was in flight. Besides, the medication made him sleepy, and that's what he wanted to do more than anything else right now. Sleep would keep him from thinking about Greg. *What had happened? How could Greg be dead?*

Greg Williams and Roberts had been buddies since they were ten years old. They had met at Morton Street School when they were in the fifth grade. They both had lived in the Stella Wright Housing Projects until Mr. Roberts got a promotion to supervisor at Westinghouse, and the family had to move out because their income became too high. That happened when Roberts entered the tenth grade. He and Greg saw each other every day at school, though, and had remained best friends all through high school. They were together when the rebellion first started in Newark. It was Greg who made sure Roberts got home safely after the bottle hit him. It was Greg who talked him into waiting a little longer to enlist in the army.

"Man, things can't get any worse in Newark now," Greg had said at the end of the summer of 1967 when Roberts still had not found a job. "Wait awhile, things are going to get better. If they don't get any better, I'll enlist with you," he had promised. It wasn't until the summer of 1968 that Roberts enlisted. He was only nineteen years old. He had no job, or even the prospect of a job, no money, no girlfriend, nothing.

Roberts remembered the day he had gone to enlist at the recruiting office on Broad Street in downtown Newark. From the looks of downtown, no one would have suspected that a year ago there had been a five-day bloody rebellion in the city. Twenty-six people had lost their lives in those five days, including an innocent mother of twelve children who had been shot by National Guardsmen shooting recklessly at the windows of Hayes Homes, a housing project in the Central Ward. Businesses had been burned, looted, and completely destroyed. Most of the damage had been in the Central Ward. The only noticeable changes to the downtown area were the newly installed riot-proof gates all of the stores had installed.

At the recruiting station, a middle aged White man who was overly friendly had interviewed Roberts. He was given an aptitude test to determine what his talents were and later was told that the test had revealed that he would make a good mechanic. He signed all the necessary paperwork, made an appointment to have a physical examination, and then went home to tell his family that he was now an enlisted man.

Roberts looked up into the face of a pretty flight attendant who was asking him what he wanted to drink. He asked for a ginger ale, then reclined his seat and lay his head back on the pillow he had been provided. *Greg dead! Why can't I remember?* He let his mind wander back to the days before he had been shipped out to basic training.

Mr. Roberts had been upset with his son's decision to enlist in the Army. "Boy, hasn't anything I've been saying to you sunk into that skull of yours? You don't know what you're getting into. Why couldn't you be a little more patient? Things are going to get better here. There's talk about putting a Black mayor in office. Even President Johnson is talking about giving more aid to the cities." He had thrown his hands up, exasperated.

"What am I supposed to do in the meantime, Dad? It's going to be another two years before there's a municipal election and then more time for any aid to come into the city. I need to be doing something now." He had looked to his mother for support.

"Leave the boy alone," she had said. "He's nineteen years old now. He can make his own decisions. Besides, he already has enlisted. There's nothing that can be done to change that now."

His buddies had mixed feelings about his enlistment, too. Big Man told him to his face that he was a fool.

"Man, are you crazy?" he had asked. "Why would you enlist to go off somewhere and fight a war that has nothing to do with us? We are meeting with hell right here in Newark, New Jersey, and no one is sending in any troops to free us. The only time they sent troops into Newark was last summer, and you saw what they did to us. Well, those people in Vietnam are going to feel the same way about you that we felt about those troops that were sent into Newark. Are you crazy, man?"

"Why couldn't you wait until they drafted you?" Jeff had asked. "They're mostly calling guys that are twenty-one years old. My brother knows his time is up, and he's talking about leaving the country and going up to Canada. I don't know any nineteen year olds that are being drafted. Why couldn't you just wait?"

Greg, the only one in the group who had found something productive to do, looked dumbfounded when he learned that his best friend had enlisted. Greg was training to become an emergency medical technician at The University of Medicine and Dentistry. He had the promise of a job when he finished the training.

"I didn't believe that you were going to do it," he had said. "I didn't forget my promise to you. As soon as I finish the training, I'll enlist, too." He looked at Roberts with a sincere look on his face.

"You don't have to do that." Roberts had insisted. "This was my decision; I don't expect you to live up to that promise. Things are going well for you, man. You just keep on doing what you're doing."

"A promise is a promise." Greg had said. Two weeks after he finished his EMT program, Greg had enlisted in the army. He had requested that he be assigned to the same company as his best friend.

Roberts remembered the surprise he had received while having dinner at the mess hall at Fort Jackson, South Carolina, about three weeks into his basic training. He had looked up from his plate to the sound of a familiar voice saying "Move over man and make room for me." Greg had just grinned at the stunned look on his face.

If they had been close before the enlistment, they became even closer afterwards. They formed a real buddy team, taking advantage of every opportunity to be together during basic training, helping each other out whenever they could. Roberts graduated three weeks before Greg, at the top of his class.

Roberts had gone home for a one-week leave before he was sent to Fort Benning, Georgia for combat training. Three weeks after he arrived in Georgia, he looked up and there was Greg again, waving from across the field where Roberts had been assigned to apprentice as a mechanic.

Both Roberts and Greg received orders to be deployed to Vietnam on the same day. At Fort Benning, Greg received further training as a medic, and Roberts trained to become an expert mechanic, although he spent more time driving trucks than fixing them once he landed in Vietnam. They both trained for combat at Fort Benning and remained in Georgia for about a year. Now they were going to fight together in Vietnam. They were twenty years old, in great physical shape, well-trained, and scared.

"Would you please return your seat to an upright position?" Roberts heard the flight attendant ask, drawing him out of his sleep.

"Where are we?" he asked, still groggy.

"We will be landing in Newark in about twenty minutes. I need you to pull your seat up, please."

Roberts obeyed, and then he looked around the plane. This was a commercial flight and although most of the passengers were returning soldiers, there were many civilians on the plane as well. In twenty minutes, he would be back in Newark. He hadn't been home since he and Greg had come home together from Fort Benning, Georgia, before their deployment to Vietnam. They had both received a two-week pass before being sent into combat. What a great time they had had.

They'd decided to surprise their families and had come into Newark unannounced. They'd caught a cab and rode up Springfield Avenue together. It had been two years after the rebellion and things did not look any better. The streets were still littered with trash. Burned out, abandoned buildings and boarded up businesses were in abundance.

People walked the streets like zombies with no place to go. He and Greg had stared out the cab windows, shaking their heads.

When they got to Greg's Street, the cabdriver had stopped to let him out at the cross street, a main thoroughfare. "Come on home with me, man. I'll borrow my mother's car and give you a ride home."

"Okay." Roberts had grabbed his bag and gotten out of the cab.

They had walked the block or so to Greg's house, taking in the familiar sights. Greg's neighborhood still looked intact. He had waved to some of his neighbors, who smiled, glad to see him home. When they'd gotten to Greg's front porch they both thought they saw someone looking out the window. When they'd gone into the house everybody had yelled "surprise." They had intended to surprise their families, but they were the ones who had gotten the surprise.

Roberts' mother had called his commanding officer to inquire as to why she had not heard from him. She was told that both he and Greg were due to arrive that day. The families had worked feverishly to get the party together before they got home. Now both families and their friends were there to greet them. What a wonderful surprise.

For two glorious weeks, Roberts and Greg had visited friends and families, eaten home cooked-meals until they were stuffed, and hung out with pretty girls who had nothing but love for the soldier boys.

Again, Roberts had come home unannounced, only this time he was alone. His heart was heavy. Was Greg really dead? Could Frank have been wrong? Why hadn't someone told him before now that Greg was dead? Sure, it was true that he had been in a Hawaiian hospital for almost six weeks and had had no contact with anyone from his company. The letter from his mother had not mentioned anything about Greg. Did they know?

The cab ride to his parents' home was solemn. Roberts paid little attention to the scenes he passed. This time the cabdriver drove up Elizabeth Avenue. His parents had moved. They had purchased a home in the Weequahic section that had been completely abandoned by the Jewish population that had thrived there before the rebellion four years earlier. This section of Newark had pretty much been untouched by the rebellion; it was one of the better areas of the city. Many single family homes with large, well kept lawns lined the streets. Services in the city had fallen off, though, and Roberts couldn't help but notice that the streets weren't as clean as they used to be.

When the driver pulled up to the house on Pomona Avenue, Roberts got his first look at his new home. It was a nice house. He paid the driver and went up the stairs. He rang the bell and waited. His mother came to the door. She screamed when she saw him. His father came running. They were so surprised to see him. His mother hugged him, crying uncontrollably. His father was full of smiles. Then his mother spoke. "Honey, we are so sorry about Greg."

It's true. He began to cry.

CHAPTER

7

Roberts had been home for a full week before he even considered leaving the house. His extended family dropped by to welcome him home, but he'd been non-communicative and on a few occasions had asked his mother to tell them he was sleeping or resting. He was in mourning for his best friend, and he was just too distraught to talk about it with anyone.

The newly purchased house that was now his home was quite comfortable. His parents had converted the attic into a small apartment just for him. His quarters consisted of a large bedroom, a sitting room, and his own private bathroom. Roberts spent most of his time in his apartment, sleeping, reading up on the local news, and eating the home delicious meals his mother prepared daily, but mostly he thought about Greg.

Roberts learned from his parents that the funeral had been held six weeks ago. The last letter he'd received from his mother didn't mention Greg's death because she had not known when she wrote it that Greg had died. She had been notified of her son's injuries, but had been told nothing about Greg. Greg's mother hadn't found out about his death until a week after the incident.

Army military officials told Greg's mother that he'd died as a result of sniper fire, and that Roberts had tried to save his life. Roberts was carrying Greg's body to safety when members of another company had come upon them. Roberts had been injured himself by the sniper, but despite his injuries he had carried his dead friend's body to safety. Greg's family considered Roberts a hero.

"Out of respect for Greg's family, you should go and visit them to offer your condolences in person," his mother said late one afternoon after he had been in his apartment the entire day.

"What will I say to them?"

"Tell them how sorry you are that Greg died. Tell them how close the two of you were, how much you loved him, and how much you miss him. That's what you say to people when they're in mourning. That's the same thing your family has been saying to you."

"Suppose they ask me how it happened? What am I going to say?"

"The truth, that you don't remember, that you were also injured, and that your recollection of the whole incident is lost to you for now. That will have to be enough." Mrs. Roberts put her arm around her son and tried to console him.

"Would that be enough for you, Mom? What if I had been the one that died, wouldn't you want to know more?"

"Not if that was all someone had to give. I don't think Greg's family will pressure you once they see how distraught you are. Your father was right; I never should have encouraged you to enlist. 'War is hell.' They send all of you boys thousands of miles from home to fight a war that you don't even understand. Then they send you home all scarred, emotionally and physically. I'm sorry I ever let you go."

"You didn't let me go, Mom. I wanted to go. Greg went because of me. I'm sorry, too, now."

"Well nothing that we say or do will bring him back. We can only help to ease the pain of those who loved him. Go and see his mother today." Mrs. Roberts practically demanded.

ALL DRESSED UP in his dress uniform, Roberts paid a visit to his best friend's family. He was surprised at the welcome he received. Greg's mother and two younger sisters hugged him and cried with him for Greg. Their living room was covered with photos of Greg in his high school graduation cap and gown, and in his army dress uniform. They even had pictures from the funeral with photos of the casket draped in the American flag.

Greg's sister hugged one of the pictures to her bosom. "We were so proud of him. We miss him so much."

"I loved him, too. He was my best friend for twelve years. I'll never forget him." Roberts stroked one of the pictures of Greg in uniform.

"He always spoke highly of you," Greg's mother said. "Why don't you keep that picture? We have plenty more just like that. Greg loved the way he looked in uniform. He sent us dozens of pictures that we will always cherish. He loved being in the Army. He wrote about how much he was learning in all of his letters." She dabbed at her eyes with a white handkerchief.

"He was one of the best medics in the company. Everybody thought so." Roberts hoped his words would console Greg's family a little.

When Roberts was ready to leave, Greg's mother walked him to the door. She thanked him for being there for Greg and asked in a soft, low voice, if he would share some memories of Greg with her one day. She didn't ask how he died, but Roberts sensed that was what she wanted to know.

When he left Greg's family's house, Roberts went to find his buddies. He went to the old haunts looking for them. The Felix Fuld Neighborhood house was still there, but the courtyard and the basketball courts were littered with trash. Young teenagers were hanging out on the grounds smoking cigarettes and weed. They eyed him suspiciously as he looked around the facility for familiar faces. There was no one there that he recognized.

Roberts took the number 5 Kinney bus to West Market Street, the last place Big Man had lived with his mother and six other siblings. Big Man had gotten married in the last year or so and had had a new baby, a boy. Roberts was looking forward to meeting Big Man's new family. When he rang the bell, Big Man's mother answered the door.

"Who are you?" she asked as though she was angry with the world.

"Don't you recognize me?" Roberts took off his cap.

"Is that you, David?" The heavyset woman grabbed him and gave him a bear hug. "I'm so glad to see you, honey. You really are all grown up now, a soldier boy." She held him at arm's length, giving him a thorough look-over. "So are you home to stay?"

"Yes, Ma'am," Roberts said. "Is Big Man still living here? I heard he got married."

"Yeah, he got married all right, but he hasn't gone anywhere. They're staying down in my basement. Come on through the house. You sure do look good in that army uniform." She led him to the stairwell leading to the basement.

As Roberts descended the basement steps, he heard Big Man yelling, "Girl, can't you shut that baby up, I can't even hear the television."

"You're the daddy, why don't you see after him?" a pretty young woman said as she emerged from the bathroom directly across from the stairwell. She looked startled when she saw Roberts coming down the stairs.

"Hi," Roberts said to the woman. He wanted to put her at ease.

"You must be looking for Big Man," the woman said, eyeing his uniform. "Come on in. He's just watching television."

Roberts followed her to the doorway of a large room. A floor model television set was against one of the walls, and a big overstuffed sofa sat across from it. Big Man sat on the sofa in his boxer shorts, absorbed in a wrestling match. Roberts watched as the woman crossed the room, heading in the direction of the crying baby sounds. Big Man looked up, and then stood up to his full six-foot four-inch height when he saw his buddy standing in the doorway. "Man, look at you. How long have you been home? No one told me." The two men embraced each other.

Smiling for the first time in a week, Roberts said, "I've been home a week now." He stared at Big Man who looked like he had gained twenty pounds since Roberts last saw him and was now sporting a beard.

"Sit down, man. Tell me how you are. How long are you home for? I heard you got hurt, but you look all right to me." Big Man was all smiles. "Man, I missed you." He sat back down on the sofa and motioned for Roberts to take the seat next to him.

Roberts sat in the armchair next to the sofa. "So, it's true. You got married." Roberts looked around the basement apartment.

"Any young man with good sense got married and had kids right away to avoid going to Vietnam. I never understood why you were so hell bent on enlisting." He got up again to turn down the volume on the television.

"It was different with me. I didn't have anyone to marry, and I didn't have a job, no money. I didn't have any options," Roberts followed him with his eyes.

"There are always options, man. When there aren't, you make them. I did," Big Man said turning the television down and then changing his mind and flicking it off altogether.

"How? How could I have made some options?" Roberts sat back in his seat and crossed his legs.

"You and Rachel had just broken up. Man, you could have gotten back with her long enough to knock her up. That's what a lot of guys did," Big Man said, lowering his voice. "Jeff did the same thing when they sent him a letter talking about the draft. He put a hole in the next condom he used; three months later he got married and then got a letter from the obstetrician saying that his wife was expecting a baby."

"I couldn't do that, man. I couldn't make a decision about someone else's future; it was hard enough making a choice about mine. *Besides, Rachel wasn't giving it up back then,* Roberts thought to himself, but did not say. "I couldn't do that to Rachel." He shifted in his chair, uncomfortable with the conversation.

"Well, what about what she did to you, dropping you two weeks before the prom? What about that?"

"That was her choice. She's entitled to make her own choices just like me." Roberts uncrossed his legs and leaned up in his chair.

"What about Greg? What about his choices? Do you think he would have chosen to die in Vietnam?" Big Man's look of outrage caused Roberts to feel guilty.

"He didn't have to go. I tried to tell him that," Roberts said softly, looking down at his hands, which were folded in his lap.

No one spoke for a few minutes. Both men sat looking at the floor. Then Big Man said, "It was the saddest funeral I ever attended. He was the first one of our graduating class to die in Vietnam. Practically the whole class came to the funeral; everyone loved Greg. A few of the guys came in uniform; they had finished up their basic training and were home on leave before being shipped out." He put his face in his hands and became silent again.

"God, I loved that boy," Roberts said. "I keep hoping that this is a dream and that I'll wake up and he'll be here." He stretched out his legs and leaned his head back in the chair, closing his eyes.

"Well, he's not coming back, he's gone forever. You didn't see him in that coffin, I'll never get over...." Big Man stopped, realizing what he was saying. "Man, I'm sorry. I forgot you were with him when it happened. Tell me about it, I'd like to know how he died."

"That's the strangest thing," Roberts said, sitting up in the chair. "I don't remember. All I remember is that I was driving Greg and another medic, along with some medical supplies, to a field hospital in the jungle. The next thing I remember is waking up in the same hospital that I was making the delivery to, only I was wounded, and they were treating me. I stayed in that hospital for three weeks but I barely remember any of it. I don't even remember being lifted out of there in a helicopter, and boarding a plane for a hospital in Hawaii. I must have been drugged. I didn't find out that Greg was dead until the day I was coming home, man, nine weeks later." Roberts leaned back in the chair again.

"That's rough, man, being a hero and not even remembering it." Big Man shook his head in disbelief. "The Ledger did a story on it, you know. Local boys, childhood friends, fight together, and one is killed while the other becomes a hero. I would have thought that the mayor would have given you a hero's welcome home. Well, he's new and just learning his way around. I know you heard we have our first Black mayor; things are going to change in this town."

"I'm not really a hero, man. I didn't save Greg's life; he's dead."

"Yeah, but you tried to save his life. I hear you carried him through the jungle to safety even though you were injured. You're still a hero as far as I'm concerned. I'm proud to call you my friend."

Roberts got up from the chair and stretched, then said, "I'd better get out of here, let you get back to your family. When are we going to get together again and play a little ball?" He smiled; remembering the old days and then threw his arms up as though shooting a basketball.

"I haven't played ball since you and Greg left. That was kid stuff; we're men now. Let's get together for a drink, you, Jeff, and me. I'll call him and let him know you're home." Big Man stood up and walked over to Roberts. He put his arm around Roberts' shoulders, and they started to walk slowly towards the door.

Suddenly remembering, Big Man said, "Hey wait, you haven't met my wife and baby, yet." He yelled for his wife to come in and to bring the baby to meet his friend.

Roberts couldn't help but feel a little envy when he looked at the baby, a beautiful little boy about a year old. Big Man's wife, Marsha, appeared to be a devoted mother. She looked to be about twenty or twenty-one. Roberts wondered if she knew that Big Man had deliberately gotten her pregnant to avoid being drafted.

WHEN ROBERTS' GOT home, he found his sister's fiancé visiting with his parents while waiting for Deneen to get ready for their date. They'd been high school sweethearts, much like he and Rachel had been, only Deneen was madly in love and fearful that Derrick might get drafted. She wanted to get married and pregnant. All smiles, she came into the living room shortly after Roberts entered.

"I'm glad you got home before we left," she said, giving her brother a hug. "Derrick wants to ask you something." Deneen took Derrick's hand in hers.

"What's up?" Roberts asked.

"I want to know if you'll be my best man," Derrick said, all smiles. "I've never had a brother before, and now that Deneen and I are getting married I feel that I'm inheriting a brother, as well as getting a wife. I'd be really honored if you would consider it."

Roberts considered it for all of about five seconds, and then said, "I'd be honored to be your best man. I've never had a brother before, either; it will be good to have another male in this family. Finally, the men in the family will be the majority. Maybe we'll get listened to more, now." He shook Derrick's hand and then embraced him.

"The men will only be in the majority until you find yourself a wife," Deneen said. "Then we'll be evened out again."

When Roberts was finally alone in his attic apartment he thought about Dorothy Campbell. Before he left Hawaii, on that last night when they had gone out to dinner, she had given him her address and phone number in Ohio. She'd told him that she would be finishing up her tour of duty in six months, and that she would love to hear from him then. *Six months is a long time,* Roberts thought as he searched for a pen and some stationary to write her a letter at the hospital in Hawaii.

KILL . . . OR BE KILLED

CHAPTER

8

The next few weeks were quite hectic for Roberts as he settled down and tried to readjust to civilian life. His father took a day off from work, at his insistence, to go with his son to the VA Hospital. Roberts had been instructed to have a prescription filled for his medication as soon as possible after he returned home. Dr. Mallard also had written a referral to the resident psychiatrist at the East Orange VA Hospital, explaining Roberts' mental condition along with his recommendation for treatment. Roberts listened as his father described the politics of the VA Hospital on the drive to neighboring East Orange.

"These doctors at the VA don't take a personal interest in anyone. They treat us like we are some damn albatross around the government's neck. After we've fought their wars and come home wounded in mind, body and spirit, they behave as though they wished we would disappear off the face of the earth." Mr. Roberts shook his head and sighed loudly.

"Why do you keep going to them, Dad? Why not find a good private doctor who will give you the personal attention that you deserve?" Roberts looked at his father and waited for an answer.

"Where am I going to get the money for that? The best thing about the VA is that you don't have to pay a penny. I've been coming up here for over twenty years now, and I've never had to pay for anything. I've had a hernia surgery, a dislocated shoulder, bouts with the flu and other things, and I've not had to pay a dime out of my pocket."

Roberts listened while his father continued to ramble about the advantages and disadvantages of receiving treatment at the VA hospital. He also observed the changing landscape of East Orange. East Orange had apparently been affected by the rebellion in Newark as well. Many of the more affluent residents had put their homes up for sale or rented them out to former residents of Newark who wanted to escape the fallout of the rebellion but were unable to go too far. The East Orange community had definitely become more Black since he had been gone. The quality of municipal services had certainly declined as a result.

Pulling into the parking lot of the VA Hospital, Mr. Roberts cautioned his son to be careful in dispensing information about himself. "Don't volunteer any information, just answer the questions. Make sure when you fill out the forms that you don't volunteer for any experimental treatments. These places are known to use veterans as guinea pigs; a lot of the veterans complain that many of the symptoms they are experiencing didn't appear until they started using some of these experimental drugs."

"Okay, Dad. I'll be careful."

"Don't be surprised if they keep us up here all day. They act like we don't have no place else to go. Because they're not charging us any money, they think our time is their time."

After a two-and-a-half-hour wait, Roberts finally got a chance to talk to the doctor.

"The pills make me drowsy," he said to the short balding white man, wearing a starched white jacket. "Isn't there any other treatment for the night terror?"

"None that I know of other than, perhaps, long-term psychotherapy that may help you deal with the issues that are causing them, but, something that we don't have available." The doctor kept writing prescriptions without even looking up from his pad.

"I want to find a job," Roberts told the psychiatrist. "How am I going to work if the medication makes me drowsy?" He didn't want to take pills for the rest of his life.

"The side effects will subside in time," the doctor told him. "In the meantime, you just keep taking the medication until I tell you to stop. Make sure that you make an appointment to come back here in a month. Take these prescriptions to the pharmacy." He handed Roberts the prescriptions, dismissing him.

LOOKING FOR A JOB was a job in itself. Roberts made all the rounds that he had made before he enlisted in the Army. He went to banks, the post office, insurance companies, the telephone company, and numerous other places. After being handed an application to fill out at the post office he asked the receptionist, "Why do I have to fill out another application? I never heard anything regarding the one I filled out three years ago." Roberts' frustration was evident from the look on his face.

"We only keep applications on file for a year," the pleasant looking older woman told him. Her smile was genuine.

"Do you think I'll get called this time?" Roberts asked, taking the application from her, quickly glancing at it.

"I don't know," she said politely. "With so much money being spent on the war, there's sort of a freeze on hiring right now." She directed him to a desk where he could fill out the application.

At Prudential Insurance Company, headquartered in Newark, he was told practically the same thing. "We'll keep your application on file for a year," a tall blond woman told him. "If something comes up that we feel you'll be suited for, we'll give you a call."

Every evening Roberts came home disappointed. Finally, his mother suggested that he look outside of Newark for a job. "You'd think that with so many White people fearful of coming into Newark to work now, the job opportunities would be better for Blacks. That just goes to show you that things are not always what they appear to be. Maybe you should go into some of their areas to look for a job."

She gave him a reassuring look.

"I don't want to be spending a half day on a bus just getting to and from work, Mom. Besides, I'll probably just fall asleep on the bus and never get to work on time anyway."

"Honey, why don't you just use some of that money I saved up for you while you were in the Army and buy yourself a car?"

"Now that sounds like a plan." The idea of owning his own car was enough to lift Roberts' spirits. He jumped up, grabbed his mother around the waist and spun her around the kitchen floor, both of them laughing loudly. They didn't even hear Deneen when she came into the house.

"What are you two so happy about?" Deneen asked upon entering the kitchen.

"I'm going to get me some wheels," Roberts said, grabbing his sister and dancing her around as well.

"Well, this is something to dance about; the Roberts' family is going to be a two-car family. We are moving up in the world." Deneen laughed with her mother and brother.

THREE WEEKS LATER Roberts was driving his brand new, at least to him, three year old, fire engine red Mustang to Hudson County, New Jersey. His father had told him that some of his co-workers had mentioned that Send By Us, a large trucking company that delivered packages all over the world, was hiring and that they were giving preferential treatment to Vietnam veterans and minorities. Roberts sang along with the radio as he headed north on McCarter Highway toward Route 3. He couldn't be happier. Finally, things were going right for him. He was out of the Army; he had his own place, well almost his own place; he had a car; and now it looked like he might be getting a job. The best thing of all, though, was that he had received a letter from Dorothy that he carried in his shirt pocket for good luck.

After he filled out the application at SBU, he sat and waited for an interview with four other applicants. He pulled Dorothy's letter out of his shirt pocket and reread it for the hundredth time.

> *Hi, Soldier,*
>
> *I guess I should refer to you as a civilian now that you are out of the Army. I must tell you that I was pleasantly surprised to hear from you so soon. I was hoping that you wouldn't forget me, but I didn't expect to hear from you until I, too, became a civilian again.*
>
> *This war is not getting any better. I can't wait until my time is up and I am back in the real United States. Every day more and more wounded are coming in. It is becoming very disheartening, I'm glad to hear that you are picking up the pieces of your life.*
>
> *I will never forget the time I spent with you, especially the last night that we spent together in Hawaii. Continue to do good things with your life, but save a little corner for me. I'll be home before you know it.*
>
> *Sincerely, Dorothy*

Roberts folded the letter and put it back into his pocket. He had a smile of confidence on his face when they called him in for his interview. He had that same smile of confidence on his face as he drove the red Mustang back to Newark; he couldn't wait to tell his family that he was now back in uniform as a driver for SBU. He would begin work on Monday.

DRIVING THE TRUCK for SBU was a breeze compared to driving the truck with medical supplies for the Army. First of all, there were no jungles with Viet Cong lurking around to hijack his truck and, secondly, once he finished delivering the packages on his. route, he was finished for the day. Roberts reported to work in the morning at 7AM and generally finished up by 3PM. Sometimes he had to work an hour or so past three and sometimes he finished a little before three. It all balanced out in the long run, he figured.

The greatest difficulty he experienced was staying awake after lunch. He generally ate lunch in the truck, occasionally grabbing a bite at a local delicatessen or diner. His prescription called for him to take two pills in the morning with food, and two at dinnertime. He fought the urge to fall asleep in the mornings, as he had become accustomed to since he began taking the medication. Drinking lots of coffee during the day helped him stay awake. But after lunch the urge to sleep was too great.

One day Roberts had given into the urge to sleep, and it was almost three o'clock when he heard someone banging on the door of his truck. It was a customer who had been waiting for him to deliver a package. He had noticed the truck parked in front of his house for an hour and forty-five minutes before going out to investigate.

"I'm so very, very sorry. I must have dozed off," Roberts apologized profusely to the irate customer.

"I've been waiting all morning for this delivery, and here you are sleeping on the job. I'm not surprised. You people!" the irate customer said angrily.

"I'm sorry," Roberts said again as he jumped out of the truck and started walking up the driveway, carrying the package.

"Where are you going?" the customer asked in an angry tone. "Just give me the damn package."

"I can't do that," Roberts said. "I have to ring the bell and get a signature. It's company policy. We have to make sure the packages are put into the right hands."

The man stormed up the driveway and opened the door as Roberts rang the bell. He quickly signed for the package, snatched it out of Roberts' hands and then slammed the door in his face just as Roberts was about to apologize again.

Roberts decided then that he would adjust the medication himself and then talk to the doctor about it on his next visit. The adjustment seemed minor enough. In the mornings, he now took only one of the pills, but continued to take two in the evenings with his dinner. Roberts didn't notice any vast changes in his behavior once he altered the dosage, except that the urge to fall asleep during the day lessened considerably.

Eventually Roberts changed his evening dosage of medication, too. Normally he would fall asleep shortly after dinner. He would go up to his apartment with the intention of watching television, but he would always nod off shortly after the evening news. The war news generally depressed him so much that he was glad that the medication caused him to sleep, so that he would not have to think about it. Roberts' work and sleep routine caused him some concern. He knew this was no life for a bachelor.

ONE SATURDAY NIGHT Big Man called and suggested that he, Roberts, and Jeff get together for a rare night out on the town. "There's a boxing match going on later tonight at this gym on Springfield Avenue," he said. "A friend of mine knows the fighters. He said it should be a good match. It'll be fun anyway," Big Man said as though he had to convince Roberts.

Roberts and Jeff met Big Man at the pool room on West Market Street, around the corner from his house, at 6PM. Before they left for the gym, Roberts played a game of pool with Big Man while Jeff watched.

"I see you haven't lost your touch," Big Man said to Roberts after he sank his fifth consecutive ball into a pocket.

"This was the only form of recreation I had on the base for the last three years," Roberts said. "I've been waiting to show off my skill to you guys." He smiled and put another ball into a pocket.

They left the pool room and headed up to Laurel Gardens, a bar and grill on Springfield Avenue. Behind the bar and grill was a gym where aspiring boxers trained. Once a month it featured an amateur boxing match that cost ten dollars. They paid their ten dollars and went into the gym. The fight had just begun when they arrived. While they were still trying to decide where to sit, keeping their eyes on the fighters in the ring, the fight was over in the first round. The favorite fighter won by a knockout.

"Man, what a rip-off," Big Man said. "You pay ten hard-earned dollars to see a fight, and then the fight is over before you can even find a seat."

"Oh, well," Jeff said. "Let's go to the bar and have a beer. The whole night doesn't have to be a total waste."

At the bar, they met a couple of other guys that they had known through the years. They all sat together at the bar drinking beer, eating barbecued ribs, and laughing and talking the night away about the good old times in their twenty-two years of life. It turned out to be one of the best nights Roberts had had in a long time. As they were leaving the club, Big Man said, "We should do this on a regular basis; you know, a boys' night out."

Jeff was quick to agree. "Man, let's get together on Wednesday nights to shoot some hoops like we used to and go out for a few beers. I need some excitement in my life. My wife wants me to reserve Saturday nights for her, and my mom insists that we do the Sunday dinner thing with the family at her house. Weekends are for family as far as they're concerned." Jeff looked to his buddies for a commitment.

"Sounds good to me, man. What about you, Roberts?" Big Man was agreeable.

"I'm the bachelor here," Roberts said, laughing. "Any night is good for me. I don't have any family commitments. I thought you said shooting hoops was kid stuff?" Roberts reminded Big Man of his previous comments.

"We don't have to shoot hoops all the time. We can shoot pool or go to a movie, anything to break the monotony and have a chance to get together like old times."

Before the trio parted for the evening they had decided that Wednesday nights would be their night out. It was close to midnight when Roberts got home. He hadn't taken his dinner time medication. He took it before he went to bed.

THE BOYS NIGHT out was the beginning of a social life for Roberts. That first Wednesday night out, they went to the movies to see "Shaft." After the movie, they stopped at the Key Club on Halsey Street where Sarah Vaugh was singing to a packed audience.

"I didn't know she was going to be here tonight," Big Man said.

"If I'd know she was here, I would have skipped the movie," Jeff said. "Belinda is going to be mad when I tell her I saw Sarah at the Key Club. She loves Sarah Vaughn."

"Then don't tell her." Big Man looked at Jeff with a quizzical expression on his face. "Do you tell your wife everything?"

"Yeah," Jeff said, ignoring the look on Big Man's face.

Roberts enjoyed the time he spent out of his apartment so much that going out after work became his new routine. He seldom went directly home from work, choosing instead to eat his meals out where he could talk to other single people. He stopped taking the medication with his evening meal. Occasionally he would go to the gym at Felix Fuld Neighborhood House and get into a basketball game, or have a few beers at a neighborhood bar. Sometimes he would go the movies alone, but he would always meet the guys on Wednesday nights.

ONE WEDNESDAY NIGHT, the three men had parked their respective cars on Springfield Avenue and were walking in the direction of Laurel Gardens when a gun-toting teenager accosted them and asked them for their wallets. Roberts and Jeff tried to talk the teen into putting the gun down and avoiding the trouble such behavior would bring. The teen was tough, though. He got into Jeff's face and said "I'm the one with the gun; you're the one that's in trouble. Now just give me your wallet before I blow your brains out."

While the kid was in Jeff's face, Big Man circled behind the kid and grabbed his arms, Roberts acting quickly disarmed him and put the gun in his pocket. They held the kid for a while contemplating whether or not to call the police. Finally they let him go with a stern lecture.

"Are you going to give me back my gun?" the kid asked after Big Man released him.

"Are we on Mars?" Big Man asked the kid before he attempted to grab him again. The kid took off running up the street. Halfway up the block he stopped, then turned around and shouted out at them, "I'll have another gun by tomorrow. You better hope that I don't run into you guys again."

Over fried chicken sandwiches and glasses of Heineken, Big Man filled Roberts in on what had happened in Newark since the rebellion. "This place has become a war zone in the last four years. Guns are coming into the community at about the same rate they are going into Vietnam. Every kid can get his hands on a gun now." He shook his head in disbelief.

"Suburbanites wearing suits come into Newark and sell guns out of the trunks of their cars to teenagers," Jeff said in disgust. "They're not going to be happy until we all kill ourselves, at least the young men."

"They're no jobs in the city, no money; more businesses are moving out everyday," Big man said. "Despair is setting in, you know what that means? Drugs will be coming in droves. I hear that they have a new form of cocaine out in California that's very cheap. It's moving its way across the country. They're calling it "crack." Once it hits here, things will really get bad. Marsha is already talking about moving our family out of the city." He took a bite of his chicken sandwich and washed it down with a gulp of his beer.

"My mom is hopeful that the new mayor will make a difference," Roberts said.

"What difference can he make?" Big Man said. "White people

are offended. We will have to pay for this. Does your mother think that they will invest in a city that they were literally chased out of? They will make sure that they do everything in their power to bring this city down to its knees before they invest any money here." He finished up the last of his sandwich.

"Yeah," Jeff said. "We will have to hit rock bottom before any money comes into this city again. Even then it will only come if Whites feel that they can come back and be in charge again. That will be a long way off, at least forty or fifty years." He drained the last of his beer and stood up, signaling the others that it was time to go.

"Work day tomorrow," Big man said, getting up, too.

On the way to their respective cars, Roberts remembered the gun. "What are we going to do about the gun?" He fingered the weapon in his jacket pocket.

"You keep it," Big Man said. "You're the single man out on the town. You might need it one day."

"Yeah," Jeff said. "After our run in today with that little thug, I might just keep my black ass home from now on, where my old lady wants it to stay anyway." He laughed at his own words.

ROBERTS DIDN'T EXPECT to find anyone still up when he got home, but the soft dim light coming from the living room window let him know that someone was having a sleepless night or perhaps his sister was still entertaining her fiancé. He stopped in the living room before going up to his apartment. He was surprised to find his father still awake. "Can't sleep?" he asked from the doorway.

"No, I was just waiting up for you."

"Is everything okay?" Roberts took a seat in the armchair near the doorway.

"I heard on the news that there's been another shooting in Newark. I just wanted to make sure that you were all right."

"I'm all grown up now, Dad. You don't have to stay up worrying about me. I can take care of myself."

"I know all of that, David, but it doesn't stop me from worrying. This city is getting so dangerous."

Roberts couldn't help but smile. "That's the same thing the fellows and I were just talking about." He didn't tell his father about the incident with the gun, though.

"Things in this city are going to get a lot worse before they get better," Mr. Roberts said. "It don't sit well with White people to lose something that they considered theirs. I don't care if we do have a Black mayor, now. Political power without economic power is useless. White people have all the economic power and they will see to it that it stays that way. They won't allow us to accomplish much in this city."

"Don't you think that Blacks can empower themselves economically, Dad?" Roberts gazed at his father across the room.

"Sure, we can, but by the time we get things together enough to do that, they will have found a way to get control of this city again. We need a lot more than a Black mayor to maintain control in this city.

Black men came to this country in chains, and that's the way White people want to keep them."

Roberts took his medication before getting ready for bed. As he hung his clothes in the closet he felt the gun that was in his jacket pocket. He placed the gun high up in his closet, hidden in a hatbox under his army hat. He had no intention of ever using either of them.

Before he lay down he reread the latest letter he had received from Dorothy. He conjured up a picture of her in his mind. She was wearing the yellow sundress. He could see her face, a radiant smile lighting it up. He remembered the softness of her hand as he held it across the table. He remembered her scent; it was a nice gentle scent like the smell of spring flowers in the air. Roberts lay back on his pillow and allowed sweet memories of their time together to lull him to sleep.

CHAPTER

9

S pring was on its way out in Newark; the rains had ceased, the air smelled cleaner, and the trees were in full bloom. Driving the red Mustang up Central Avenue to the VA Hospital Roberts thought about how well his life had come together since his discharge from the army. The night terrors had not returned and he'd successfully adjusted his dosage of medication so that it did not interfere with his lifestyle.

He'd mentioned to a psychiatrist at the hospital – he got a different one each month – that he was only taking one pill in the morning and two at night before going to sleep. The psychiatrist had only nodded and asked if he was experiencing any night terrors. When Roberts told him no, he only nodded again and dismissed him until the next month.

It was still early when Roberts left the VA Hospital, only four o'clock. He'd finished work early enough to take care of a few things, and the doctor's visit had been his first order of business.

Now he headed up to Bloomfield, NJ, where he had an appointment for a fitting for a tuxedo for his sister's wedding. Deneen wanted everything right for her wedding, which was only two weeks away. She wanted to make sure all the groomsmen had well fitted-tuxedos to go along with the perfectly attired bridesmaids.

Since the Newark rebellion, it appeared that most orders of business had to be taken care of out of the city. There were no more shops where one could go for a fitting for formal attire. No more supermarkets, no more car dealerships, and only a few neighborhood drugstores were left. He wanted to get some stationery to write a letter to Dorothy. Her last letter to him had made him so happy. She was coming home. Her tour of duty would be over the middle of June. She expected to be back in Ohio by the beginning of July.

A wrong turn off Bloomfield Avenue caused Roberts to get lost. He drove around looking for familiar streets that he thought would get him to the shop, only to become more confused. Before he knew it, he was in the South Mountain Reservation. *How did I get here?* he wondered. For a brief moment he thought he was lost in the jungles of Vietnam again. Panic set in, and he started to perspire excessively.

Roberts looked around and realized that he was in a park of some sort. He could not ever remember being there before. The park was deserted, and he felt panic building up in him again. He drove the car frantically, looking for a way out. His imagination began to play tricks on him. He heard a loud booming sound. *Bombs*, he thought.

The car was speeding through the park now. Suddenly he heard sirens. He was still sweating and in a state of panic. He looked in the rearview mirror and saw a police car with a lone officer following him. He was signaling him to pull over.

The officer, a tall White man who appeared to be in his mid to late forties, asked Roberts to step out of the car. Roberts obliged. The officer asked to see his license and registration.

"There're in my wallet, in my back pocket, sir," Roberts responded politely just as though he was speaking to an army officer.

"Reach with your left hand behind you and pull out your wallet, boy," the officer said.

Obliging again, Roberts handed the officer his wallet.

Ignoring the gesture, the officer said "now take out your license and registration,"

While Roberts fumbled through his wallet, looking for the requested documents, the officer took notice of his dog tags that had come from under his open collared shirt.

"You a soldier, boy?" he asked gruffly.

"I was, sir; I was just discharged a few months ago."

"Was it an honorable discharge?" The officer eyed him up and down.

"Yes, sir, I was wounded in Vietnam."

"My son is serving in Vietnam now. How was it over there?" The officer appeared to be softening.

"It was hell over there, sir."

"Hmm," the officer said. "I can imagine."

The officer let him off with a warning after telling him that he could have killed someone driving so recklessly. Roberts expressed his gratitude and drove slowly off the reservation, following the directions the officer gave him to get to the formal wear shop. He was still shaken from the incident, though, and noted that he would tell the psychiatrist about it next month.

DENEEN'S WEDDING WAS beautiful. Over one hundred guests were at the reception held in the upstairs banquet room at the Laurel Gardens on Springfield Avenue in the Central Ward of Newark. Roberts had the time of his life; all of his friends were there along with extended family members from as far away as South Carolina and Florida. He danced, ate, and drank with his friends, maybe a little too much.

At the end of the reception, after the bride and groom had departed for their honeymoon, a slight altercation took place between two of the groomsmen. It appeared to be over the attention of a particular bridesmaid. Roberts stepped in to help resolve the situation. Somehow he lost focus of his surroundings. He looked at the two men in tuxedos and saw soldiers.

"Be quiet," he yelled at them. "Do you want them to hear us? If they hear us, they'll kill us, so shut up."

"What are you talking about?" one of the groomsmen asked.

"Yeah, man," the other one said. "You need to go home and sleep it off."

"Shhh," Roberts tried to quiet the two. "They're all around us. Do you want to die?" His eyes moved about the room in a frightened manner.

"Man, you're crazy."

Roberts pounced on the groomsman and began choking him, "Didn't I tell you to be quiet?"

Big Man and Jeff pulled Roberts off the groomsman, dragging him outside, while explaining to the remaining guests that Roberts had had too much to drink.

THE DAY AFTER THE reception, Sunday, Roberts woke up with a severe headache and no memory of the incident that had taken place at the reception. He had no idea how he got home or who helped him get out of the tuxedo. He showered and dressed and went downstairs to get something to eat. He was glad that his parents were at church, he didn't feel like talking to anybody.

Roberts fixed himself some toast and eggs, made some instant coffee and sat down to eat. No sooner had he put the first forkful of eggs in his mouth than the doorbell rang. He picked up his cup of coffee, took a sip and went to answer the door. He was surprised to find Big Man and Jeff leaning on the bell. "What the hell are you two doing here so early on a Sunday morning?" he asked, looking at them with a surprised look on his face.

Big Man was the first to speak. "Man, after what happened at the reception yesterday, we were worried about you." He walked past Roberts and into the house. Jeff followed him.

"Come on in," Roberts said sarcastically, still holding the door.

Big Man walked straight to the kitchen. Jeff and Roberts tagged along behind him. He looked around and asked, "Where are your folks?"

"Church, I guess." Roberts sat down at the kitchen table and resumed eating his breakfast.

"What happened to you?" Big Man asked, grabbing a piece of Roberts' toast.

"What are you talking about?" Roberts gave him a puzzled look.

"Man, he doesn't know," Jeff said in total disbelief. "You went off last night, behaving as though you were still in Vietnam. We had to pull you off one of the brothers."

"No way," Roberts stopped eating and stared at his two friends, his mouth hanging open.

"Man, I thought you were going to kill him," Jeff said, searching for something to eat.

"Did my parents see this?" Roberts was concerned; he didn't want his parents to worry.

"No. They had already left the reception. We drove you around for awhile until we figured they were in bed," Big Man said. "Then we helped you up to your apartment and put you to bed. You had passed out by then."

"I really don't remember," Roberts said. "My memory has been playing tricks on me. There's so much that I can't remember, yet every now and then I remember something."

"They're flashbacks," Big Man said. "I've been reading that some of the Vietnam veterans are experiencing these flashbacks. Is that why you're going to the VA Hospital?"

Roberts told his friends about his stay in the hospital in Hawaii. They'd wondered why he was in the hospital for so long when they'd been told his injuries were not life threatening. He told them about the medication he was taking and the affect it was having on him. He told them about the incident at the South Mountain Reservation. When he finished, he was relieved. He no longer felt alone with his problem.

"After the trauma you've gone through--fighting a war thousands of miles from home, killing people that you didn't even know, and watching your best friend die right in front of you--you would think they would provide you with more than a few pills every month." Big Man shook his head, disgusted. "Are you talking about this to the psychiatrist, is he helping you to put things in perspective?"

"Not really," Roberts said. "They just want to know how the medication is working, whether or not I still have the night terrors. I haven't really talked about the war with anyone."

"Maybe you should, man," Jeff said. "I think you need to be deprogrammed or whatever. Look at what happened to that rich White girl from California. When the Symbionese Liberation Army released her, they said that she had to be deprogrammed. She needed extensive psychotherapy to function normally again. Maybe that's what you need, man."

"They're not going to provide extensive psychotherapy to a Black man," Big Man said. "The entire emotional trauma that we've experienced and continue to experience in America at the hands of White people, including slavery, discrimination and racism, has gone untreated. We're supposed to just get over shit. People believe that Black people are equipped to handle trauma without any help, but White people need valium and psychotherapy just to get through a normal day." Big Man stood up, ready to leave.

"What you need is a woman," Jeff said. "The love of a good woman will make you forget all kinds of trauma, trust me," he laughed and stood up with Big Man. "Haven't you met anyone, yet?"

Roberts lead the way to the front door. "As a matter of fact I have met someone, a nurse I met in Hawaii. We've been writing to each other."

"You need someone in Newark, man," Big Man said. "Hawaii is in the middle of the Pacific Ocean, and letters do not comfort you at night between the sheets."

"She's coming home. She'll be back home in Ohio in less than two weeks." Roberts had a big smile on his face as he led his friends to the front door to let them out.

"Ohio?" Big Man said. "That's almost as bad as Hawaii. With all of these pretty women in Newark, why can't you find a Newark woman?"

"She's the one for me, Big Man. I can just feel it," Roberts said, watching his friends leave the house.

"Maybe you should talk to your dad about the war," Jeff said on his way out the door. "He experienced World War II. He may just be able to relate to what you're experiencing."

"Good idea," Big Man said, giving Roberts a pat on the back as he left.

AT 4PM ROBERTS heard a soft knock on the door to his apartment. He had spent the time following his friends' departure reading the newspapers and watching the tennis matches on television. Arthur Ashe, an African American, was the favorite to win Wimbledon this year. Roberts wasn't a tennis enthusiast, but he liked showing support for African-American athletes; they so seldom got a chance to make it to the big times.

When he opened the door, he was surprised to see his father holding a plate of food covered with one of his mother's dishtowels. His mother was a frequent visitor to his little attic apartment, bringing him clean sheets and towels every week. His father, though, had not been up to the apartment since he had helped him bring some of his things up from the basement where they had been stored while he was away. He considered the visit an omen. Maybe Jeff was right, and he should talk to his father about his war experiences.

"I hope I'm not intruding," said Mr. Roberts as he entered the apartment. "Your mother wanted you to have some of her meatloaf; she knows how much you like it." He handed his son the plate.

"Thanks, Dad." Roberts took the plate, pulled the dishcloth off, and savored the aroma of the food.

"Are you busy, Son?" the older man asked. Something was obviously on his mind.

"No, what's up?" Roberts placed the plate on the coffee table, made himself comfortable on the sofa and then dug into the food."

"Your Aunt Louise shared something with me today that I found very disturbing. Your cousin Cynthia told her about this thing last night." Mr. Roberts avoided eye contact with his son.

Aunt Louise was Mr. Robert's older sister, and Cynthia was her youngest daughter. They had both been at the reception yesterday. Roberts wondered if perhaps one or both of them had witnessed the incident.

"What is it, Dad?" Roberts chewed slowly on the tasty collard greens his mother had put on the plate with the meatloaf.

"Cynthia told her mother that she witnessed an incident involving you at the reception. She said that your behavior was bizarre, like you were still in the war. What happened, Son? Can you tell me about it?"

Roberts told his father what Big Man and Jeff had shared with him. He also told him about the incident at the South Mountain Reservation. Again he felt a sense of relief when he got the story out. He looked at his father when he finished giving him all the information and saw the look of concern on his dad's face.

"I don't want you to worry about this, Dad. It's my problem. I'll handle it. I hope you didn't tell Mom."

"I didn't have to; Louise told us the story in the car when we gave her a ride home from church. Your mother is just as concerned as I am. Any serious problem that our child is having is our problem, too. You'll understand this when you become a father."

"I'm glad you know, Dad. I was going to tell you anyway. I wanted to know if you had experienced anything like this when you got out of the service after the war."

"I don't think that I experienced any flashbacks like what you're experiencing, but I had memories that I wanted to forget. It took me a long time to bury those memories, but I've kept them buried for a long time now. Taking care of my family has consumed my energy for the past twenty-something years. I haven't thought about the war in a long time. I hope that with time you'll be able to forget, too. Maybe once you have some responsibility, it will help you to forget."

Long after his father had left the apartment and the tennis matches were over, Roberts pulled out a copy of the last letter he had received from Dorothy. He read the last line of the letter over and over again. *It would be wonderful if you could drive up to Oxford, Ohio, for the Fourth of July holiday. I would love to see you again.* She had signed the letter *Love, Dorothy.*

When Roberts turned in for the night, his thoughts were on Nurse Dorothy Campbell. He made up his mind that he would be in Oxford, Ohio, for the Fourth of July.

KILL . . . OR BE KILLED

CHAPTER

10

The drive from Newark to Ohio was long, scenic, and relaxing. Route 80 runs right through the Delaware Water Gap, a beautiful sight. From the water gap, the drive winds through Pennsylvania, a mountainous region with rolling hills, lush foliage, and clean and refreshing air. Roberts sat back in the Mustang and took in the sights for the next ten hours. His mind was on Dorothy. He pictured her in the yellow sun dress, with her beautiful golden skin radiant and glowing.

Dorothy's letters to him had been sweet and encouraging. He imagined he could have a future with her. Since his return from the military, he had not met anyone that he could get serious about. There were a few women that he had met on his evenings about town in Newark that appeared interested in him. Roberts would sometimes buy a drink for a woman that he met in a bar, or talk to women that he met at Laurel Gardens. They often gave him their phone numbers, but he never called. None of these women excited him the way that Dorothy had.

The drive through Pennsylvania was the longest part of the journey. *This must be one of the largest states in the Union,* Roberts thought as he approached a road sign stating that he was leaving Pennsylvania. The sign welcoming him to Ohio made him smile. *Not much longer now.* He popped another cassette into his tape deck. The sounds of *Earth, Wind, and Fire* permeated the car.

Before he left Newark, Roberts had telephoned Dorothy to let her know what time he expected to arrive. She had appeared just as excited about their meeting as he was. She had asked him about his treatment, though. She wanted to know if he was still taking his medication and if the doctors were helping him. *She must be worried that I might have had another episode*, Roberts had concluded. He was at the VA Hospital the week after the incident at the reception. The doctor told him not to drink alcohol while he was taking the medication. He had offered no other recommendations and did not appear to be concerned that Roberts had attacked someone at his sister's wedding reception. Roberts did not tell Dorothy about the incident; he didn't want to worry her.

It was 5PM when the red Mustang finally pulled up to a white farmhouse with green shutters sitting on a beautifully landscaped front yard. There were three vehicles already parked in the driveway, so Roberts parked his car on the road in front of the house. He slowly got out of the car and opened the trunk to take out gifts he had bought for Dorothy and her mother. He was bending over the trunk of his car, while getting the packages out, when he felt a hand on his arm. He turned around and looked into the beautiful, smiling face of Dorothy.

Roberts swept Dorothy up into his arms and swung her around. Her laughter was like music to his ears. He held her in his arms, feeling the warmth of her body for almost a minute before she pulled away. He put her down, but continued to look at her.

"Did you have any trouble finding us?" She stood back to get a good luck at him. "You look thinner, are you eating okay?"

"No, I didn't have any trouble finding you at all; and, yes, I've been eating just fine. The reason I've lost weight is because I'm getting plenty of exercise working. I'm not just lying around in a hospital bed all day." He grinned at her.

Dorothy looked at the two colorfully wrapped boxes he had taken from the trunk and said, "Aren't you going to bring your bag into the house?"

"I didn't know where I would be sleeping tonight. I don't want your parents to think I'm being presumptuous coming into their home with an overnight bag."

"You'll spend the night with us, of course, silly," Dorothy said, reaching for the overnight bag.

Roberts grabbed her arm, "I'll come back for it once I've had a formal invitation from your parents," he said, closing the truck.

"What's in the boxes?" Dorothy asked, eyeing the gifts.

"This one is for you." Roberts handed the smaller of the two boxes to her. "The other one is for your mother."

"You didn't have to buy us gifts," Dorothy squeezed his hand and gave him a warm smile, then she tore the paper off the box.

"My mother taught me never to go on a visit to someone's home empty handed," Roberts said. He smiled at the look of delight on her face when she opened the box.

"I like your mother already." Dorothy said looking at the gift, a bottle of her favorite perfume. Then she took his hand and led him to the house.

ROBERTS LIKED DOROTHY'S mother right from the beginning as well. She had a pleasant disposition and made him feel right at home. Mrs. Campbell was about the same age as his mother. She was a little shorter than Dorothy, and Roberts could tell that she had been just as pretty as Dorothy when she was younger. She was still a good-looking woman, even with graying hair and being slightly overweight.

Mrs. Campbell went out of her way to make him feel at home. She had homemade lemonade and freshly baked tollhouse cookies awaiting his arrival. She was delighted with the crystal candleholders that he had given her. She sent him right back out to his car to get his overnight bag so that Dorothy could show him to his room where he could freshen up for dinner. Mr. Campbell would be home shortly and they would all sit down to dinner.

The room Dorothy showed him looked as comfortable as the rest of the house. A handmade quilt with matching pillow shams made the bed look very inviting. Roberts put his bag on the floor and sat on the bed. He was tired from the long drive.

"The bathroom is down the hall on your right." Dorothy said as she opened the window and let a fresh summer breeze enter the room. "Why don't I leave and let you get some rest?" She turned toward the door.

"Not yet." Roberts grabbed her hand and pulled her down next to him on the bed. "I'm so happy to see you again." He kissed her gently on the lips. "I've been dreaming about this moment." He pulled her against his body.

"I'm just as happy to see you. But right now I've got to help Momma get dinner ready. Daddy will be here any minute. You just rest until I call you to come down for dinner." She stood up, still holding his hand. Roberts kissed her hand and watched her go out the door. He lay down on the bed with a big grin on his face and thoughts of Dorothy on his mind, before he drifted off to sleep.

DINNER WAS SCRUMPTIOUS. Dorothy and her Mom had cooked a meal fit for a king. There was baked ham, smothered chicken, and pot roast with roasted potatoes. Cabbage, green beans, and asparagus accompanied the entrees. Mrs. Campbell uncovered a basket of home-made dinner rolls that were soon melting in Roberts' mouth. He hadn't seen so much food since he first came home from the army. He complimented Mrs. Campbell on her cooking.

"I didn't think anyone could cook as good as my mother, but in a contest I don't know which of you would come in first. It would probably be a tie."

"I've never tasted your mother's cooking, but if it tastes anything like my wife's then you are a very lucky man, indeed," Mr. Campbell said, unbuckling his belt.

"Both of my daughters have turned into fine cooks, too," Mrs. Campbell said, looking at Dorothy.

"Sandra is a much better cook than I am, Mom," Dorothy said, referring to her older sister.

"You're both good cooks," Mr. Campbell said. "Sandra just has more experience cooking than you because she got married early and concentrated her efforts on being a good wife and mother. She never had an interest in pursuing a career that would take her away from her family like yours did."

"Like I already said, both my daughters are fine cooks." Mrs. Campbell hoped to put an end to the discussion that she feared was taking them away from her point. "A good portion of this meal was prepared by Dorothy and we'll have an opportunity to sample Sandra's cooking tomorrow at the Fourth of July celebration. When will you be leaving to go back to New Jersey, Mr. Roberts?

"Since the holiday falls on a Sunday, I have Monday off from work. I thought I'd leave on Monday, right after breakfast if that's all right with you." Roberts looked at Mr. Campbell for his approval.

"I've always said that the men who get to marry my daughters are getting a prize. Not only are they both beautiful, like their mother, but they are great cooks like her, too." Mr. Roberts finished off the last of his carrot cake made with cream cheese icing.

Following dinner, Mr. Campbell stood up rather abruptly. He wasn't a very big man, only about five-feet-ten inches tall, but he had a commanding appearance. His gray hair and mustache gave him a distinguished look. He seldom smiled, but he had a twinkle in his eyes that let you know he was smiling inwardly. He invited Roberts into the living room for an after dinner brandy while the women cleaned up the dinner dishes. Once they were in the den, Roberts declined the offer of brandy, instead asking for a ginger ale.

Pouring himself a glass of brandy, Mr. Campbell asked, "Are you a non-drinker?"

"I drink occasionally." Roberts chose not to elaborate on the question.

"I admire men that control their drinking." Mr. Campbell handed Roberts a glass of ginger ale on the rocks. "I make it a habit of having a glass of brandy after dinner every night, and that's my total consumption of alcohol." He sat down in the comfortable looking armchair that Roberts surmised was his own personal chair.

"My daughter tells me that you're a Vietnam veteran, and that you were injured in the war. Have you fully recovered from your injuries?" Mr. Campbell took a sip of his brandy.

"My physical injuries are healed, but there are still some emotional scars that I am dealing with." Roberts wanted to be as truthful as possible, without divulging too much information. "I'm being treated at the VA Hospital in New Jersey." He sat back on the sofa admiring the décor of the room. There were family pictures on the mantle above the fireplace and lots of framed family portraits covering the walls. He was particularly taken with a portrait of Dorothy in a graduation cap and gown. She looked beautiful.

"The emotional scars take the longest to heal, if they ever do heal," said Mr. Campbell. "Mine have never fully healed."

"Are you a World War II veteran?" Roberts sat on the edge of his seat.

"I most certainly am. I served in the 35th infantry division of the United States Marines. An experience I will never forget and never get over." Mr. Campbell took another sip of his brandy. "Even though the Marines were integrated by then, the racism was almost more overwhelming than the war. Since then I try to have as little to do with White people as possible. I stay here and run my little farm getting pleasure from my family and friends. They're the only people that I come in contact with 29 or 30 days of the month.

"Are you saying that you never leave the farm, Mr. Campbell?"

"I mean that I rarely leave Oxford. I try to limit my contact with the outside world as much as possible. The war did that to me, you know."

"My father is a lot like that. He's a World War II veteran, too. He limits his relationships to family and friends, too. He never goes to restaurants, movies, or large social events outside the community."

"It sounds like your father and I have a lot in common. But here in Oxford, there's little reason to leave the area. I don't know if

Dorothy told you, but Oxford is a Black town. Founded by free Blacks and escaped slaves in the middle of the 19th Century. My grandfather was one of the founders. Is the racism in the military as prevalent now as it was back then?"

"I don't think so; at least it is not as overt as it was back in the forties. The army has changed a great deal from what my father tells me. If it were not for war, I think I could have made a career of the army, but I could never be in another war."

"War is hell," Mr. Campbell said. "Killing people for reasons you never fully understand is something you will never get over. I never could understand why my little girl wanted to be involved with war, even if she never saw any of the action. There are plenty of places right here in Ohio where she could have gotten a job as a nurse. She didn't have to join the army."

"I'm glad she did," Roberts said, looking up to see a smiling Dorothy enter the room.

"What are you glad about?" She asked, sitting down next to him on the couch.

"I'm glad you wanted to be an army nurse, otherwise I never would have met you." Roberts reached for her hand.

Standing up and pulling Roberts up with her, Dorothy announced to her father, "I'm taking my guest on a tour around the farm. We'll be back later, but don't wait up for us." She pulled Roberts toward the front door.

The tour of the Campbell farm was a new experience for Roberts.

In all his twenty-two years he had never been on a farm. Dorothy drove her father's pickup truck, and the first place they visited was the fields. They grew corn, potatoes, soybeans, broccoli, peppers and other organic vegetables. Mr. Campbell was convinced that organically grown foods were healthier and reduced the chances of contracting cancer and other diseases. Dorothy told him that her father worked on the farm from sunup to sundown most days. He didn't mind the long hours because he was the boss. He loved the farm that had been in his family for over one hundred years.

Dorothy's great grandfather escaped from slavery in Alabama in 1863, he was only nineteen years old. He crossed the Ohio River with the help of the Underground Railroad and settled in Oxford before it was even a town. He managed to elude slave hunters for two years until the Emancipation Proclamation. By then he had managed to save enough money from his earnings as a farmhand to buy a piece of land for himself. Twenty-two years later her grandfather was born on the farm in 1885.

"My father was born on this farm in 1918," Dorothy said, as they sat in the truck looking out at the fields. "We have 140 acres here," she said proudly. "This farm is in our blood. Sometimes I think my father is so disappointed that he never had a son to pass the farm down to; but, my sister has two boys that make up for it a little bit." She laughed happily.

"Do you think your nephews will be interested in farming?" Roberts breathed in the fresh country air, feeling better than he had in years.

"I don't know. Their father owns the farm adjacent to us. It's been in his family for a very long time. Over twenty Black farm families founded the town of Oxford. Most of them still live here along with countless other Black farmers that have moved here in the last fifty years or so. Farming is in their blood. My nephews adore their father and will probably want to follow in his footsteps."

"What about you, Dorothy. What is it that you want to do with your life? Do you want to be a farm girl forever, like your mother?"

"Oh, my mother was never a farm girl, not until she married my father. My mother grew up in Dayton, Ohio. Dayton is a city, you know."

"I've heard of Dayton," Roberts said, looking at the sun as it positioned itself to make its descent.

"My mother met my father at a church social. He was visiting some friends in Dayton at the time. They've been together since 1950."

"You still haven't answered my question. What do you want to do with your life?"

"I'm a lot like my mother; the lure of the city is in me. I love visiting my grandparents and cousins in Dayton, but I love the farm too. I'm going to move to Dayton in a few weeks to look for a job. I don't anticipate any problem; nurses are in high demand everywhere." She put the truck in gear and headed in a westerly direction.

The final stop on the tour was the barn. It looked just like the pictures of barns that Roberts had seen in his childhood books. He waited in anticipation, expecting to see farm animals in the barn.

"Where are the animals?" he asked after Dorothy opened the door, and held it for him to enter.

"We don't have many animals any more." She laughed at his surprise. "Daddy concentrates on growing organic food now, but we have a grass fed cow for milk and a few free-range chickens Momma keeps around for eggs." As they walked through the barn, Roberts noticed the haystacks.

"Why do you keep hay, if you don't have animals?"

"Most of it is left over from when we did have animals. Some of it is for the cow; she still likes to chew it." Dorothy climbed a ladder leading up to a loft. Roberts followed her.

"This is my favorite spot in the barn. We can watch the sun make its final descent from that window." She led him to her favorite spot.

They lay on a bed of hay and watched the sun set. The sky was magnificent, hues of red, yellow and orange exploded in a kaleidoscope of color. Roberts pulled Dorothy into his arms. He kissed her forehead, her chin, her cheeks, her neck and then her mouth. She eagerly returned his affection. Without a word, they undressed slowly. Then they continued exploring each other's bodies with their hands, lips and tongues. He removed a condom from his pants pocket that he had brought along just in case he would need it. Later, they lay entwined in each other's arms, caressing and feeling satisfied beyond their wildest expectations.

"That was a first for me," Dorothy said as she lay in his arms gazing through the window at the moon that now lit up the sky.

Roberts smiled. He wasn't sure if he should tell Dorothy that it was a first for him, too. The closest he had ever come before was with Rachel. But she wanted to hold out until marriage. Opportunities for sexual encounters were plentiful in the military; there were always women willing to sleep with a soldier, some for money, some for free. But the movies and lectures Roberts saw during basic training, warning of the dangers of sexually transmitted diseases had discouraged him from having casual sex with anyone. He, too, was waiting for the right lady.

"Me, too," he finally whispered in her ear.

KILL . . . OR BE KILLED

CHAPTER

11

*T*hree weeks later Roberts was driving up Route 80, heading to Ohio again. In the past three weeks, he had spoken to Dorothy on the telephone a total of nine times and written her three letters. He was falling in love. From the telephone conversations and letters that she had written him, it appeared that Dorothy was falling in love, too.

Dorothy had landed a nurse's job at Dayton General Hospital and was moving into her own apartment near the hospital that same morning. Roberts was going to spend Saturday night and Sunday morning with her; leaving in the early afternoon to return to Newark to prepare for work on Monday morning. He was happier than he could ever remember being before, or at least for a very long time.

The drive to Ohio seemed to fly by. He'd brought along his favorite cassette tapes to listen to, helping to pass the time and keep him company. The music of The Drifters, Marvin Gaye, Diana Ross and the Supremes, and the whole Motown Revue blared in the car as it rolled past the mountains of Pennsylvania. It wasn't until Roberts was turning off the highway into the city of Dayton that he realized he had misplaced the directions Dorothy had given him to her new apartment. He started to panic. *I must have dropped them when I stopped at that last rest stop in Pennsylvania,* he thought.

Dorothy didn't have telephone service in her new apartment yet, so he couldn't call her. He thought about calling her parents, figuring *they'll know her new address.* Then he remembered that Dorothy had told him that her parents would be at a weekend church revival until Sunday night. He wished he had taken the address and phone number of Dorothy's sister while he was visiting at her home three weeks ago. He didn't know anyone else in Ohio that he could contact.

Once in Dayton, Roberts drove up and down the side streets off the main street, thinking if he saw Dorothy's street he would recognize the name. After an hour of this, he was becoming frantic. What could he do? He certainly didn't want to turn around and head back to New Jersey, and he didn't want to spend the night in a motel when he knew Dorothy was waiting for him with a home-cooked meal and a warm bed.

Just as he turned the corner, putting him back on the main street for the fourth time, Roberts noticed two soldiers in dress uniform heading up the street. His heart began to pound, and he began to perspire profusely. He stared at the two men, convinced that one of them was Greg. *Greg isn't dead,* he thought. What was happening?

Was he hallucinating in broad daylight again? He followed the two soldiers to a silver Chevrolet, Impala. He watched the men get into the car, they were laughing and kidding around just like he and Greg used to do. He followed them when they drove off.

The two soldiers drove in a circuitous route, looking behind them every few minutes. Roberts kept up with them. He followed them into an alley and panicked when he thought he lost them, but then he spotted the Impala parked at the end of the alley, it was empty of driver and passenger. Roberts pulled over and parked behind the car. He got out of the Mustang and walked over to the Impala. He looked inside the vehicle; he even tried to open the door. Finally he turned away, scratching his head in disbelief. He was totally confused.

When he reached his car, he noticed the two soldiers standing in the shadows of a nearby building looking at him. They approached him.

"Is that you, Greg?" Roberts asked the taller of the two emerging figures.

"Who are you and why did you follow us?" The shorter of the two soldiers asked.

"Don't you know me, it's Roberts?" Roberts smiled at the soldier. "They said you were dead, killed in Vietnam."

"He's not Greg, mister. You have him confused with someone else."

"Greg, it's me, Roberts. We went to school together. We fought together in Vietnam."

"Are you a Vietnam veteran?" The taller soldier spoke for the first time.

"Why are you asking me that? You know that I am. What are you trying to pull?" Roberts shook his head as though trying to clear it.

"What are you doing in Dayton?" the shorter soldier asked after noticing the New Jersey plates.

"I'm here to visit my girl. She's a nurse. She lives in Dayton, but I got lost. I can't find her house, and she doesn't have a phone yet."

"Where does she work?" the taller soldier asked.

"Dayton General Hospital," Roberts said. "In the emergency room."

"What's her name?"

"Dorothy Campbell," Roberts said, beginning to relax a little more now.

"My mom works there," the shorter soldier said. "Maybe she can help us." He spoke to the taller soldier in a whisper for a few minutes.

"Get back into your car and follow us," the taller soldier said.

Roberts climbed into his car and followed the two soldiers as they had requested. They pulled up to the emergency entrance of Dayton General Hospital. The shorter soldier got out of the car and went into the hospital. The taller one got out and walked up to the Mustang. "You got any identification," he asked.

Roberts gave him his drivers' license and his military honorable discharge card.

"Wait here," the taller soldier said before following his buddy into the hospital.

A half hour later they both came out of the emergency entrance together. They walked up to the Mustang, and the taller soldier gave Roberts his identification back.

"Follow us," the taller soldier said before he and the other soldier climbed into the Impala again.

Roberts followed the two soldiers for a five-minute ride to a five-story apartment building on a quiet, tree-lined street. The sun had set, and Roberts was already three hours late.

"Wait here," the shorter soldier said over his shoulder as he and the taller soldier went into the building.

Five minutes later Roberts looked up and saw Dorothy running from the building with the two soldiers walking behind her. Roberts opened the door and rushed into her arms.

"I was so worried about you. What happened? Where were you?" Dorothy looked frantic; she had tears in her eyes.

"Take care of him," the taller soldier said to Dorothy as the two men walked to their car. "He still appears a little confused."

"How can I ever thank you?" Roberts asked, fully cognizant now.

"Just stay out of trouble and always help a fellow soldier when you can." They got into their car and started the engine.

"What are your names?" Roberts called out just before they pulled off.

"Just call me Greg," the taller one said to the laughter of the shorter soldier. They drove off down the street.

DOROTHY'S APARTMENT WAS spacious but sparsely furnished. They entered a foyer, right next to the living room. Only a credenza and chair furnished the large room.

"I know it looks bare right now, but I plan to get a sofa and some tables soon. My parents let me take the credenza and the chair from their attic. Come and let me show you the kitchen." She took him into the roomy kitchen.

The kitchen was cheery, the walls were painted a bright yellow, and the cabinets and counter tops were white. A center island served as a table and there were two barstools for sitting. There was a large window in the kitchen, and Roberts could tell that it would be dark shortly. He could see the sky from the window and what remained of a sunset, which let him know that the kitchen faced west. Dorothy hadn't gotten around to putting up curtains yet, but there were two potted African-violet plants sitting on the windowsill.

"Something sure smells good in here, and I'm starving," Roberts said, walking over to an apartment sized stove.

"When was the last time you ate?" Dorothy asked, standing back and watching him.

"I left home at 5AM without having any breakfast. I stopped in Pennsylvania and had a hot dog and a root beer, that's where I think I lost the directions you gave me to your house." Roberts took the lid off a pot and looked into it.

"So that's what happened." Dorothy breathed a sign of relief.

"What did you think happened?" He replaced the lid and looked into another pot.

"I didn't know. I was getting panicky by the time the soldiers showed up. They told me that a very confused young man was downstairs in a red Mustang asking for me. I asked them how they found me, and they said they went to my job. Luckily, one of the soldier's mother knew someone at the hospital that knew me. What did they mean when they said that you were confused?" She looked at him for an explanation.

"I'll tell you over dinner." Roberts continued snooping in the pots and savoring each smell, prompting Dorothy to wash her hands at the kitchen sink and begin fixing plates of food for them.

While they ate steamed cabbage with hot corn bread and barbecued chicken at the center island, sitting on the tall bar stools, Roberts told Dorothy all about his confusion with the two soldiers, holding nothing back. When he finished he felt as though a large burden had been removed from his chest.

"That must have been some experience," she said, and then got up and started to clear away the dinner dishes. "Has it ever happened before?"

Roberts told her about his getting lost at the South Mountain Reservation and the incident that occurred the night of his sister's wedding reception.

"I've met other soldiers that I nursed in the hospital who were suffering with flashbacks of memories they wanted to forget. Some of them seemed to be undergoing such torture. Do you have painful memories, too?"

"That's just it; I can't remember much of anything. I couldn't even remember Greg's death. He was my best friend since childhood. We served together in Vietnam. At home, they consider me a hero for trying to save his life, but I don't remember any of it." Roberts dried the dishes while Dorothy washed.

"Maybe the flashbacks are your memory trying to come back. You can't suppress stuff like that forever, even in the recesses of your mind. What do the doctors say?" She hung up the dishtowel and began putting away the dishes.

"You don't think I'm crazy, do you?" Roberts looked at her in all earnestness.

"No, I just think that you will have to learn to deal with each painful memory as it materializes. Luckily, they are coming back one at a time. Do you think you can deal with them?" She stopped putting away the dishes and faced him, a concerned look on her face.

Roberts took Dorothy in his arms and held her tight. "Baby, as long as I have you, I can deal with anything." He kissed her passionately.

Finally Dorothy showed him the bedroom. The bedroom was the most furnished room in the house. There was a queen-size bed all made up with a beautiful pink and white comforter and at least a half-dozen accent pillows in various colors and sizes tossed about. On each side of the bed was a matching night table. A triple dresser took up almost one whole wall, and a large armoire completed the set.

Roberts fell backwards on the bed, pulling Dorothy down on top of him. "What do you think, Dorothy? Do you think you could grow to care for a mixed-up guy like me?"

"I already care a great deal for you. I don't see that changing anytime soon." They kissed and slowly began to undress each other on top of the queen-size bed where they spent the remainder of the weekend.

CHAPTER

12

*D*riving the SBU truck five days a week for eight hours a day, and then driving six-hundred miles each way to Dayton, Ohio, every weekend became Roberts' routine over the next few weeks. He rarely missed a weekend being with Dorothy. He lived for the weekends, and the thought of being with her was enough to keep him in smiles all week long. He stopped hanging out after work and spent most of his time in his apartment talking to Dorothy on the telephone, listening to music, or watching television.

Roberts avoided the evening news. War stories made up 90 percent of the news on television and he tried to avoid them as much as possible. *Dorothy is right--the flashbacks are my memory trying to come back,* he convinced himself. Watching news of the war on television would oftentimes trigger a flashback, and on a couple of occasions Roberts found himself cowering in a corner of his room trying to fend off the memories. He learned to replace those memories with thoughts of Dorothy. The war memories would go away, and he could smile again.

Once he chased away a particularly bad memory with thoughts of him and Dorothy at a county fair in Oxford. It was Labor Day Weekend, and he'd had three days off from work, meaning he could spend Saturday and Sunday nights at Dorothy's apartment in Dayton. Dorothy had promised her nephews that she and Roberts would come to the county fair in Oxford, where they were showcasing their prized calf.

On Sunday, they had gotten up early in the morning and had drove the two hours from Dayton to Oxford. Dorothy's sister, her husband and the boys were already at the fair, along with Dorothy's mother. Mr. Campbell had opted to stay home. Roberts could not remember the last time he had had so much fun. He participated in sack races, rope climbing, and he even wrestled a bull to the ground. He became an instant hero to Dorothy's nephews.

It was memories like these that sustained Roberts during the week until he got to Dayton. The other thing that sustained him was the boys' nights out Wednesdays when he, Jeff, and Big Man would get together. Big Man and Jeff would ride him continuously for information about Dorothy.

"When are we going to get to meet this mystery woman?" Jeff asked one Wednesday as they sat at the bar in the Bridge Club having a drink. Roberts drank only ginger ale now.

"Yeah, man, you think she won't like you anymore once she meets your handsome, witty friends?" Big Man asked.

"I'm not worried. Besides, you're both married; Dorothy would never get involved with a married man." Roberts took a sip of ginger ale, sounding very confident.

"Was married," Big Man said. "As of Saturday, I'm a single man again." He stared down into his beer.

"What? When did this happen?" Both Jeff and Roberts looked up in astonishment.

"She just packed up and left. Said she was tired of living in my momma's basement, tired of worrying about whether or not I was going to have a job when she got home, and tired of picking up behind me all the time. She just took my baby and ran back to her momma's house."

"So what're you going to do?" Jeff asked.

"Nothing, I'm just going to enjoy being single again. No responsibility, no wife nagging me all the time. I was getting sick of her anyway. The only reason I married her was to keep from getting drafted. If I'd been drafted, I'd be getting out of the military in a few months. I was beginning to feel like I was trapped in this marriage thing forever."

"What about your marriage vows?" Jeff asked. "Marriage is for better or worse. If you had gotten drafted, you could be dead now, like Greg. You made a commitment to Marsha. Besides, you deliberately got her pregnant. You interrupted her life plan."

"So, what? She's better off without me, and I'm better off without her. Some people are just not cut out for marriage, and I'm one of them. What about you Roberts, do you think you're cut out for marriage?" Big Man said, then both he and Jeff looked at Roberts.

"I know I'm cut out for marriage," Roberts said. "I'm going to ask Dorothy to marry me." He surprised himself by saying it out loud.

"Oh, man." Big Man said. "You're making a mistake, just like you did when you enlisted." He stared at Roberts incredulously.

"Bring her to Newark, man. Let us at least meet her before you go popping the question," Jeff said. "Give your parents a chance to look her over, too. Marriage is nothing to be taken lightly. I was just lucky. I love my wife and my daughter, and I love being married. Roberts, your luck has been bad. Get the blessings of your family and friends before you just go off and make another mistake."

"I plan to do just that. I plan to invite Dorothy to Newark to meet my family and my friends. You guys just be on your best behavior." He chuckled loudly.

ROBERTS LEARNED THAT his parents' thinking was similar to that of his friends when he had dinner with them on Thursday night, two nights before he was to leave for Dayton. The Thursday night dinners had become a pattern since Roberts had started visiting Dorothy every weekend. His mother would always fry his favorite catfish, porgies, or whiting fish. She would make hush puppies or cornbread and make her famous steamed cabbage and potato salad. It was at these Thursday night dinners that his parents would catch up on the happenings of their son's life.

"How long is this long distance relationship been going on now?" Mrs. Roberts asked as she put food on the table. "Aren't you tired of all this driving every weekend? I worry about you spending so much time on the road. You barely get a chance to rest after working all week." She sighed before sitting down at the table.

"There's nothing to worry about, Mom. The drive has become routine to me now; as a matter of fact, I enjoy it. I just listen to my music and munch on some junk food, and before I know it, I'm in Dayton, Ohio." Roberts sprinkled hot sauce on his fish and popped a forkful into his mouth.

"Yeah, but you're spending twenty hours or more each weekend on the road driving just to be able to spend a few hours with this girl. That doesn't make sense to me." Mrs. Roberts passed the cornbread to her husband with a look of concern on her face. "Honey, you drive a truck for a living forty hours a week. You don't need to be spending another twenty hours driving back and forth to Ohio every weekend." She looked at her husband to garner his support.

"She's not just a girl, Mom. She's the woman that I want to make my wife."

"So it's that serious, huh?" Mr. Roberts asked, buttering his cornbread.

"Yes, it is." Roberts looked from his father to his mother, wanting their approval.

"Have you asked her to marry you, yet?" Mrs. Roberts asked.

"Not yet."

"How do you know she wants to get married?" Mr. Roberts asked.

"She just got out of the military after spending two years in Hawaii. Besides from what you tell us, she appears pretty happy in Ohio. Are you planning to move to Ohio if she says yes?" Mr. Roberts made eye contact with his son over their plates.

"I'm going to feel the situation out this weekend. I just want to find out how she feels about me. I'm not going to ask her to marry me until I'm sure it's what she wants, too. If it is, then we'll go from there." Roberts gave his parents a reassuring smile. "Don't worry," he said again.

"When are we going to get a chance to meet her?" Mr. Roberts asked, taking a sip of his iced tea.

"Thanksgiving is in two weeks," Mrs. Roberts said. "Do you think she'll come to Newark and have dinner with us?" She got up and started to clear the table without waiting for an answer.

"I'll ask her."

ON FRIDAY, ROBERTS mechanically delivered packages along his route with thoughts of Dorothy and his impending visit to Dayton on his mind. *What if my Dad is right,* he wondered. *What if Dorothy doesn't want to get married? Will she feel that I'm rushing her? Suppose she says no when I ask her to marry me? That would kill me.* The very thought made Roberts break out in a cold sweat.

At 4PM Roberts was making his last delivery of the day to a small manufacturing company in a remote area in the meadowlands. He had just dropped the package off in the office and returned to his truck when he put the gears in reverse and looked behind him. There were bushes and high weeds, and instantly he was transported back to the jungles of Vietnam. He saw three men with AK7 rifles come out of the bushes. *The Viet Cong,* he thought. They wanted to hijack his truck. He quickly backed up, then put the gears in drive and sped off, driving like a maniac. In the rearview mirror, he could see the three men chasing him.

When Roberts got out of his truck at the SBU depot, he was perspiring like crazy and apparently had a look of alarm on his face. A couple of drivers asked him if he was okay.

"Yeah, man," was all that he could say to them, but he was asking himself, *Did I see three men with guns or was it my imagination?*

Lying in his bed that night, waiting for sleep to overtake him, Roberts thought about what Dorothy had said to him about his war memories returning, one memory at a time. *Was today's flashback a returning memory?* If it was, Roberts wanted to deal with it. He thought about the episode; three armed Viet Cong coming out of the bush towards him as he sat in his truck. He searched his memory until he could remember.

Whenever he had been on a mission in the military truck, there had always been at least two other men with him. It was the policy. Most of his missions involved driving medical supplies, combat soldiers, and sometimes medics from his base camp at Cu Chi to the base camp at Tay Ninh. Cu Chi was about 20 miles northwest of Saigon. Each time he went on this mission, there was an armed soldier in the cabin with him, looking out for snipers or hijackers. One or two soldiers would ride in the back with the supplies, ready to fire if an incident should occur.

He remembered most of those missions up and down Highway 13 as being uneventful; however, as he lay there, he remembered a particular mission that could have been deadly. He was driving the truck; the soldier in the cabin beside him was a mid-westerner from Iowa. Roberts couldn't remember the soldier's name, but he remembered that the guy loved to talk. He was running his mouth a mile a minute and Roberts was thinking, *he's a lousy lookout; he needs to shut up and pay more attention to our surroundings.* Thick jungles were on each side of the highway and there was no telling when a surprise attack might occur. Roberts had to concentrate on the road in front of him, as well as on the jungles on each side of the road. He was dependent on the drivers in the back to look out behind them.

Roberts remembered his thoughts being interrupted when an unidentified truck drove up next to them and succeeded in running them off the road. He fought for control of the vehicle, but it traveled several yards into the jungle before coming to a stop when the front wheel landed in a ditch and became lodged in the mud.

Roberts and the Iowan got out of the truck to investigate. The two other soldiers got out of the truck to assist. Roberts got back in the truck and gunned the engine, while the three soldiers tried to push the truck out of the ditch, but their effort was futile. Finally they tried to get enough traction by putting twigs and dirt under the wheel, hoping that would help. Roberts remembered that he had looked up and seen three armed Viet Cong coming out of the jungle in front of them to the left.

Roberts quickly gunned the engine, put the clutch in drive and drove out of the ditch. In the mirror, he saw his two comrades running behind the truck. He braked. Still looking behind him, he saw the Viet Cong aim their guns. Roberts stopped and backed up the truck, allowing the other two soldiers to jump into the back of the truck just as gunfire exploded. Roberts drove like a mad man getting the truck back on the main road. They arrived at their destination with their cargo and their lives intact.

Roberts had been teased about this incident. It appeared that his three comrades had been fearful that he was going to drive off and leave them in the jungle. Roberts took a lot of ribbing from the guys, but he was able to assure them that he never would have left them. His military record had been impeccable; his honorable discharge was evidence of that. Besides, he was under consideration for a purple heart and a medal of honor for his effort to save Greg's life.

When Roberts finally dozed off, he was one step closer to regaining his memory. He was grateful that he had Dorothy to talk to and that she was such an intelligent and sensible woman. She was definitely the woman he wanted to marry. He looked forward to the trip to Dayton the next morning. He was anxious to explore her feelings.

KILL . . . OR BE KILLED

CHAPTER

13

The drive through Pennsylvania was even more beautiful in the fall. The foliage had changed from green to various shades of red, orange, brown and yellow. As the red Mustang cruised along the highway, Roberts thought about the questions he should ask Dorothy to help him discern if she was ready for marriage. He tried to anticipate her responses. *Maybe she'll think that we're too young,* he thought.

They were young; he was almost twenty-three and Dorothy had just turned twenty-two. His sister was only twenty when she had gotten married just a few months ago. Robert's parents had been in their early twenties when they got married. Most of the married people he knew had gotten married in their early twenties. Roberts remembered, though, that Dorothy had told him that her parents were close to thirty when they got married. *Farm people get married later,* Roberts concluded. *There are fewer opportunities for them to get together to socialize. No, age should not be a factor,* he decided.

Maybe she doesn't think that I'm the right guy for her, he wondered. Dorothy never told him about any previous boyfriends. *Maybe she hasn't had enough time to look around. No, that can't be it,* he determined. Dorothy had been in the military for two years and had come in contact with hundreds of American soldiers, and she never mentioned anyone to him during any of their conversations. He was the one she picked to take a special interest in. He was the one that she chose to date after her military commitment was over.

When Roberts pulled up to Dorothy's apartment house, he was convinced that she loved him as much as he loved her, but he still wasn't sure if she wanted to get married, though. It was a holiday weekend, Veterans Day, and Roberts had two whole nights to find out.

Dorothy had big plans for the weekend. She had accepted an invitation to attend church in Oxford with her parents and her sister's family. They would be spending Sunday night in Oxford and Roberts would be leaving from there to drive back to Newark on Monday morning. Dorothy planned to spend an extra day with her parents and take the train back to Dayton on Monday night. Roberts wasn't too happy about spending the night in Oxford. He knew he would have to sleep in the guest room at Dorothy's parents' house. He didn't like this at all.

"Why can't we drive back to Dayton after church?" he asked Dorothy, as they lay cuddled up on her new buttery leather sofa.

"Because my sister is cooking dinner for the whole family, and she's invited guests over to meet you. It'll be late when everyone leaves and I thought it would be easier to just stay in Oxford. You need a full night's rest before that long drive back to Newark."

"When I'm in Ohio, I want to sleep with you every night. I don't like the idea of sleeping in the guest room all by myself," Roberts whined like a spoiled child.

"Don't worry, sweetie, I've got that all taken care of. You're in for a surprise." She gave him a seductive, mysterious smile.

THE CHURCH THAT Dorothy's grandfather had helped to build, and which she attended every since she was born, looked like something out of a picture book. It had a tall steeple and a bell tower that really worked. Someone was ringing the bell as they pulled up on Sunday morning at exactly 11AM. The church was painted white and the stained-glass windows gleamed in the sunlight. Roberts looked at the people as they arrived; women dressed up in their finest clothes with hats of various shapes, sizes and colors to match their outfits. All the men wore suits or jackets and ties. Roberts felt a little out of place; he hadn't brought a jacket and was in his shirtsleeves. Dorothy had asked her father to bring an extra tie and a dark jacket for him, though.

They walked together up to the church, Dorothy holding his arm. All eyes appeared to be on them; smiling faces and nods of approval greeted them as they entered the church. An usher led them to the front of the church where Mr. and Mrs. Campbell along with Sandra and her family sat in the second pew from the front. Dorothy and Roberts slid in next to Sandra's two boys. Every one was all smiles. Roberts felt like a part of the family.

The jacket that Mr. Campbell had brought with him was much too small for Roberts, but the tie matched his shirt and trousers. Dorothy whispered to him that he looked just fine and not to feel uncomfortable. Roberts settled back in the pew and focused his attention on the pulpit.

The service was inspiring; Roberts sat up and listened to every word. The pastor, Reverend Washington, spoke of the evils of war.

"Every week we have to hear about our young men dying in a country that is foreign to us; a country where we have no legitimate business. Dr. King told us before he died that this war was wicked and that nothing good was going to come from it. We have entertainers like Marvin Gaye singing that 'War is not the answer.' We have young men right here from Oxford who came home from that war scarred and maimed. These are our children, our sons that are going off in great numbers everyday; many never make it back home; let's pray for them. All the young men in this church who have gone to Vietnam and returned and those that are thinking or expecting to go, please stand up. If someone you know is there now, or gone and not come back, stand up for them." Roberts stood up among the many.

The congregation prayed while the choir sang softly in the background. Roberts looked around the church after the prayer. People were crying. Some continued to pray, and others comforted one another. Reverend Washington called on his flock to write letters to the president, senators, and congressmen. He urged them to participate in anti-war demonstrations and do all that they could to end the war. "We need to support our soldiers and bring them home," he said. And then, suddenly, Reverend Washington said, in a thunderous and resounding voice, "War, what is it good for, absolutely nothing," ending his sermon.

Following the service, Roberts and Dorothy drove the short distance to Sandra's home where Reverend Washington and his wife along with Mr. and Mrs. Campbell joined them. They ate a delicious dinner of roasted turkey, barbecued spareribs, green beans, potatoes, and salad. For dessert there was sweet potato pie and home-made ice cream. After dinner, they all walked the reverend and his wife to their car. The men then sat on the front porch listening to crickets and enjoying the quiet, while the women cleaned up the kitchen. Dorothy was the first one out of the kitchen. She took Roberts' hand and said goodnight to her sister's family. She turned to her parents and told them that she would see them in the morning for breakfast. "Don't worry about us," she said. "We'll be just fine," she chuckled.

Dorothy is an amazing woman, Roberts thought as he let her lead him to the car. Once at the car, she surprised him by getting behind the wheel.

"Where are we going?" he asked.

"You'll see soon enough. Just give me the keys."

Dorothy drove back to her family's farm, only she didn't head to the house, but went directly to the barn. Roberts followed her as she entered the barn and climbed the ladder leading to the loft. He smiled as it dawned on him what she had in mind.

Lying in the hay where they first made love, they satisfied the passion that had been building up in them for a week. After they both had their fill of delicious love-making, they lay in each other's arms looking through the little window at the moon and the stars that they both agreed shone a little brighter just for them.

"What did you think of my church?" Dorothy rolled over on top of him, her curls tickling his forehead.

"Nice; very nice."

"I'm glad you liked it because that's the church we're going to get married in." Dorothy laughed at the shocked look on Roberts face.

Roberts couldn't believe what had just come out of Dorothy's mouth. All the time that he had spent worrying about whether or not she wanted to marry him, and here she was bringing up the subject of marriage. "And just when will we be doing that, my dear?" he asked. He tightened his arms around her waist.

"I've always wanted to be a June bride." She kissed his nose and his eyes. "Unless you think that's too far away. I don't know how much longer you want to continue this long-distance romance."

"You never cease to amaze me." He smiled at her. "I'll try to hold out until June, if you agree to do some of the commuting. My parents and friends are anxious to meet you. What do you think?"

"How about if I come to Newark for Thanksgiving?"

Roberts burst out laughing. He couldn't believe what he was hearing, and that he had worried needlessly. He never had to ask Dorothy one question to feel her out. He was relieved and overjoyed. A huge smile lit up his face.

BREAKFAST WITH MR. and Mrs. Campbell the next morning provided Roberts with further evidence that he was already considered a member of the family. It was ten o'clock before Roberts and Dorothy entered the cheery country kitchen smelling of sausage, ham, eggs, biscuits, and coffee. There was a working fireplace in the kitchen; a simmering teakettle hung over the burning logs. Pretty white chiffon curtains with big yellow and orange butterflies hung from the window over the kitchen sink. There was a breakfast nook with a bench for two on each long side of the table.

The table was set for four, with brightly colored platters stacked with food serving as the centerpiece. Mr. Campbell, already seated at the table, sipping a glass of orange juice, looked up when Roberts and Dorothy came in the door. "Come and sit down so we can dig into this food before it gets cold," he said.

Roberts squeezed into the seat opposite Mr. Campbell, grateful that he hadn't asked where they had been. "This looks wonderful," he said.

Dorothy went over to the stove to help her mother, and soon came to the table carrying a coffeepot. She poured coffee into a mug that was in front of Roberts and then poured coffee for the others before squeezing into the seat beside Roberts. Mrs. Campbell arrived at the table with a bowl of steaming grits, which she placed on the table with the other food. After she was seated, they all joined hands, and Mr. Campbell said the grace.

The sound of flatware scraping stoneware plates that Mrs. Campbell used for informal dining was the only sound in the room for several minutes as the foursome filled up on the delicious country breakfast.

"I'll bet you don't get to eat food this fresh at home," Mr. Campbell said, breaking the silence.

"No, the sausage, eggs, and ham that we eat at home come from Shop Rite Supermarket," Roberts said.

"Well, the sausage and ham you're eating this morning came from Sandra and her husband's farm. The eggs come from our chickens right here," he said proudly.

"I can certainly tell the difference," Roberts said, savoring a mouthful of delicious eggs.

"Wait until Thanksgiving," Mrs. Campbell said, while passing the biscuits to Roberts. "We're going to have a country dinner at Sandra's house, with just about everything coming right off the farms. We have a turkey that we've been fattening up just for the holiday. You will be joining us, won't you?" She looked at Roberts for him to confirm.

"I'm going to Newark to have dinner with the Roberts family," Dorothy said, all smiles.

"Oh," Mrs. Campbell said, raising her eyebrows as she looked at her husband.

"Oh, indeed," Mr. Campbell said. "I guess I won't be having a serious talk with the young man after all," he chuckled at Roberts' bewilderment, as the ladies giggled. "I thought we needed to talk so that I could question you about your intentions with my daughter. You've been keeping company quite steady with her now, and her mother and I were curious to know where this was leading. But, now that you've decided to take her home to meet your family, it puts us at ease. I suspect that your intentions are honorable."

"Yes, sir," Roberts said. "My intentions are honorable. I love your daughter, and she loves me." He leaned forward in his seat and smiled across the table at Dorothy's parents.

"We're planning to get married," Dorothy said, her face breaking into a big smile. "We're going to get married in June."

"Well, that's just wonderful," Mrs. Campbell said. "I'm happy for both of you."

"Yes," Mr. Campbell said. "Welcome to our family, Son. Let's say a prayer for this young couple and this occasion." He looked at his wife who had tears in her eyes.

The four of them joined hands once again and Mr. Campbell prayed. "Dear Lord, our beloved daughter, Dorothy, has decided with this young man to let you join them in holy matrimony and to live their lives together as a family. We ask that you give them your blessings as we have given them ours, and bless their union with prosperity, good fortune, and lots of children."

KILL . . . OR BE KILLED

CHAPTER

14

*D*orothy had wanted to drive to Newark from Oxford; she wanted an opportunity to see the fall foliage in Pennsylvania that Roberts had described to her. But Roberts and her parents had persuaded her to take the train; they thought it would be safer for a woman traveling alone. Dorothy enjoyed the train ride; she read Toni Morrison's *Beloved*, enjoying it tremendously. She also slept intermittently catching up on some much needed rest. She'd been busy the week before her scheduled departure, shopping for gifts for Roberts' family.

It was late morning when the conductor announced that the train was approaching Newark Penn Station. Dorothy had taken the midnight train out of Ohio; she was well rested and full of anticipation. She hadn't seen Roberts since his Veterans Day visit, and she had missed him tremendously. The love between them had grown so deep so quickly that she literally felt swept off her feet.

It had been almost a year since she first met him in that hospital in Hawaii, but the time had gone by so quickly that she sometimes felt completely overwhelmed by all that had occurred in such a short time. So much had happened since she got back to Ohio less than six months ago.

Within six months, Dorothy had started a new job, moved off the farm and into her own apartment, and fallen in love. As if that were not enough, here she was getting ready to meet the family of the man she loved, and at the same time planning a wedding that would take place in a little over six months. As the train pulled into the station, Dorothy wondered if perhaps she was rushing things just a little. The only thing she was really sure of was that she loved Roberts.

Just before the train pulled into Newark, Dorothy went into the bathroom to freshen up a bit. She wanted to look her best when Roberts saw her. As she looked in the mirror, putting on a dab of blush and a little lipstick, her thoughts returned to how fast things had happened, and she wondered again if perhaps she was rushing into marriage.

Afterwards Dorothy gathered her luggage and, with the assistance of one of the porters, she got off the train. Walking through the train station toward the door that Roberts told her he would meet her, she looked up and to her surprise there he was, smiling broadly.

"I parked the car and came in to help you with your bags. I wanted to surprise you." He kissed her lightly on the lips.

"I only have two bags." She handed the heavier one to him. "I took your suggestion and packed light."

"You won't be needing many clothes." He smiled seductively.

They walked the two or so blocks from the train station to the parking lot. Everything looked pretty normal to Dorothy. But, as Roberts drove through downtown Newark, not the site of the rebellion four years ago, Dorothy realized that Newark was nothing like what she had imagined it to be. She had been a senior in high school when the rebellion broke out in the city. The teachers in the regional high school she attended had not spent much time talking about the rebellions that appeared to be sweeping across the country in major cities; therefore, her knowledge about them was limited to what she'd seen and heard on television.

The downtown Newark area was pretty empty even for Thanksgiving Day. All of the stores had iron gates up to the windows. There were no visible holiday displays like there were in Dayton. The streets were littered with trash and there appeared to be a few abandoned stores. As they drove up Springfield Avenue, in the Central Ward, Dorothy saw devastation like she had never seen before. There were burned out buildings. Trash and filth littered the streets. Roberts showed her the spot where a "flying bottle," as he referred to it, had injured him. He drove along Avon Avenue where a fire had taken place shortly after the rebellion and had burned down an entire city block.

Dorothy shivered at the sight of idle youth walking the streets, stopping cars. "What are they doing?" she asked.

"Making a living, selling drugs for the holiday."

"In broad daylight?"

"That's the way it is in this city now. No one cares."

The Weequahic section of the city, where the Roberts family lived, looked like another city from the one they had just passed through. Dorothy felt a little more at ease when Roberts pulled the car into the driveway of a nice colonial-style single-family home on a quiet tree-lined street. The house was painted blue with white shutters. The front lawn was neatly trimmed with bags of recently raked leaves waiting to be hauled off.

"Well, we're here." Roberts jumped out of the Mustang, coming over to her side of the car to open the door. He took her bags out of the back seat. Handing her the smaller bag, he put an arm around her waist to escort her into the house.

The Roberts' home was comfortable and nicely furnished, though it lacked the country, informal style of the Campbell's farmhouse. It was more sophisticated like some of the homes she'd seen on television. There were shiny wood floors and heavy upholstered furniture in the living room. There were custom-made draperies in both the living room and adjoining dining room. Mrs. Roberts came in from the kitchen to greet her. She was wearing an apron and a big smile that put Dorothy at ease.

"Welcome to Newark," Mrs. Roberts said, giving her a warm embrace. "I hope you had a comfortable train ride." She gave Dorothy a thorough assessment and then smiled warmly again. "You can put her suitcase in Deneen's room," she said to her son.

"She's staying upstairs with me." Roberts gave his mother a stern glare as though this was something they had already discussed.

"I give up." Mrs. Roberts threw her hands up in despair. "You can't tell these young people anything today."

"I'll sleep wherever you put me, Mrs. Roberts," Dorothy said politely.

"He insists that you stay upstairs with him," Mrs. Roberts said. "You're both grown ups over twenty-one. I know things have changed with this generation. My parents never would have allowed unmarried people to sleep together in their home."

"You're right, Mom, things have changed." Roberts steered Dorothy toward the steps that would take them up to his apartment. "We'll be down for dinner." He gave his mother a quick kiss on the cheek and a mischievous smile.

"Do you want me to help you with dinner?" Dorothy asked over her shoulder as Roberts practically shoved her up the steps.

"No, honey, you just relax from that long train ride. Deneen is coming over to help me. I'll call you when dinner is ready."

DOROTHY WAS IMPRESSED with the neatness of Roberts' apartment. The sitting area was quite comfortable. A brown leather sofa with a matching armchair and ottoman created a comfortable seating arrangement. The coffee table was loaded with neat stacks of magazines. There was a long stereo with a shelf above it holding a huge collection of albums and stacks of forty-five RPM records. The floor was shiny oak like the ones downstairs, but Roberts had a nice beige and brown throw rug in front of the sofa. Dorothy was most impressed with the artwork hanging on the walls.

There was a picture of Malcolm X, with his finger up to his temple as though he was in deep thought, hanging over the sofa. A picture of a very dark man embracing a beautiful woman of about the same hue was particularly eye catching. The woman wore a white dress of chiffon looking material. Her hair was in braids. The man wore white slacks with an open collared white shirt and a beautiful gold chain. They were looking at each other so intensely it was obvious that they were in love.

"I bought that picture shortly after I got back from Hawaii. I saw it at a local art gallery and it reminded me of us. Do you like it?"

"I love it. It reminds me of us, too."

"Come on, I'll show you the bedroom." Roberts picked up the suitcase and ushered Dorothy into the bedroom.

The bedroom was neat, masculine, but with a slight female touch. There was a bouquet of fresh daisies on the dresser. A comfortable looking rocking chair near the window had a beautiful embroidered seat cover. The full-size bed looked comfortable. The bedspread was plain, but there was a ruffled bed skirt that gave it a soft impression. There was a nice sized bathroom next to the bedroom; it smelled like the aftershave that Dorothy loved to smell on Roberts. There were fresh towels and a lovely jar of scented soap, as well as a few more daisies in a small vase on the vanity.

"Everything looks so nice." Dorothy smiled at Roberts.

"I wanted everything to be perfect for you."

"And it is."

"Come and sit down, I'll fix you a drink. Are you hungry?"

"No, I ate breakfast on the train."

Roberts opened a small refrigerator and took out a pitcher of juice. He filled two glasses and carried them over to the coffee table on a tray.

"I have a lot planned for you this weekend. I'm hoping to convince you that you'll be happy living in Newark." He sat the tray down, then handed her a glass of grape juice. "What do you think so far?"

"Well, it was a little frightening. All the iron gates and boys blatantly selling drugs in the streets, that was scary."

"Things are going to get better. We have a new mayor. This is the first African-American mayor that Newark has ever had. Most of the White people have fled the city. The new mayor will put some of those idle youth to work; that's what they need, jobs. I was born in this city, Dorothy; I want to be a part of bringing it back."

"But you don't even work in the city. How far away is your job?" She had a concerned look on her face.

"That's something else that I wanted to talk to you about. Beginning next month, I will be working in Newark. A couple of things happened at work that I think led up to me being transferred to a route in Newark."

"What happened?"

Roberts told her about the incident where he fell asleep in the truck

143

and about the incident where he thought he was back in Vietnam and saw three Viet Cong coming after him.

"After the Veterans' Day holiday, I was called into the administration office at work. I was told that a customer had complained about me falling asleep on the job, and then another complaint came in about me speeding through residential streets in the truck. This is still a probationary period for me; I've been driving for the company for less than a year."

"Does this mean that you may get fired?"

"I was offered a transfer. A lot is going on in Newark right now. Drivers are afraid to come into the city. They offered me a route in Newark. They tried to make it sound as though they thought I could handle it because I'm familiar with the city and know my way around, but I'm sure it's because it's risky and they don't want to risk one of their fair-haired boys getting hijacked."

"What about the flashbacks, are they getting worse?"

"I get them every once in a while. I never know when I might get one but I'm taking your advice and handling them as they come, one at a time."

"Are you still seeing the doctor?"

"I'm still going to the VA Hospital every month, if that's what you mean. They're not doing anything more for me than giving me the medication. I still take it, but I think I'll be able to handle things myself in due time. I don't want to take the medication for the rest of my life." Roberts moved closer to her on the sofa. "Are you finished with your juice?

Dorothy drained the glass, "Yes."

"Let's go into the bedroom. I missed you."

"What about your parents? Your mother might come up or call for us."

"She won't come up; she said she will call us for dinner." He looked at his watch. "I figure we have at least three hours before that turkey is done."

IT WAS 5PM when Mrs. Roberts called upstairs that dinner was about to be served. Dorothy and Roberts had just showered and dressed. Dorothy was brushing her hair in the bedroom mirror while Roberts tidied up the bedroom. He knew that some of his nosy cousins would want to see his apartment and didn't want them making any off-the-wall remarks about the bed being unmade.

"How many people did your mother invite?" Dorothy finished brushing her hair and slipped on a pair of casual black mules to match her black and white mini-dress.

"Wow, you look good." Roberts gave her a low whistle as he checked her out from head to toe. "Counting us, there will be fifteen people, my parents, my sister and her husband, my father's sister and her two kids, and my mother's brother, his wife, and their two kids."

"I counted thirteen."

"Two of my cousins are going steady, they'll probably stop by and bring their significant others. Are you ready to meet the clan?"

"As ready as I'll ever be."

KILL . . . OR BE KILLED

CHAPTER

15

The Friday after Thanksgiving was a marvelous day in Newark, New Jersey. It was one of those balmy fall days where a sweater or light jacket was all that you needed to feel comfortable outdoors. The sun was streaming through the bedroom window in Roberts' attic apartment when he woke up. He looked next to him at a sleeping Dorothy, all curled up hugging her pillow. *This is as good as it gets,* he thought.

The Thanksgiving Day holiday had been wonderful. His mother and sister had prepared a marvelous meal, and his family had been so receptive to Dorothy, making her feel welcome. Right from the beginning, Deneen had embraced her and told her how happy she was that her brother had finally met the right girl. Deneen had teased Roberts about being the favorite child. "Mom would never allow Derek to spend the night in my room before we were married," she had said. "You see the double standard when it comes to the favorite child."

Deneen had laughed and playfully punched her brother's arm.

All of the Roberts clan had made Dorothy feel at home. They had complimented Roberts on his taste in women, remarking on Dorothy's good looks and her intelligence. Roberts could not have been more proud. Dorothy was charming as she helped Deneen set the table and then helped to serve the meal. Everything had gone just wonderful.

Roberts nudged Dorothy slightly, causing her to stir and stretch on the bed. He kissed her gently on the lips and face until she opened her eyes. "Wake up sleepy head. I have a big day planned for us."

"What time is it?" Dorothy looked around the room, searching for a clock.

"It's ten o'clock, time for us to get started." Roberts got out of bed and headed for the bathroom. "Come on and take a shower with me," he said and then grinned.

"What do you have planned?" Dorothy lazily stretched one leg out of the bed.

"I'm going to introduce you to Newark. I want to convince you that you can be happy living here," Roberts shouted over the running water. "Nurses are in demand here, just like everywhere else."

They had a lovely shower together where Roberts gently lathered Dorothy with lavender body wash and shivered from her touch as she did the same to him. "I love the way your skin looks all shiny and golden with these tiny white bubbles all over you."

"I love the way you feel, all smooth and slick and hard," Dorothy purred.

"Just think, in a few months, we'll be married and we'll have the rest of our lives to enjoy each other like this." Roberts pulled her into his arms and kissed her deeply on the lips.

"Not after the children start to come." Dorothy said and smiled after he released her.

"Children? That's something we'll have to talk about, but not now." He ran his hands all over her silky smooth body.

BY ELEVEN O'CLOCK Roberts and Dorothy were in the Mustang heading downtown. "We'll start in the East Ward, then drive to the North, Central, and South Wards. I want to show you all the hospitals in the city so you'll get an idea of what's available. That'll help you when you start to look for a job here, okay?" He glanced at her for a reaction.

"What about the West Ward, don't they have a hospital in that ward?"

"No. That's the only ward in the city without its own hospital, unless you want to count United Hospital. That may be considered the West Ward, but I think it's the Central Ward. "

Saint James Hospital in the East Ward was nice, small but sufficient to service the needs of that community. They went into the hospital to look around and Dorothy was impressed with the apparent efficiency of the staff, but not with the antiquated look of the interior of the structure. She was also impressed with Children's Hospital, another small hospital in the North Ward of the city located on the corner of Park and Clifton Avenues.

University of Medicine and Dentistry of New Jersey, referred to as UMDNJ, in the Central Ward, was a teaching hospital and still growing according to the information Dorothy had researched on her own. The hospital, as well as the teaching facility, was expanding every year with the potential to become a state-of-the-art facility when completed.

"This is the hospital I was born in," Roberts said, pointing out the old building behind the Martland Medical Center building. "It was called City Hospital back then. My mother was born there as well."

Finally they visited Beth Israel Hospital in the South Ward, the community where the Roberts family home was located. It, too, was a growing hospital facility. "It's within walking distance of my parents' home." Roberts told her.

"Where will we be living after we're married?" Dorothy asked.

"That's another thing we'll have to discuss. I know my apartment is too small for us to live in; besides you'll need your own kitchen. We'll have to find a bigger apartment before the wedding. It appears we have a lot to do before then." Roberts looked at her, and they both nodded in agreement.

ROBERTS AND DOROTHY were invited to Jeff and his wife, Belinda's, home for dinner on Saturday. They had recently purchased a house in the Weequahic section of the city, not far from the Roberts' home. They had had their first Thanksgiving dinner in their home and were hoping to get rid of the leftovers. Big Man had been invited, too. He had a huge appetite, and both he and Jeff were anxious to meet Dorothy.

"Nice neighborhood," Dorothy said when they pulled up to the house Saturday evening around five.

"Yeah," Roberts said, admiring the house. "I wonder how much money they had to lay out for this place."

It was a one family, colonial-style house with a big front porch and a long driveway with a detached garage in the back. The street was lined with huge maple trees that had almost completely shed their leaves. Jeff apparently had not gotten around to raking up any leaves. Dorothy and Roberts laughed as they heard the crunching of leaves beneath their feet as they made their way up the walkway.

"I love fall," Dorothy said, pulling her wrap a little tighter. The air had turned a bit cooler over the weekend.

"Me too. I love the crisp air and the colors of the leaves. I even like raking leaves. You probably noticed that all the leaves in front of my parents' house are raked and bagged. I did that. That's one of the chores around the house I relieved my dad of."

"I'm glad to know that you aren't lazy." Dorothy deliberately stepped on a pile of dry leaves. She smiled when they crunched.

"Me, lazy, no way. I like to keep things orderly. I like to keep busy."

"I noticed how neat and orderly your apartment is." Dorothy gave him a smile.

"That's something we have in common," Roberts said, ringing Jeff's doorbell.

Belinda answered the door and greeted Roberts with a big warm smile and a affectionate hug. He was a little surprised since he had only seen her on a few occasions. On those occasions, she had appeared a little standoffish. She was a very attractive woman, tall and thin. She wore her hair in a short Afro style, and wore a loose-fitting African garment. She also wore beautiful African jewelry that perfectly accessorized her outfit. Belinda didn't wait for an introduction.

"You must be Dorothy," she said, giving Dorothy a hug equal in affection to the one she had given Roberts. "I'm so glad to finally meet you. I'm so happy that you two are getting married. I'll feel better knowing that my husband is hanging out with a married man rather than single guys out on the town." She laughed as she led them into the house.

Jeff and Belinda's home was beautiful. There was a nice size foyer with a huge living room to the left and a dining room to the right. Directly in front of them were steps leading up to the bedrooms. French doors separated the living room from the entrance hall. After hanging up their jackets, Belinda opened the French doors and escorted them into the living room where Jeff was busy trying to get a fire started in their beautiful stone fireplace. He stopped what he was doing when his guests entered the room.

"You must be Dorothy," he said, giving Dorothy a big smile. He extended his hand to her.

Taking his hand, Dorothy said, "And you must be Jeff." She smiled back at him.

"Come on in and make yourselves comfortable." Jeff held on to Dorothy's hand for a few seconds before leading her to a comfortable looking couch directly in front of the fireplace. "Roberts do you know anything about making a fire?" He walked back to the fireplace and resumed poking the logs with a poker.

"I grew up in the projects like you, man, what would I know about making a fire? We weren't boy scouts, you know. By the way, I love this house." Roberts looked around and focused his attention across the foyer on the dining room. All kinds of goodies had been placed on the table, waiting for the guests to arrive. "Whoever thought we'd be living in houses with wood-burning fireplaces, wood floors, and staircases like this?" The house resembled the home the Roberts' family now lived in.

"It's our time," Jeff said. "White flight from this city has enabled us to move on up. Whites in this neighborhood were so anxious to get out of Newark after the riots they were practically giving their homes away. There are only a few holdouts left, hoping they can get more money. You should look around this city for a house to buy before thinking about renting an apartment. They are having what they call a buyer's market in Newark."

"You think we can find something this nice in Newark that we can afford?" Roberts asked Jeff while looking at Dorothy for her reaction.

"I'm sure you can, man. Even if you don't have the money for a down payment, I know you'll be able to raise it."

"I love this house," Dorothy said just as the doorbell rang.

Belinda left the room to open the door. A few seconds later, she returned with a smiling Big Man directly behind her. Big Man was his usual charming self with the ladies. He had a bouquet of flowers for Belinda, and he held Dorothy's hand for several minutes after he'd been introduced, gazing into her smiling eyes.

"You are more lovely than Roberts described you," he said, bringing her hand up to his lips and kissing it. "Meeting you makes me almost sorry that I didn't join the army myself. Who knows? I might have met you first." He kissed Dorothy's hand again.

"That's enough," Roberts said, gently pulling Dorothy away from him. "This is my fiancée, show a little respect."

"I didn't mean to be disrespectful," Big Man said. "I just get so overcome when I'm in the presence of a beautiful woman. Forgive me." He gave Dorothy a charming smile.

"Come on, Dorothy," Belinda grabbed Dorothy's hand and started leading her through the dining room and into the kitchen. "I'll let you take a peek at our sleeping daughter, and show you the rest of the house while the guys try to get a fire going in the fireplace."

Roberts and Dorothy were both stuffed when they left Jeff and Belinda's house. They had feasted on left-over turkey, chicken salad, macaroni and cheese, cheesecake, and a number of other delicious foods. They had been impressed with Jeff and Belinda's insights on marriage and responsibility sharing. Belinda was a working mother with a two-year-old, yet she maintained a beautiful home and had a happy family.

Roberts and Dorothy were positive that they would have the same strong marriage. Jeff and Belinda had convinced them that they could find a house in Newark before the wedding rather than look for an apartment.

Roberts loved seeing the happy look on Dorothy's face. "What are you thinking?" he asked as he opened the door of the Mustang for her to enter.

"I'm just happy that I came to Newark for Thanksgiving. I'll be leaving tomorrow, satisfied that I have a family here and a new girlfriend. I love Belinda already, and Jeff and Big Man are delightful. I think I'm going to like living in Newark. Maybe you can send me an application for a nursing job at Beth Israel. I love this neighborhood, and I think I want to live and work here." She gave Roberts a smile that just melted his heart.

IT WAS 9AM on Sunday morning when Mrs. Roberts called her son and his fiancée to come downstairs for breakfast. Roberts and Dorothy had agreed to attend church with the family before she would board the train heading back to Dayton. They were already up and dressed when the call came. When they got downstairs the dining room table was already set with Mrs. Roberts' finest china and flatware. Mr. Roberts, who was seated at the table skimming through the Sunday papers, glanced up when the couple entered the room.

"You two certainly look nice," he said, laying the paper aside.

"Yes, you do," Mrs. Roberts said, coming into the room from the kitchen carrying a platter of hot cakes. "Sit down before the food cools off." She put the tray down and took the seat opposite her husband. "I'm so happy that you two are coming to church with us today. I don't want to pressure Dorothy, but she will need a church family when she comes to Newark. I want her to see our church first before she makes a decision."

"Sounds like pressure to me," Mr. Roberts said.

"We've been members of this church for almost twenty-five years," Mrs. Roberts said, ignoring her husband. "It has served our spiritual needs well. David and Deneen were raised in our church. I'm sure you'll enjoy it, Dorothy." They joined hands to say the grace.

St. Johns African Methodist Episcopal Church on Lyons Avenue looked stately sitting in the sunlight as the family approached it from the bottom of the hill where they had parked the family car. There was a small parking lot adjoining the church, but Mr. Roberts liked to leave those few parking spaces for the elderly and the handicapped.

The AME church had once been a Jewish synagogue, but after the Jewish congregation had fled the city, St. John's parishioners had taken advantage of the opportunity to buy the building at a very reasonable price. The synagogue had been converted to a church, and the parishioners were as proud of the stately building as if they had erected it from scratch. The building they had moved out of had been much smaller and ill equipped for the church's growing congregation.

Reverend Coleman was a good pastor; St. John's congregation loved him. On this Thanksgiving Sunday, he preached about abundance. "We have so much to be thankful for," he told his flock. "Even in the midst of despair, high unemployment, high crime, a war in full force where many of our young men are dying everyday, we have a lot to be thankful for. How many of you over-ate these last three days?" he asked. Nearly everyone raised his or her hand. "That's abundance. Look around this church, is there anyone here that isn't clothed and looking good?" he asked. "That's abundance. "When you accept God as the head of your life, then abundance is yours."

Roberts looked at his fiancée and saw tears in her eyes. He squeezed her hand. "Are you all right?" he asked.

"Yes," she said. "I'm just happy."

When Reverend Coleman announced that he was opening the doors of the church for people to join the St. John's family, Dorothy was among those who moved to the altar. She looked back at her future husband, his parents, and the rest of the congregation of smiling faces aglow with love and knew that she was where she was meant to be. She had worried needlessly. Roberts was the man she was meant to be with, the man she wanted to spend the rest of her life with.

THE AMTRAK TRAIN sped out of Newark Penn Station heading to Ohio at exactly 1PM. Roberts stood on the platform waving to his fiancée with a big grin on his face. Dorothy's first visit to Newark, New Jersey, had been more than he had anticipated. Everything had gone exactly as planned. The short visit had put them on track for a wonderful future. She was leaving with the knowledge that she had a loving fiancée, a new family, new friends, a new community, and a new church family all waiting for her return. *What could be better than this?* Roberts asked himself as he watched the train speed away from Newark.

CHAPTER

16

Filled with anxiety, Roberts reported to the SBU depot in Newark on Monday morning to receive his new assignment. To his surprise, he was no longer the only African-American driver reporting to the depot, there were four others. One of the drivers looked familiar to him. After he completed the short orientation session, a supervisor introduced him to the African-American that he thought he knew. "Billy has been driving this route for three years now, he'll be riding with you today just to help get you acquainted with the route," the supervisor said.

Once they were settled in the cab of the truck, Roberts told Billy that he looked familiar and thought he might know him. They ruled out the military, Billy had gone to work for the trucking company right out of high school.

"What high school did you graduate from?" Roberts asked.

"Central."

"Me, too." Roberts smiled. "What year did you graduate?"

"1965."

"Two years before me. I probably saw you around the school before you graduated. Man, how did you luck up and get a job like this right out of high school. I had to put in three years in the military before I even became qualified."

"A high school diploma and a driver's license is all you need to qualify for this job," Billy said. "The salary is great, that's why these jobs are pretty much reserved for White boys. The personnel director's son was a friend of mine. We sang together in the New Jersey All-State Chorus. He asked his dad to give me a job when I asked him, and I got it. I guess I was just lucky that I had a White friend who had a father that was connected. In the five years that I've been here, the company has only recently started to hire more African-Americans. I've been promoted to supervisor to work with the drivers that will be working the Newark routes. Man, these White boys are scared to go into Newark. We're hiring new Black drivers every day to work the inner-city routes."

"That bad, huh?" Roberts said, all the while thinking to himself, *So, that's the real reason they transferred me.*

"I've heard some say that the only difference driving a delivery truck in Vietnam and Newark's inner-city is that you're permitted to carry a gun in Vietnam," Billy said.

The first day on the new route was not uneventful. Most of the deliveries were in the housing projects in the Central Ward. Stella

Wright Housing Projects was where Roberts had grown up so he was familiar with the layout of the buildings. He even knew a couple of the families that he delivered to that day. He chatted with some of his old neighbors who peeked from behind chain bolted doors, afraid to open them too wide.

At the Baxter Terrace Housing Project, Roberts and Billy came out of a building and discovered two teenagers trying to break into the truck, but they were having a difficult time budging the burglar-proof door. One of the boys had a brick that he was preparing to throw through the window when Billy came up on him with his hand in his pocket, looking as though he was about to pull a gun. The teenagers ran.

They made deliveries at two other housing projects that day before they went to lunch. Sitting in the truck, eating the sandwiches they had purchased, and sipping hot coffee, Roberts listened while Billy told him about the three years he had driven the route. "It was a lot safer here before the riots," he said. "I was handling packages inside the depot when the riot broke out. I didn't become a driver until later. I replaced a White boy that refused to come into Newark to work. They gave him some plush route delivering packages to small companies in Secaucus, New Jersey.

Roberts laughed. "That's where I'm coming from," he said. "I've only been working with the company for a few months now, and they think that I'm ready to be thrown into the lion's den." He laughed again.

They completed the route without any further incidents. Roberts went to bed that night thinking about Dorothy and their impending wedding, but his mind kept wandering to the poverty he had seen that day; it reminded him of Vietnam. He had never thought that he was poor the whole time his family had lived in the projects. They were never hungry and never afraid. People were not afraid to come out of their homes. Things had certainly changed after the rebellion.

The poverty of the city became even more evident in the subsequent days. Roberts delivered what he began to think of as "care packages" to some of the neediest families in the city. Many of the packages contained clothes, food items, and household goods that were not coming from some mail-order house, but from out-of-town relatives that had been solicited by their more needy kin.

After Roberts had been making the deliveries on his new route for about a week, he had an episode that caused him some concern. It occurred on a Friday. He was entering the courtyard of a housing project when he noticed three or four young boys sitting on a broken bench near the entrance to the building where he had to make the delivery. They all appeared to be about eleven or twelve years of age. They watched him as he entered, but they said nothing.

When Roberts came out of the building, the boys were nowhere to be seen. He walked to the truck that was parked outside the courtyard on the street. Just as he opened the door, the boys seemed to reappear out of nowhere. Each boy had a rock in his hand. Roberts stood looking at them and they looked at him. For a moment, he was transported back to another time and similar circumstances.

He and several comrades had entered a village in Vietnam where they had come to look for wounded soldiers. As they entered the village, several kids began throwing rocks at them. Many Vietnamese kids had an intense dislike for American soldiers. They had been told that the Americans meant them no good, and that they would kill them if provoked. These boys, apparently, wanted to find out if it were true.

Roberts remembered the biggest of the boys throwing the first rock. The others followed suit and threw their rocks. Roberts and another soldier started to approach them; they wanted to talk to them, perhaps put a scare into them. This caused the boys to back up. Just as the boys began to turn and run, three of Roberts' comrades opened fire on them. All of the boys were killed. Roberts remembered women screaming, people running, and complete chaos. He and his comrades managed to get the wounded out of the village and back to their camp without further incidents. They were never reprimanded for this act and somehow it had receded into the recesses of Roberts' mind.

Just as quickly as the memory had entered Roberts' mind, it left. He was back in the present, and he stood there looking at the boys for what seemed like an eternity when, for no reason he could immediately understand, they suddenly dropped their rocks and started to run. Roberts looked around and saw a police car coming up the street. He climbed into his truck and drove off. Now that he had recaptured the memory, he would deal with it.

Later that night as Roberts prepared for bed, he thought about the memory. He remembered the men in his company calling the Viet Cong gooks, slanty-eyed gooks to be more specific. The combat training they had received led many soldiers to believe that the Viet Cong were less than human. The Americans were there to save them from Communism, something they were incapable of doing for themselves.

Roberts remembered a conversation he'd had with Greg while they were in Vietnam. They were eating dinner one evening, listening to some of the soldiers openly bragging about killing civilians. There were many stories circulating about American soldiers raping and killing women and children. Roberts remembered telling Greg about the boys throwing rocks at them. He had referred to the boys as "little gooks."

"Don't call them that." He remembered Greg reprimanding him. "They are human beings just like us." The anger on his face had been quite evident.

"Okay, I'm sorry. Everybody calls them that, it's just a name."

"Just a name, huh. So is nigger and nappy-headed coons. If we were fighting in Africa right now, that is what they would be calling the people. Would you use those same words?" Greg looked directly in Roberts' eyes. "Don't let them drag you down to their level. These are human beings that we are killing. Don't ever forget that."

Greg had always been the race conscious one in the group. He often pointed out to them the racist incidents that took place daily in their lives. Roberts remembered a time in high school when Greg had shown concern that all of the literature they were required to read for English II was written by White authors. "You would think that Blacks never wrote anything," he had said to Mrs. Bernstein, their English teacher. "Why can't we read books written during the Harlem Renaissance or one of the books by J.A. Rogers?"

"How did you hear about these books?" Mrs. Bernstein had asked.

"My father told me," Greg had said.

Roberts went to sleep that night thinking about Vietnam. Throughout the night, he was consumed with dreams of little boys chasing him through the Vietnam jungles, throwing rocks at him. He ran and ran. Even though he had his gun with him, it never occurred to him to fire on the boys and end the chase.

WEDNESDAY NIGHT OUT with the boys, Roberts talked about the rock throwing incident that occurred on his delivery in the housing project. He didn't tell his friends about the war memory, though. Since Jeff and Big Man were both products of the Newark housing projects, he thought they might have some ideas as to how to handle future situations of that nature.

"What did you do with the gun we took from that kid?" Big Man asked. "Maybe you should start carrying it with you. You never know when you may encounter some bigger kids carrying guns and not rocks."

"Yeah," Jeff said. "What did you do with the gun?"

"I still have the gun, but I would never carry it on the job. I could get fired, and I need this job. I'm getting married, don't forget."

"You can't get married if you're dead," Big Man said. "I'm telling you, man, guns are pouring into this city. These kids think you have money collected from delivering packages, and they want it. Carry the gun."

"But I don't collect money on deliveries," Roberts said. "The company policy has changed; no more C.O.D. I just get a signature indicating the customer has received the package." Roberts looked at his friends, still seeking advice.

"These punks don't know the policy," Big Man said. "Carry the gun, man, you never know."

TWO WEEKS AFTER Thanksgiving, Roberts was yearning to see Dorothy. They'd agreed that with all they needed to do before the wedding, they would have to limit the time they spent with each other. They decided to see each other twice a month until the wedding. Dorothy agreed to visit Roberts in Newark one weekend a month, and he would do the same, visiting her in Ohio once a month. The last time they had spoken on the telephone, they'd even decided to forget about spending Christmas together.

"I have to work on Christmas day anyway," Dorothy had said. "I think I'll just drive out to my parents' home after work and have dinner there with the rest of the family."

"I have to work the day after Christmas," Roberts had said. "We'll make next year our first Christmas together."

"Let's just make the most of the time that we do get to spend together," Dorothy had said.

It was his turn to visit, and now she was telling him during one of their daily telephone conversations what she had planned for them for the weekend.

"We'll have to go to Oxford to meet with Pastor," she said. "I've reserved the church for June 11, but he wants to meet with us once a month for premarital counseling."

"Does that mean that we'll have to spend every weekend that I come to Ohio at your parents' house?" The disappointment was evident in Robert's voice.

"Unless you want to drive back and forth from Dayton to Oxford while you're here."

"Why don't you arrange a Saturday evening visit with Pastor. I'll meet you in Oxford, and after the counseling session we can drive back to Dayton together."

"That might work. I'll call him tomorrow and see if I can arrange it. How are you coming along finding a house for us?"

"I have an appointment with a realtor to see a house after work tonight. I'll call you when I get home to let you know how it went."

"I have a book of wedding invitations that we have to look through and make a selection, and I want you to help me pick out the colors for the bridal party."

"I trust you to do that without me. If I do all the things you have planned for the weekend, I'll be too exhausted to do what I want to do."

"And what might that be?"

"As if you don't know," he said with a smile that she could feel through the phone.

"Well, you better get plenty of rest before you get here, because we've got a lot to do, including satisfying your needs." Dorothy's laugh was low and sexy.

"I'll try," he said. "I've been waking up really exhausted every morning."

"Why?" She was concerned.

"Bad dreams. I'll tell you about them when I see you."

"Are you okay?"

"Yes. Don't worry. I'll see you on Saturday."

On Friday, Roberts woke up early. He had dreamed the same dream throughout the night. The boys chased him through the jungle, throwing rocks at him. He felt exhausted, as though he had actually been running instead of sleeping in his bed. He was wet with perspiration and the sheets were damp, too.

I'll be glad when the wedding is over, and Dorothy is here with me every night, Roberts thought. *The dreaming and all this travel are taking their toll on me. I'm exhausted and I have a ten-hour drive tomorrow morning. I hope I can make it until June.* He jumped out of bed and started to get ready for work.

CHAPTER

17

*T*he drive to Ohio went by quickly on Saturday. Roberts left Newark at 5AM and he arrived in Oxford at 3:32PM. He went directly to the church and was pleasantly surprised to find that Dorothy was early, too. She and the pastor had been sitting in his study chatting about the impending wedding. She got up when Roberts entered and gave him a quick hug.

"You remember my fiancé, David Roberts, don't you, Pastor?" she asked.

"Of course, I do," Pastor said, coming around his desk to shake Roberts' hand.

"Take a seat and let's get started. You two are a good looking couple, and I want to advise you both in every way that I can to make sure that you have a long and happy marriage."

"Yes, let's get started." Roberts wanted the session to be over so that he could have Dorothy all to himself. He was anxious to get on the road to Dayton so they could be alone.

Reverend Washington talked to them about the sacredness of marriage. He recited the vows that he would be asking them to make to each other and listened to their explanations of what each vow meant. "Love, honor, and cherish should not just simply be words that you say to get through the ceremony. You should embrace each word and commit yourself to living up to its meaning."

"There are some other vows that I would like included in the service," Dorothy said. "I want my husband to promise that he will be faithful, honest, and caring 'til death do us part as I will promise as well." She looked at Roberts to see if he agreed with her.

"Yes, I will vow to do all of those things in sickness and in health 'til death do us part." Roberts met Dorothy's gaze. "I am committed to keeping those vows."

"I don't believe in divorce," Dorothy said. "I want a marriage that is grounded in trust, and that will last for eternity like my parents' marriage."

"My parents have that same kind of marriage, and it's what I want for myself." Roberts looked at pastor with a sincere expression on his face.

"Good, you're both of the same mind when it comes to marriage. You're off to a good start." Pastor's smile was warm and genuine.

An hour later, they were heading for the car. "Are you sure you don't want to stop by the farm? I know my mother probably has dinner ready with enough for us."

"I'd rather drive straight to Dayton and pick up some takeout, if you don't mind."

"Okay. I'll drive; you rest. Take a nap so that you'll be refreshed when we get to the apartment." Dorothy walked around to the driver's side of the car.

Five minutes after Dorothy got on the highway Roberts was fast asleep. Two hours later he felt a hand on his shoulder. Roberts jumped at the touch and cowered against the door on the passenger side of the car. He was confused for a few seconds when he first opened his eyes. He felt exhausted, and he noticed that he was wet and sticky with perspiration. He looked out the window of the car and noticed that they were in the city.

"Are you all right?" Dorothy said gently.

"Yes. Where are we?"

"We're around the corner from my apartment. I want to know if Chinese food is okay with you. I'll go in and get us some if you want." She looked concerned.

Roberts looked out the window and saw that they were parked in front of a Chinese restaurant. "Chinese is fine."

"Moo goo gai pan all right?"

"Whatever you get will be fine with me."

While Dorothy was in the restaurant, Roberts tried to compose himself. He'd had the dream again. The Vietnamese boys were chasing him through the jungle. He'd run and run until he was exhausted. How long is this going to go on, he wondered. What can I do to make it stop?

At Dorothy's apartment, while she set the table, Roberts showered and put on a new pair of lounging pajamas that she had purchased for him. When he entered the dining area, she had lit candles everywhere creating a romantic setting that helped to further relax him. Dorothy had purchased moo goo gai pan, shrimp fried rice, egg rolls, and won ton soup. Roberts was starving.

"Where are the utensils?" He looked for a fork so he could dig in.

"Chinese food is better when you use chopsticks." She handed him a pair of bamboo chopsticks.

"I've never eaten with chopsticks before."

"Not even while you were in Vietnam?"

"I don't even know if they use chopsticks in Vietnam." Roberts fumbled with his.

"I'll teach you." Dorothy showed him how to hold the chopsticks and demonstrated their use by picking up a piece of chicken from her moo goo gai pan."

Roberts tried to imitate her. The chicken fell in his lap. They laughed. He tried again, succeeding this time. "You're a good teacher."

They ate in silence for a while. Roberts was consumed with thoughts of the dreams although he tried to push them out of his mind.

"What happened in the car?" Dorothy asked.

"What do you mean?"

"While you were sleeping. You appeared frightened when I tried to wake you. Were you having a bad dream? Is that what you wanted to talk to me about?"

"Yes." Roberts took a few sips of water. "I've been having this recurring dream." He told her about the dream.

"Have you associated the dream with a memory from the war?"

"Yes." Roberts told her about the incident in Vietnam where the boys had thrown stones at American soldiers and paid with their lives. "We were trained to believe that the Vietnamese were uncivilized, not like Americans."

"That's awful," Dorothy said, when Roberts finished the story. "I remember from philosophy class that a famous philosopher once said that 'civilization is the victory of persuasion over force.' Who are the uncivilized ones, really now?"

"I'm just afraid that there are many more stories like that. I almost wish my memory wouldn't come back. I don't know if I can handle this."

"Don't worry. We'll handle it together one memory at a time. Remember?" She got out of her seat and came behind him. She massaged his shoulders and the back of his neck.

"That feels wonderful. You know, the soldiers were right. They would always say that nurses make the best wives. They know all the right places to touch to make a man feel good all over."

Dorothy laughed. "This is just the beginning. I have some surprises that I'm saving until after we're married."

"I'm looking forward to it." Roberts laughed softly. "Right now, though, I'm thinking about the dreams. What do you think I can do to make them go away?"

"I think maybe you have to atone for what happened. Let's pray together and ask God for forgiveness. I think you should ask those boys for forgiveness, too. Maybe if you lit a candle in church for each one of them and asked for their forgiveness they would stop chasing you. It might just help." She massaged deeply into his shoulders.

"It can't hurt. That's for sure."

Before they went to bed, Dorothy and Roberts knelt at the foot of her bed and prayed. Roberts asked for forgiveness for the deaths of the Vietnamese boys. Even though he had never pulled the trigger of his gun he felt responsible somehow for their death. He asked for forgiveness for his comrades as well. He asked God to show him what he could do to make up for the waste of those young lives.

When they finished praying Roberts lay down on Dorothy's bed and let her give him a full body massage. He could never remember feeling so relaxed. She managed to hit all the right spots.

"Ooh, Ah, Ooh, Ah," was all that Roberts could say.

"You're so tight. Every one of your muscles is as tight as the skin on a drum. Just relax and let me work my magic." She dug her palms into the small of his back.

For the first time since Roberts began visiting Dorothy in Ohio, he fell sound asleep without making love to her. He had a restful sleep, free of frightening dreams. He dreamed of Dorothy, beautiful, loving, caring, and gentle.

ON SUNDAY MORNING Roberts awoke to the sound of rain hitting against the windowpanes to Dorothy's bedroom. He reached for her, but she was not in the bed. The smell of coffee wafted in from the kitchen. Roberts stretched his body the full length of the bed. He let his feet dangle over the edge of the bed. He could not remember the last time he woke up feeling so refreshed.

"You finally woke up, sleepyhead." Dorothy came into the room with two mugs of coffee. She was dressed in a sexy white negligee with a matching robe that was untied. She set the coffee mugs down on the night table and lay down beside him.

"You let me fall asleep so early last night and sleep through the night without waking me." Roberts gently scolded her.

"You needed the rest; you have a long drive in front of you today." She reached across him to get what appeared to be a picture album on the night table next to him. "These are the invitations that I want you to look at. We have to make a selection and put in our order soon. I want the invitations to go out in plenty of time for people to make plans to attend our wedding, especially those that will be traveling a distance. You want your coffee now?"

"I want my buns," he said, grabbing her buttocks and pulling her on top of him."

She slapped his hand playfully. "We don't have time it's already nine o'clock and you have to leave by noon if you want to get back to New Jersey before midnight."

"I'm not doing a thing until I get my buns. If you want me to look at invitations, you'd better come here and give me some morning sweetness."

AT TWELVE-THIRTY on Sunday afternoon, Roberts was on his way back to Newark. He and Dorothy had had a wonderful morning making love, looking at invitations, eating breakfast, and then making love again. Dorothy had made him feel so good, not only physically but emotionally as well. Her suggestion to make atonement for what had happened in Vietnam with the boys had been a wonderful suggestion. She was a wonderful woman and she was going to be his wife. *Things can't get any better than this.* Roberts thought as he listened to Diana Ross' voice blaring through the Mustang.

CHAPTER
18

C hristmas week found Roberts busier than ever. Christmas packages were packed in the delivery truck at three times the normal rate. He was working longer hours than usual to complete his route. He wanted to make sure that every one of his customers got his or her packages in time for the holiday. So many people were expecting gifts for their kids from grandparents, aunts, and uncles. Some were expecting mail order gifts they had ordered, but the majority was expecting "care packages" from absentee boyfriends, husbands and fathers, many serving in the war. Every day forlorn looking women would meet him coming into the buildings, anxious to see if he had a package for them.

Roberts loved to see the smiles on the faces of those he made deliveries to. It was as though he were Santa Claus. Once he delivered a package to an elderly woman living on the third floor of a building in Baxter Terrace Housing Project. The old woman started to unwrap the present as soon as he gave it to her.

"You have to sign for it, first," he told her.

"You don't know how glad I am to get this package," she said. "My son is sending me a winter coat as a Christmas gift, and I need to put it on and go shopping for Christmas gifts for my grandkids. It's been so cold that I haven't gone out because I don't have a coat that's warm enough."

Roberts was touched by the spirit of Christmas. It was his favorite time of the year, but it was also sad because the spirit of Christmas only lasted for a short season. When he made his last delivery of the day it triggered another war memory. From the moment he knocked on the door, he sensed that something was about to happen.

The woman in apartment 3C in the housing project was slow to answer the door. Roberts stood waiting. It was his last package, and he was a little anxious to get home. He was hungry. He had been thinking of picking up a hot pastrami sandwich at Coopers, his favorite place for deli sandwiches. He looked forward to eating his sandwich in front of the television set in his apartment. He wanted to call Dorothy, too.

When the door finally opened, the first thing Roberts noticed was the sound of a baby crying in the background. The woman, about twenty-five years old, had on a shabby bathrobe, and her hair was uncombed. The package weighed about thirty-five pounds, so Roberts offered to carry it into the house. When he entered, he noticed three small children sitting on the floor of the living room, which was in shambles. Clothes were strewn all about. The woman disappeared for a minute and returned with the crying baby. Robert asked her to sign for the package. She laid the baby on a chair and reached for his pen.

Roberts jumped at the sudden gesture; he was thrown back in time to a similar setting in Vietnam. He and his comrades had gone into a village looking for Viet Cong who were said to be hiding out and holding hostages. Some of the hostages, reportedly, were wounded. Their orders were to get all of the civilians out of the village and then to look for hostages before burning the village down. They were ordered to shoot anything that moved while conducting their search. The Viet Cong were not to be trusted; they were tricky. Kill or be killed, they were told.

Roberts remembered going on the search, hooch by hooch, ready to kill anything that moved. He entered a hooch that appeared empty. He was just about to set it ablaze when he heard what sounded like a baby crying. He moved cautiously toward the sound and saw a flurry of movement from a corner of the room. For a split second before he fired he saw a woman with a knife. Her face was thin and shallow. He heard her fall and then he heard the sound of a whimpering baby. He approached her and saw her lying in a pool of blood. Her eyes were wide open with a look of terror in them. She still had the knife in her hand. The baby was injured, but not dead. He could still hear the whimpering sounds it was making. Roberts stepped outside the hooch, took out his lighter and set the thatched roof on fire.

"What's wrong, I only want to use your pen," he heard the woman from the projects saying to him.

Roberts struggled to let go of the memory and come back to the present. He shook his head a couple of times trying to clear it. "What do you want?" he said shakily.

"I only want to use your pen."

"I'm sorry; a headache just came on me." He handed her the pen, trying to push the memory further back into the recesses of his mind.

When Roberts delivered the truck to the depot, he walked to the parking lot to get his car, thinking about Dorothy. She was due to come to New Jersey for a couple of days before the holiday. Even though she would be leaving before Christmas he would get to see her for two whole days. He didn't want anything to spoil this visit. He would not think about the memory.

Roberts went on with his plan to get a sandwich from Coopers. He went home and ate his sandwich while watching "Jeopardy" on television. Then he called Dorothy.

"Pack that white negligee that I like," he said, barely giving her a chance to say hello.

She laughed. "You have a one track mind. I want to beg off coming this week. I'm so tired from shopping for Christmas gifts. I've been working overtime because so many nurses are taking time off to shop; I'm exhausted. Would you mind if I just waited and came after Christmas?"

"I'm disappointed, but I understand. I'm exhausted myself; I've been working longer hours too. When do you think you can get here?"

"Well, I get the weekend after Christmas off, and I don't have to work on New Year's Day because I'm working Christmas, so I figure I can take an extra day or two off and stay until after the New Year."

"That sounds great because I have a couple of houses that I want you to look at. I'll try to use some of my vacation time. Maybe we can stretch the weekend into four or five days together." Roberts was full of anticipation.

"I'll work on it from my end," Dorothy said. "By the way, have you had anymore of those dreams?"

"No. Maybe I've made atonement to those boys." Roberts did not mention his latest memory.

"Good. Don't forget to keep praying, though; and think good thoughts before you go to sleep."

"I won't forget to pray," Roberts said, chuckling. "And I'll definitely think good thought before going to sleep."

Although he prayed and asked for forgiveness, Roberts was not given any respite from the dream that had to be dreamed in order to bring that memory back into focus. He had to deal with it. He stayed awake long after the talk shows went off the air. He lay in bed listening to the radio hoping that the music would lull him into a deep sleep, free of dreams of the war. He stayed awake until his body gave into the much-needed sleep it required.

The dream started soon after he fell asleep. He wasn't in Vietnam though; he was in his apartment taking a shower. The dream seemed so real that Roberts could feel the warm water cascading off his body. He was whistling and singing in the shower. Everything was so lovely until he turned the shower off. He opened the curtain to step out and standing there glaring at him with those terror filled eyes was the Vietnamese woman. She had the knife and was coming after him. He ran.

The dream was so real and so frightening it abruptly woke Roberts, causing him to jump out of bed. He ran through his small apartment and then down the stairs. He ran smack into his mother's Christmas tree, knocking it over. He ran into the room his sister slept in before her marriage. He crawled into her bed and hid under the covers. He wouldn't come out; he lay there shaking like a leaf. Then he heard his father's voice.

"David, are you all right?" His father was trying to coax the covers off him. "Are you all right, Son?"

Roberts let his father gently pull the covers down. He looked over his shoulder and saw the worried face of his dad. He started to cry.

"What's the matter, Son? Tell me about it."

Roberts sobbed and sobbed while his father held him in his arms and stroked his back. Roberts felt like a child again. He remembered his father doing that when he was a little boy upset about something that had happened in school or in the neighborhood. "She was chasing me, Dad," he said.

"Who was chasing you, Son?"

"The woman I killed in Vietnam."

"So your memory is coming back. I remember having those kind of dreams when I got home from World War II. They were horrible; I understand how you must feel."

"What did you do about them?"

"You have to learn to live with them. You've got to learn to live with yourself."

"But, Dad, I killed people, women, children, human beings. How am I going to live with that?"

"You take one day at a time, Son. Things will get better with time. You're getting married and hopefully there will be children. They will help you to put things in perspective. They will help you to love yourself again. I know having a family helped me a great deal."

Roberts spent the night in his sister's bed. The next morning he got up early, before his parents arose, and straightened out his mother's Christmas tree before going back upstairs to his apartment. He cautiously entered the apartment, looking around expecting the woman to jump out at him again. He kept the shower curtain open as he showered, knowing full well that he would have a mess to clean up when he got out. He didn't care; he just wanted to feel safe.

The dream would not subside and kept recurring for the next two nights. Roberts was beside himself. Every night, as soon as he dozed off she would appear. He would wake up in the middle of the night believing he was being chased. He found himself running up and down the stairs through his parents' apartment and back upstairs to his quarters. Then back downstairs again until he was exhausted.

Two days before Christmas, his father woke up to use the bathroom and found him sitting on the floor against his parents' bedroom door. He had a kitchen knife in his hand.

"What are you doing with that knife?" Alarm was evident in his father's voice, though he spoke softly.

"She won't leave me alone. She wants to kill me. I've got to protect myself."

"David," his father said commandingly, what you've got to do is get some help. Get dressed, I'm taking you up to the VA Hospital." Mr. Roberts helped his son up, gently taking the knife out of his hand.

The resident psychiatrist at the VA Hospital listened as Roberts told him about the dreams that had been plaguing him since his last visit. "I can't go on like this." Roberts said. "I'm getting married. I can't let my fiancée see me like this. I can't keep disturbing my parents. Can you help me?"

"What is it that you want?" The doctor looked at him, concerned, but baffled as to what he could do.

"I want my life back. I want to be whole again, like I was before going to Vietnam."

"You can't go back there," the doctor said. "This will always be with you. You will just have to learn to accept it and go on."

When he left the VA hospital, he had more medication. The doctor had said that the sleeping pills he was prescribing would keep him from waking up during the night. They would not stop his memory from returning, but they would help to keep him from acting out the dreams. Roberts felt a little relieved, but he knew he still had to atone for everything he had done. Before going to work, he stopped at the Catholic church on Belmont Avenue. Catholic churches were always open. Even after the rebellion, they kept their doors unlocked. Roberts lit a candle for the Vietnamese woman and her baby. He also asked God for forgiveness.

After work on Christmas Eve, Roberts went shopping at Valley Fair on Chancellor Avenue at the Newark Irvington line. The store was not that far from his parents' house. The stores in downtown Newark had closed early. But, Valley Fair remained open to catch those last-minute shoppers and to collect those last few holiday dollars. Roberts had already done his Christmas shopping, but he couldn't stop thinking about the forlorn looking woman with the three children in the housing projects. This was the same woman that had triggered the memory of the Vietnamese woman and her child that he had killed.

At 9PM, Roberts was knocking on the door to apartment 3C, loaded down with professionally wrapped Christmas gifts. The woman was surprised to see him when she opened the door. She looked at him, waiting for an explanation.

"I bought these for you and your children." He handed her a shopping bag filled with gifts, mostly for the children.

"Why would you do this? I don't even know you. Who are you, anyway?"

"Just call me Santa Claus," Roberts said and then smiled.

"Come in, I just got the kids to sleep."

Roberts entered the apartment and couldn't help noticing that it had been cleaned up and decorated for the holiday. There were lights in the living room window and a small Christmas tree stood in front of it. There were a few gifts under the tree.

"My parents sent me new winter coats for the kids," the woman said. "They also sent something for me. I don't know what it is, but it's awfully heavy. That's the box you delivered. I bought the kids gloves and hats; that's all I could afford."

"Let's put these gifts under the tree for your kids to open tomorrow morning." Roberts took the gifts out of the shopping bag and started putting them around the tree.

"Why are you doing this?"

"Just overcome with holiday spirit, I guess." Roberts finished and began to move toward the door. He hoped that this act of kindness to a lonely woman with children would help to atone for what he had done to that Vietnamese woman and her baby.

CHRISTMAS DAY WAS QUIET. Roberts spent the morning with his parents. He ate a hearty breakfast and felt really good, better than he had felt in days. The pills were working, and he had not gotten up during the night, although he dreamed intermittently throughout the night. He barely remembered the dreams when he woke up, though. Roberts was grateful for the reprieve that he was getting from the last few awful nights he had spent.

Deneen and Derek came over after breakfast. Deneen announced that she was three months pregnant. She and Derek appeared so happy that Roberts could not help but envy them. They exchanged gifts before Deneen and Derek left to go and visit his parents. Roberts retreated upstairs to his apartment carrying his Christmas gifts--new socks, pajamas, a muffler, leather gloves, and a cashmere sweater. Despite the awful memories that had come back to haunt him, and the fact that Dorothy was in Ohio, his Christmas wasn't so bad.

KILL . . . OR BE KILLED

CHAPTER

19

*D*orothy got off the train the Saturday morning after Christmas looking like an angel. She was wearing a red wool coat with matching gloves, scarf, and hat. *Red is definitely her color,* Roberts thought. He was all smiles when she spotted him on the platform waiting to snatch her up in his arms. The plan was for her to stay in Newark for five nights, including New Year's night. They both felt that bringing the New Year in together would be a harbinger of the togetherness they wanted in their marriage.

They left Penn Station and went to a diner on the east bank of the Passaic River to have breakfast. "I hope you're hungry," Roberts said. "I haven't eaten since five last night."

"Something told me you'd be hungry," she laughed. "I only had a cup of juice on the train; I wanted to save my appetite for when we were together."

They ordered pancakes, turkey sausage, and coffee and held hands across the table while they waited for the food to be served.

"I'm so happy to see you, Dorothy. I hope these next few months go by quickly so that we can be together everyday. I love you so much; I hope you know that." Roberts gazed into Dorothy's eyes hoping that she could see the love he was feeling for her.

"I know you do. I feel the same way. Has there been any progress finding a house for us?"

"When we finish breakfast, we're going to look at two houses in the South Ward. I like both of them, but there's another house I want you to see that I like even more. The owners are out of town for the weekend; they'll be back on Monday. I've made an appointment for you to see that house Monday evening."

"Tell me what it is that you like so much about that particular house?"

The waitress brought their breakfast and put it on the table. Roberts poured maple syrup all over his pancakes before he spoke. "The house has character. It's an English Tudor, the only one in the neighborhood. The living room windows are stained glass, and they open out instead of pulling up. There's a fireplace in the living room and wood beams in the ceiling in both the dining and living rooms. There's a powder room downstairs, and a nice large bathroom on the second floor."

"It sounds charming. Can we afford it?"

"The two houses that we are going to see today are reasonably priced, pretty much in the range that my parents paid for their house only two years ago. I think the English Tudor may be a little more expensive, but it's been on the market for a long time. I think we can negotiate a price that we can afford." Roberts put a forkful of pancakes into his mouth.

"Do all of the houses have detached garages? They're building new homes in the Dayton area with attached garages. I'd like an attached garage." Dorothy took a sip of her coffee.

"The houses we're going to be looking at are older houses. The South Ward is an old neighborhood. They haven't built any new homes in the area. We're lucky to find a house with two bathrooms; we're not going to find one with an attached garage."

"What about the schools in the South Ward, are the schools good?"

"All of the schools in Newark were considered good at one time, but they've started to decline from what I'm being told. Jeff told me that Belinda intends to send their children to private school. We'll see what happens. We may decide to do the same thing once we have children." Roberts summoned the waitress for more coffee.

Driving across the Clay Street Bridge back to Newark, Dorothy turned up the volume on the radio when she heard the prediction of snow for the evening. "In Ohio, we have lots of sleigh rides this time of year. They're so much fun. What do people in Newark do to have fun in the snow?" she asked.

"Not much. Children have fun in the snow, you know, snowball fights and sledding, but grownups stay indoors snuggled up in front of the television sets. Don't worry, I'll make sure that you have a good time."

Dorothy appeared to like the two houses that they looked at, but Roberts could tell that she was getting homesick already, and she hadn't even moved to Newark yet. "What did you think?" he asked when they were in the car heading to his apartment.

"The houses in Newark don't have much property around them. They're all so close to each other and close to the street. I think I would be afraid for my children to play outdoors with all of the traffic." She didn't look at him as she spoke.

"But, honey, you know that Newark is a city like Dayton, and there are no farms in cities." He looked at Dorothy as though he were explaining something to a child.

"I know, it's just that I loved growing up on a farm so much, I was hoping that my children would get to experience some of the joy of having a lot of property, a place to run and hide. You know, open space."

"Weequahic Park is in this neighborhood, and they can spend holidays and summer vacations in Ohio visiting their grandparents' and aunt's farms. Our kids will be just fine, trust me, Dorothy. I grew up in Newark and, believe me, I had a great time."

"Yeah, but things have changed since the riots. You said yourself that there are more drugs and guns coming into the city all the time. I get worried."

"I don't want you to worry, sweetheart. I promise you that when our kids come along, if you don't feel that they are safe here, we'll move. Not to Ohio, but to the suburbs if you want."

It snowed, just as predicted, and Roberts and Dorothy lay snuggled up in a warm quilt, handmade by his grandmother, on the living room sofa watching television. It was so comfortable and tender that Roberts felt that his father was right. The love of a good woman and the responsibility that came with being a husband and a father would be enough to wipe away the memories of the atrocities he had committed in Vietnam that still haunted him. Since Dorothy had arrived, he felt completely content.

At 7PM, they ate the takeout that Roberts had gone out and bought, while making up the guest list for their wedding. Dorothy was determined that their wedding be perfect. She wanted it to be smaller and more intimate than her sister's was, but just as elegant. She wanted a candlelight luncheon reception in one of Ohio's most prestigious banquet halls.

"I want the table linen to be coral, to match the bridesmaid's dresses, and coral candles on each table. I want white rose buds, but the bridal bouquet will be coral to offset my white gown. I can't wait until you see my gown; it's going to knock your eyes out." She laughed seductively.

Roberts pulled her close and kissed her gently. "You can't look any more beautiful to me than you look right now."

"Do you think Deneen will want to be one of my bridesmaids? My sister will be the maid of honor, and I've already asked two of my closest friends from school to be bridesmaids. Deneen will make three. What do you think?"

"I'm sure she would love to, but she's three months pregnant. By our wedding date she'll be nine months pregnant. I don't think it will be a good idea for her to be in the wedding."

"Oh my, she may not be able to come. I'd hate for her to miss the wedding."

"You can talk to her about that. I'm sure you'll see her before you leave."

"Who else will be coming to Ohio from Newark for our wedding?"

"My parents, of course, and I hope that Big Man and Jeff will come. I'm going to ask Jeff to be my best man. I hope Derek isn't offended since I was best man at his wedding. But I've known Jeff for a long time. Next to Greg, he was always my closest friend."

"Speaking of Greg, will you invite his family?"

"Maybe. His mom invited me to a memorial service at her church on New Year's Day. She said they would be honoring all Vietnam casualties from Newark and the veterans as well. There will be a special mass for Greg; the first anniversary of his death was a few weeks ago. She asked me to wear my uniform."

"How do you feel about that?"

"A little uncomfortable. I never expected to put that uniform on again when I took it off a year ago. I hope it doesn't trigger any more memories."

"Maybe you shouldn't go."

"How can I not go? He was my best friend. I haven't been to his grave. I haven't really grieved his loss. I think I should just go. It just might do me some good." Roberts laid his head back on the sofa and sighed softly. "You'll be with me; that will make it easier."

Dorothy squeezed his arm. "I'll be with you always for better or worse."

"Good," Roberts smiled. "That's comforting to know. Once we get through the difficult times, I know the best will be yet to come."

THE FIVE DAYS went by quickly. Dorothy and Mrs. Roberts worked on the guest list for the wedding. Mrs. Roberts gave her the names and addresses of all of the Roberts' clan who she wanted to invite, with an asterisk next to the names of those she thought would travel to Ohio. Deneen came over to help them with the list. She declined the invitation to be a bridesmaid, but assured them that she would be at the wedding. The baby was due two weeks after the wedding. Mrs. Roberts was a little skeptical.

They went to see the English Tudor, and Dorothy fell in love with it at first sight. She loved the newly remodeled kitchen and the backyard. It was fairly large for a city backyard, and there was a potting house that could serve as a greenhouse. The real estate agent promised them that she could secure them a ten-percent reduction of the list price. They asked for a contract to purchase the house.

They visited Beth Israel Hospital, and Dorothy met the director of human resources. She was impressed with Dorothy's credentials. The experience she had with trauma cases as an Army nurse and her recent experiences as an emergency room head nurse qualified her for a supervisory position. The head nurse anticipated a vacancy in the next few months. Dorothy applied for the job.

They spent December 31 looking in furniture stores for decorating hints. Dorothy had some definite ideas about how she wanted to decorate their new home.

"I like light, earth colors for the living room," she said. "Maybe beige, white and brown, with a little rust to offset it. I think the bedroom should be feminine, nice, and bright, maybe green and gold. I like to wake up to bright colors. What do you think?" She looked at him, hoping he agreed.

"Nothing too bright, it may keep me awake. I like relaxing colors; green sounds okay." Roberts thought about his sleep pattern for the past four nights that Dorothy had been with him. He had taken the sleeping pill as prescribed, and although he had not gotten out of bed, his sleep had been restless. He had dreamed intermittently throughout the nights. The dreams were always about the war. The sounds of gunfire and voices speaking a language he could not understand caused him so much anxiety. He had tossed and turned.

He'd awakened each morning feeling lethargic, damp with perspiration. With dry mouth, he'd look next to him to find a sleeping Dorothy, and that had made him feel better. One morning Dorothy woke up before him and found him tossing about. When he woke up, she was stroking his back and his arms. He felt more relaxed, but he was concerned that she had found him that way.

"Did you have a bad dream?" she had asked.

"I guess so, I don't remember it though." So many of the dreams were forgotten when he woke up.

"Do you remember anything at all? Maybe remembering and talking about it will help." She had continued to stroke him, causing him to further relax. He lay there thinking. "There was gunfire and Viet Cong nearby. I heard their voices, but I couldn't understand what they were saying."

"Were you alone?"

"I don't remember."

They spent New Year's Eve with Jeff and Belinda. They drove to New Brunswick and had a late dinner at a newly opened African-American restaurant. The owner was a friend of Jeff's. They ate black-eye peas and cornbread, with greens and potato salad. Roberts and Jeff talked about the past until they saw that the women were getting bored, they then talked about the future. Belinda was so happy that they were buying a home in the South Ward. Jeff was happy to accept the invitation to be best man at the wedding. Dorothy suggested that Belinda replace Deneen as a bridesmaid so that she could sit at the bridal table with Jeff.

"Besides, it will be nice to have my first girlfriend from Newark be a member of my wedding party." Dorothy looked at Belinda, hoping she would accept.

"I'd love to be a bridesmaid in your wedding. I've never been a bridesmaid before.

I knew when I first met you that we were going to be friends." Midnight came, and they made a toast to the future.

On New Year's Day, Roberts took out his dress uniform, inspecting it as he had been trained to do in the service. He hung it over the closet door and reached for the hatbox that contained his dress hat. The box felt heavy. Roberts took the hat out and saw the gun. He lifted the gun out of the box, fingering it, remembering what it felt like to have a gun in his hand. He quickly put it back in the box when he heard Dorothy turn the shower off. He put the hatbox back in the closet.

THE CATHOLIC CHURCH on Belmont Avenue was filled with people from across the city. Most of them were strangers to Roberts. The ceilings were high and decorative, and there was a huge cross on the altar with the figure of a pale, thin Jesus nailed to it. Mrs. Williams spotted him as he and Dorothy made their way down the aisle. She ushered them to a seat in the front of the church. She had saved a spot for him in a section where Vietnam veterans were seated.

"I'm so glad you decided to come," she said. "You were Greg's best friend. You tried to save him. This mass will mean a great deal more with you here." She smiled at him, her face full of pain. After introducing Mrs. Williams to Dorothy, Roberts and Dorothy sat down among the other veterans and their families. Roberts looked around the church. There were pictures of soldiers on an easel in the front of the church. He spotted Greg's picture in the middle; he was wearing his dress uniform. Roberts felt overwhelmed with sadness.

Listening to Father Joseph talk about the atrocities of the war was difficult for Roberts. He felt warm in the uniform, his shirt collar felt tight. His knee started jumping up and down; anxiety started to take over. Dorothy put her hand on his knee to still it. He looked at her. Her eyes were full of understanding. He started to relax and listen to the service.

"All of these men that sit before me are as much victims as those behind me in picture form on that easel. They are victims of a senseless war that has claimed the lives of over 10,000 Americans and countless Vietnamese. They are victims because of the atrocities of war that they've had to experience. Many of these men sitting before me in their dress uniforms have come to me asking for forgiveness and solace. They want to be at peace with God. Today we are going to pray for them asking God to forgive them and to put an end to this war that destroys lives every day."

Throughout the service, Dorothy held Roberts' hand. She was such a comfort to him. Roberts would not look at her because the tears would not stop streaming down his face. He was so overwhelmed with grief and guilt just for being alive that he was frozen in his seat. He heard some of the veterans weeping openly, but he was quiet. Father Joseph delivered a mass for Greg.

"Greg Williams was a wonderful young man with a bright future. He had family and friends that loved him. He wanted to become an emergency medical technician; he wanted to help people. He did not want to die before his twenty-second birthday. He wanted to live. He wanted a family of his own, a home, and a future."

During the mass, Roberts kept his eyes on the picture of Greg tacked to the easel at the front of the church. He remembered when they were kids, how they would leave the housing project early in the morning on hot summer days to fish in the lake at Weequahic Park. He remembered how Greg would offer to spar with him at the gym when Roberts had hopes of becoming a boxer. He remembered Greg being jealous of Roberts' first girlfriend because she took up time that they used to spend together. Yes, Greg had been his best friend and now he was gone. The tears kept coming.

After the mass, Roberts took Dorothy to the train station. They were silent during the car ride. Roberts parked the car, got her luggage out of the trunk, and gently took her arm. They walked across the street to the station in silence. Dorothy took his hand and held it tightly. Before she boarded the train, she kissed him gently. "I understand your pain," she said. "Know that I will always be here for you, and that this, too, shall pass.

"I love you, Dorothy."

And then she was gone.

CHAPTER

20

*I*t was the coldest January on record for Newark. Snow accumulations up to thirteen inches were reported in some communities across the state on a weekly basis. Roberts became more accustomed to his route. He got to know many of the people to whom he made deliveries. For the most part, they were helpful and friendly. There were still some incidents that he regularly reported to his supervisor that caused some concern but, for the most part he felt safe.

SBU had instituted a new policy that they advertised in bold writing on all their vehicles. "Our Drivers Do Not Carry Cash." Once the thieves and other neighborhood hoodlums realized that they were not going to get any money by mugging a SBU driver, the number of incidents were drastically reduced. Roberts' still had some concern about being robbed for merchandise. He constantly watched his back as he made his deliveries. Still, at least two or three times a week, there was an incident where someone would try to test his courage.

Roberts' biggest concerns, though, continued to be the loss of his memory, the recurring flashbacks, and the haunting dreams. He knew the return of his memory was inevitable, but he didn't want to remember the war. He wished it would stay buried in the recesses of his mind. The Vietnamese woman and child that he had killed, the civilians in the rice paddy, and the taunting boys were only a few of the stories. *How many others are there?* he kept asking himself.

The haunting dreams caused him so much anxiety. The medication helped but not without side effects. The dry mouth that he experienced every morning, along with the lethargy, plagued him for a good portion of the day. Whenever he went any length of time without taking the medication, the results were even worse. Still he chose to adjust the dosage as he saw fit. Many mornings he woke up downstairs in the bed in his sister's old room. The Vietnamese woman stopped chasing him, but she still made appearances. His parents could not help but worry about him.

"Are you getting enough sleep?" his mother asked one Saturday morning, watching him as he dragged himself out of his sister's bed in an effort to get upstairs before his parents woke up.

Surprised by her presence so early in the morning, Roberts tried to give her a reassuring smile. "Don't worry about me, Mom. I really don't require much sleep to function." He started to make the bed.

"Get back in the bed and sleep a little longer. It's Saturday, and I heard you walking around all night. I'll fix you breakfast."

For a few seconds, Roberts felt like a little boy again. His mother was protecting him, keeping him out of harm's way. How he wished he could go back in time and be a little boy again. No worries, just thinking about what new adventure he would have today with his friends. If only he could be a little boy again, knowing what he knew now, this time when he grew up, he would not enlist in the military. He would not go to a foreign land and watch his friends get killed and kill innocent people. "I don't want you to go to any trouble, Mom." Roberts yawned, trying to clear his head.

"It's no trouble, no trouble at all. Get back in that bed, now, that's an order. I'll wake you when breakfast is ready." She left the room, heading to the kitchen.

Roberts obeyed. He went back to sleep, and surprisingly he slept soundly. It was almost noon when he woke up again. Both his parents were waiting for him in the kitchen. They were sitting at the table drinking coffee and talking in low voices when he entered the room. Roberts knew they were discussing him.

"Sit down, honey," his mother said. "I'll get your breakfast out of the oven. I kept it warm for you." She went to get his plate. "Pour him a cup of coffee," she said to her husband.

Mr. Roberts poured the coffee into the empty mug his wife had placed on the table in anticipation of her son's arrival. He generally carried out his wife's requests. Roberts could never recall a time when his parents spoke harshly to each other. It was always obvious that his father trusted his wife to make most of the important decisions, particularly when it came down to raising the children and household money matters. Although Mrs. Roberts made many of the family decisions, Roberts never considered his father henpecked.

"So you're still having those war dreams," Mr. Roberts said, pushing the mug of coffee across the table towards Roberts.

Although Roberts and his dad had discussed the dreams before, they had never discussed them in front of Mrs. Roberts. For some reason, he thought his mother was unaware of the difficulties he was having. Roberts looked at her waiting for a reaction.

"Your mother knows all about the dreams, Son. We don't have any secrets when it comes down to our children." He picked up his coffee mug and took a sip.

Mrs. Roberts put a plate of grits, eggs, biscuits, and sausage in front of her son before taking a seat at the table. "I'm your mother. I have a right to know what's going on with you. I want to help." She poured herself some coffee.

"I don't want you to worry, Mom."

"But I am worried. I hear you running up and down the stairs at night, pacing the floor, not sleeping. How could I not worry? You're my son and I love you."

"What did the doctor say?" Mr. Roberts asked.

"Probably the same thing that they told you twenty years ago when you left Okinawa. 'You just have to learn to live with what you've done. You'll never be the same.'" Roberts had a sneer in his voice trying to mimic the doctor. "They don't care about us when we're finished doing the dirty work. They just want to forget about us."

"What does Dorothy think about this?" Mrs. Roberts asked. "Does she know what you're going through."

"Of course, she knows. She's been very helpful. Why do you ask?"

"I wonder sometimes if you're ready to get married. Maybe the extra responsibility of marriage will put more stress on you. Maybe you should wait a while longer."

"No! I don't want to wait any longer. I need her here now. Even Dad said that marriage and responsibility is what helped him cope. I'm better when she's here with me."

"I can't offer you any guarantees, Son. I said that worked for me. That's not to say that it will work for you. I think you should give your mother's advice some thought. Maybe it is too soon." Mr. Roberts made eye contact with his son across the table.

"Please, Dad, don't change up on me now. I need something solid to hang onto. I'm suffering. I need to know that something is going to make me better."

Mrs. Roberts began to cry softly. Her husband got up and put his arms around her shoulders, hoping it would bring some comfort. She sobbed more. "I'm so sorry that I talked you into joining the military. I wish you had never gone."

"It's not your fault, Mom. I made the decision."

"But you were so young. I'm your mother. I should have known better." She sobbed loudly.

"Don't cry, Mom. Things will get better. I just know they will."

BOY'S NIGHT OUT continued to be a highlight of Roberts' existence. Sometimes he wished that Big Man and Jeff had been in the military, too, so they could understand better what he had been through. On the other hand, he was grateful that they hadn't experienced the war. It was something he wouldn't have wished on his worst enemy. He still felt guilty that Greg had joined because of the commitment he had made when they first got out of high school.

Super Bowl Sunday was approaching and that was the main topic of conversation the preceding Wednesday night. The three friends were at the Bridge Club on Washington Street. They were sitting at the bar drinking beer and eating fried chicken sandwiches. Roberts was drinking Ginger Ale. Among the mostly male patrons, the voices were loud, everyone trying to talk over each other.

As Jeff and Big Man discussed the upcoming game, Roberts sat silent, head bowed, picking at his chicken breast and occasionally sipping his drink. He just could not get interested in the game.

"What's up with you Roberts?" Big Man asked.

"I've got a lot on my mind. The game just doesn't seem to be important to me now."

"I guess you do have a lot on your mind. These are your last days of freedom. You should be taking advantage of them. In a little while, you'll be a married man, accountable to your wife for every second you're not with her." Big Man gave him a gentle punch on the shoulder.

"I won't mind that. I love being with Dorothy. I'm sure it will be me that will want to be with her every second. She copes a lot better than I do being apart like this."

"That's bad, man. When a man can't enjoy the time he gets to spend with his buddies, something is definitely wrong." Big Man shook his head, bewildered. "I never felt like that the whole time I was married."

"What whole time, Big Man? You were only married a short time." Jeff said.

"I was married long enough to know that I didn't like being married."

"I don't feel that way." Jeff took a sip of his beer to wash the chicken down. "I love being with my wife. From what I've seen of Dorothy and Roberts together, they've got a good thing going. I think you're going to enjoy marriage as much as I do." He gave Roberts a reassuring smile.

"I did notice how supportive she was when you were at the memorial service for Greg on New Year's Day," Big Man said. "She was stroking your arm while you were crying your eyes out. You really took it hard."

"It was the first time that I really got to grieve for him. He was my best friend, and I miss him."

"I know if he was here now, I wouldn't be the one who's going to be your best man," Jeff said.

"Jeff's going to be your best man?" Big Man said indignantly.

"Yeah, it was a difficult choice, but I've known him longer. I hope you understand. I want you to be an usher." Roberts hoped that being an usher was a consolation.

"I guess I understand. Who else is going to be an usher?"

"I thought I'd ask my sister's husband, Derek, and Dorothy's brother-in-law, Brad. Dorothy is having three bridesmaids including Belinda. Deneen is pregnant and chose not to be a bridesmaid."

"Who are the other bridesmaids and which one will I get to escort?"

"I don't know any of them besides Belinda. The other two are friends of Dorothy's from school."

"Well, I don't want to escort Belinda or any other married woman. I want to see pictures first. I also want the first pick. Those are my conditions." Big Man gulped down the rest of his beer and held the glass up for a refill.

"Who's the maid of honor?" Jeff asked.

"Dorothy's sister, Sandra. She's good people and so is her husband, Brad. He can escort Belinda."

"Sounds good to me. I know that having me as best man is sort of a consolation. Greg would be your best man if he were here."

"Yeah, but he's not here, and life goes on. Let's toast to Greg," Big Man said.

CHAPTER

21

*F*or some reason, Roberts always considered Ohio southern and, therefore never thought it got really cold there like in the northeast. He was mistaken. Ohio got very cold in the winter, and snowfall was plentiful. Dorothy was right, though; people in Ohio enjoyed themselves in the snow. The February weekend that Roberts spent in Ohio took his mind completely off the Vietnam War. He had fun; rolling in the snow fun, making snowmen fun, ice skating fun. Even taking care of the pre-wedding business was fun that weekend.

He and Dorothy had gone for their pre-marital counseling session Saturday evening. It had been a good session, and Roberts had come away feeling more confident than ever that he had made a good choice. Marriage was going to be good for him; even Reverend Washington had said that they appeared to have been made for each other.

"Most of the couples I counsel on marriage have reservations either before or after they first come in to see me," he had said as they sat before him in his handsome office. But you two appear to be well aware of what you're getting yourselves into. You appear to understand the responsibilities that come along with marriage."

"Maybe it's because we both have parents who have been happily married for over twenty-five years," Dorothy said. "My parents have been my model for a good relationship and a good marriage. If our marriage is anything like theirs, we won't have a thing to worry about."

"Yeah, we've had good role models," Roberts added.

"Well, that's a factor that helps out a lot." Pastor Washington had beamed. "Are there any factors that you haven't told me about that may dampen your spirits once you have tied the knot? Have you been honest with each other and not withheld vital information that may have an impact later on down the road? Remember, 'Those whom God has joined together, let no man put asunder.' I don't want to hear that you two are ever contemplating divorce. When I marry people, it is with the understanding that it's for keeps." He looked from Roberts to Dorothy.

"I can't think of anything," Dorothy said quickly. "I've bared my soul to this man. I can't think of anything that he doesn't know about me."

"Dorothy knows as much about me as I know about myself at this point." Roberts looked at Dorothy so she could see the sincerity in his face. "But since I've come back from Vietnam, new things are being revealed to me all the time. I don't know what I might learn about me down the road. I just know that I've been as honest as I can and that I love her with all my heart." He took Dorothy's hand in his and kissed it.

"I know that there were things that you were forced to do in the war, but you're a good man, and I love you. All is fair in love and in war, so it's what you do in our marriage that will count with me." She gave him a look that she hoped would convince him that she, too, was sincere.

They left Pastor Washington's office and headed to Sandra's farm. Sandra and Brad had organized a sleigh ride. It was a fundraiser for the church. Dorothy had purchased two tickets and there was plenty of snow. "It will be fun," Dorothy had said when Roberts had balked about going.

"I thought we would drive back to Dayton after this session and relax in your apartment." He wanted so much to hold her and make love to her.

"We'll have time for that later. Let's go. I want you to experience a sleigh ride, Ohio style." She had laughed and coaxed him with her sensual smile.

"Okay," he had given in. "But no matter how late it is when we finish, you are going to drive us back to Dayton. I want to wake up in your bed tomorrow morning."

"I promise."

The sleigh ride was more fun than he had imagined. There were six large sleighs, the kind that you see Santa riding in, each with six people, a horse, and a driver. They bundled up in blankets and took off through the woods in the dark with only the moon lighting the trail. They sang crazy songs like *Found a Peanut* and *Ninety-Nine Bottles of Beer on the Wall*. Then they sang spirituals like *Wade in the Water* and *This Little Light of Mine*.

Roberts knew all of the songs. He couldn't count the number of times he had sung the crazy songs on school buses taking the wrestling team to matches across the state of New Jersey. The spirituals he remembered from singing in the church choir. He had a good voice and had sung with the junior choir when he was in junior high school. He'd quit the choir when he got to high school because there were so many other things to distract him.

All six of the sleighs lined up around a frozen pond at about 6:30PM. They built fires on the bank of the pond and roasted hot dogs, chicken kabobs, and marshmallows. Flask bottles of who knows what were passed around. Some people sat around the fires, eating, drinking and telling jokes; others skated on the pond. Roberts and Dorothy helped another couple build a snowman while Sandra and her husband skated. Then they traded places. Dorothy borrowed her sister and brother-in-law's skates and dragged Roberts out on the pond.

Roberts had never been ice-skating in his life. "It's just not something we do in Newark," he told her. "In Newark, we roller skate. I can't stand up on that little blade."

"Yes, you can," Dorothy insisted. "I'll teach you."

She taught him to ice skate. Roberts actually enjoyed it, and by the time she was ready to get off the ice, he was pretty good at it. It was something that he was looking forward to doing again.

"See, I told you you could do it." Dorothy smiled at him.

"I told you before, baby, I can do anything with you at my side."

It was after midnight when Dorothy pulled the red Mustang up to her apartment complex in Dayton. Roberts was so tired from the long drive from Newark and the activity that had followed that he had slept like a baby all the way to Dayton. He was full of energy, though, once they got inside the apartment. He barely let Dorothy open the door before he pulled her into his arms and kissed her passionately. The bulky outerwear prevented him from touching her the way he wanted. He was full of passion and couldn't wait to remove her clothing.

Without turning on the lights, they groped each other, moving slowly toward the bedroom, tossing articles of clothing along the way. By the time they reached the bed, Dorothy was wearing only her panties and bra. Roberts had stripped down to his briefs. They fell on the bed and both began tossing the throw pillows on the floor as they pulled back the comforter and crawled between the sheets. "Oh, baby, how I've missed you," Roberts said before he covered his bride-to-be with sweet kisses, taking her on another love journey.

The next morning, Roberts awoke to the smell of coffee and turkey bacon. He reached for Dorothy, but she was already up and about. He lay there in the bed with his arms outstretched, thinking about the night before. He had made love to her as though he did not have a care in the world, and when they were both completely satisfied, he had slept peacefully. He couldn't be more convinced that marriage was going to change his life. Dorothy was going to make him forget all those bad dreams about the war.

"So, you finally woke up," Dorothy said, coming into the room with a tray full of breakfast food. "I'm glad you slept well because I want to talk to you about the wedding. I have so much to tell you before you drive back to Newark." She put the tray down on the night table.

"Come here," Roberts said, reaching for her.

"Haven't you had enough? We've got other things to do." Dorothy was laughing as she let him pull her gently down beside him on the bed.

"I never get enough of you." Roberts rolled her on top of him, kissing her softly. "Besides I trust you to make all the decisions about the wedding. I know it will be perfect."

"But I need some input from you. We haven't picked out our wedding bands, and my brother-in-law asked me about his attire. What are the groomsmen going to wear?" Dorothy gave him a pouty little look that only caused him to become even more aroused.

"I talked to him about the attire last night; I'm going to send him pictures of the tuxedo I pick out so he can find a duplicate in Oxford; no need for him to come to New Jersey to get a tuxedo. As far as the rings are concerned, I heard about a guy in Manhattan that makes wedding bands to his customers' specifications, and he'll do it in six weeks time. When you come to Newark later this month, we'll go to

New York and put in our order." Roberts kissed her again. "See, no need to worry. Everything is under control."

"What about the house, how's that coming?" Dorothy rolled off him, reached for the tray of food and sat it between them.

"Oh, the bank sent me a list of things that they want before they'll consider giving us a mortgage. Jeff told me that City National Bank has a reputation for giving African-Americans who are attempting to become first time homeowners a mortgage; they're the first African-American owned bank in the city. I made a copy for you. We'll be okay."

"I'll look at the list tomorrow, then I'll gather the information I need to provide and mail it to you."

"I hope you're finished with the questions," Roberts said, reaching for her again and almost upsetting a glass of orange juice.

"Eat," Dorothy ordered, reaching for a piece of toast. "Breakfast is getting cold and you have a long ride before you. I have one more question." She nibbled on the toast, watching him gobble up a piece of turkey bacon. "Are you still having the dreams?" she almost whispered.

Roberts chewed the bacon slowly, keeping his head down. He knew she was worried about the dreams. They hadn't spoken very much about them, but he was sure she remembered how he trembled in his sleep and how he had awaked in the mornings sweaty and unnerved. He was worried, too.

"It's just that I noticed how soundly you slept in the car when I drove back from Oxford, and you slept so peacefully last night. Have the dreams stopped?"

"No," Roberts said. He wanted to be completely honest with her. "They haven't stopped. I don't have them all the time, but most nights I do. I'm beginning to remember more and more. It's not pretty, Dorothy. I saw and did some pretty awful things, but I'm taking your suggestion and coping with them one at a time. I'm trying to atone for some of the things that I did, and I'm praying for forgiveness. I don't know what else to do."

"What do the doctors say? Will you have to take the medicine forever?"

"They don't say much of anything. They say that I will never be as I was before the war, though. I'm hoping that I'll be better. I've learned a lot since that war, and the biggest lesson that I learned is that war is wrong. I didn't feel that way before I enlisted. Being in a war helped me to grow up and realize how precious life is. Not just my life, but all human life. I think I'm a better person for coming into that knowledge." He gazed into her eyes and saw the understanding.

"What about the medicine?"

"I'm hoping that once my memory returns and I have fully recollected the events that were so atrocious that I blocked them out in the first place, I won't need the drugs. That's what I'm praying for."

"I think you're getting better," Dorothy said and then smiled.

They ate the rest of their breakfast and then had a sweet dessert that Roberts felt would last him until the next time they got together.

CHAPTER

22

*F*or a while after Roberts returned to Newark, he really believed that he was getting better. The dreams were happening less frequently. A couple of days would go by, and he would not have any memory of having dreamed at all. Even when he had the recurring dream of the woman he had killed, she had stopped chasing him. She would glare at him from behind the doorway of the hooch, but she didn't have the knife anymore. She didn't want to kill him. He stayed in his own bed at night, relieving some of his parents' anxiety. He really thought he was getting better.

Even the number of incidents at work appeared to have slowed down, causing his supervisor to make an off-hand remark one day.

"Hey, Roberts, have you joined one of the gangs in Newark?" he asked one afternoon as Roberts was punching out for the day. Noticing Robert's surprise, he said, "You're the only one of my Newark drivers who's down on the number of weekly incidents. How come the gangs are leaving you alone?"

"I don't know," Roberts said. "Maybe it's because I'm considered part of the community. I talk to my customers and treat them with respect. Some of the residents, especially the elders, look out for me. They know that I care about them."

"Maybe you should be the supervisor," he said sarcastically.

"Maybe I should be," Roberts said, thinking that might not be a bad idea. Although he knew that his relationship with his customers was better than normal, he also knew that he was fortunate to have the Newark Housing Project routes in the winter months. He'd lived in the projects; he knew what it was like.

Winters in Newark could be pretty hard, but this winter was one of the most brutal.

Homelessness was high in the city and, as Roberts made his daily deliveries he saw many of the homeless huddled together around a fire, just trying to keep warm. The people living in the housing projects were some of the warmest people in the city. Heat was not something that was denied them. Some may not have had warm clothing, but they had warm apartments. Roberts thought about this as he moved from building to building delivering his packages. *It's too cold to be outside unless you really have to be. These people are unemployed for the most part; being broke and cold is not something they want to be.* He knew these factors contributed to his low incident reports.

In other areas of the city, the poor that were not living in public housing had to worry about heat. For some of these people, being outside was no worse than being indoors so they sought solace in the streets. The streets were rampant with vice. Drug addicts, rapists, thieves, or just thugs out looking for trouble found what they were looking for in the streets. In the streets, they could happen upon some unlucky person they could mug and get enough money for a quick fix or whatever else they craved.

Jeff and Big Man were both reluctant to go out in that cold winter weather even for boys' night out. "Man, it's too cold to be hanging out tonight drinking cold beer. I'm staying home in front of my fireplace with a roaring fire and sipping me a hot toddy," Jeff had said when Roberts called to find out where they wanted to meet. "You can come over here if you want," he'd said. "Belinda is working upstairs on some report for her job, so you're quite welcome."

"What about Big Man?" Roberts asked.

"He called to say that he's keeping his 'Black behind home tonight.' He's got a new main squeeze that's cooking dinner for him. Why don't you just come on over."

"Okay," Roberts said. "I'm starving; I'll bring a pizza." He didn't want Jeff to think he was expecting dinner.

"I've eaten dinner already, and you know we always have leftovers. But I might be able to put away a couple of slices of pizza," Jeff said and then laughed.

Jeff was watching the news on television when Roberts arrived. The lights were dim in the living room, and the fire was burning low in the fireplace. It was a nice, warm, cozy setting. Roberts sat the pizza down on the coffee table and plopped down on the sofa. While Jeff went into the kitchen to get plates, Roberts tuned into the television set.

There right in front of him was someone from his old outfit. He only saw him for a second or two, but he knew that it was his former lieutenant. The newsreel kept moving, trucks were rolling, and he recognized Cu Chi Highway 13; how many times had he driven down that highway? Roberts was spellbound.

"You all right, man?" Jeff asked, placing the plates on the table. He noticed that Roberts was tense as he watched the newsreel about the war in Vietnam, mesmerized.

"Yeah, I'm all right. I never watch this at home. I've been home for a year now, and I have never watched a newsreel of the war."

"We can turn it off if it upsets you."

"I just saw my old lieutenant; he looks the same. Everything looks so familiar," Roberts said, keeping his eyes glued to the television set.

"How does that feel?" Jeff took a slice of the pizza out of the box, placed it on a plate and handed it to Roberts. "Want something to drink?"

"For a minute, it felt like I never left. Now I feel like I'm in the real world, and that was just a dream." He kept watching the television, holding the plate in his hand.

Jeff got up to leave the room again. "I'm going to get me a beer. I don't like pizza without beer. You want a coke?"

Two minutes later Roberts said, "Yeah." He was completely oblivious that Jeff had even left the room.

"There he is," Roberts yelled out just as Jeff was returning with the beer. "That's him, that's him!"

Jeff put the coke and the beer down on the table and looked at the television screen. A soldier, about 35-years old, blond, wearing army khakis and an army green T-shirt was being interviewed.

"My men are facing the most dangerous situations everyday," he was saying. "The Viet Cong are everywhere; we have to flush them out anyway that we can."

"What about casualties?" the interviewer asked. "How many troops did you lose this week?"

"More than I could afford to. But my men know that we are here to do a job, we are here to make the world safer for democracy. Each one of them is prepared to give their life for that cause."

The newsreel moved along. Explosives going off in the background illuminated the television screen. "So, this is what it looks like from home," Roberts said.

"What was it like from there?" Jeff asked.

"From the war zone, it was frightening, not knowing when one of those explosives was going to go off catching you in the midst. I never knew when I would run into a Viet Cong and get blown away. I felt like every minute could be my last."

"Did you kill anybody?"

"I don't want to talk about it." Roberts stared at the television in silence until Jeff turned the channel to a basketball game.

"You didn't have to do that," Roberts said.

"I don't want to make you uncomfortable. You're my guest."

"I'm trying to deal with all of this, Jeff. It's so hard, though. Just when I think things are getting better, and I think that I'm all right, something happens to take me back."

"I'm sorry. I didn't know."

"It's not your fault. It's just the way things are." Roberts looked up and for the first time noticed a picture of Greg on the mantle above the fireplace. "Where'd you get the picture?" he asked, getting off the sofa and walking over to the mantle. "I have one just like it." It was the picture of Greg in his dress uniform. The one Mrs. Williams had given him when he had visited her shortly after he came home from Hawaii.

"Mrs. Williams was giving them away at the memorial on New Year's Day," Jeff said, reaching for another slice of pizza.

Roberts walked back to the sofa and sat down, still holding the framed 5x6 photograph of Greg. "I sure do miss him," he said.

They sat eating pizza and sipping out of their respective cans for several minutes, not saying anything. "Has the memory of how Greg died come back?" Jeff asked.

"No. No, a lot of my memory has returned, but for some reason I can't recall that last day I was in the war." Roberts looked teary-eyed at the picture. "It's as though it never happened."

"It'll come back, man. Just be patient. It's probably too painful for you to remember watching your best friend get killed and all. Just brace yourself for when it does come back. It's going to bring all that pain back on you."

"If and when it does happen, I just hope that I can handle it," Roberts said.

"Remember that you have family and friends that love you and are supporting you. We'll help you get through this." Jeff reached over and hugged his friend.

When Roberts got home, the first thing he did was to look for his picture of Greg. He found it in the bottom of the hatbox where he had put the gun. He fingered the gun for a minute before carefully placing it back under his cap. He stood the picture against the lamp on the end table next to the couch. *Why did I put it in the hatbox in the first place?* he asked himself as he stared at Greg's picture. *I've got to get a frame for this.*

Greg had a nice smile. He had smiled often Roberts recalled. Between the two of them, Greg had always been the most popular among their high school crowd. He was good looking, with a flawless pecan complexion. Greg had barely begun to shave when he enlisted in the army. He'd tried to grow a mustache in their senior year, but only a few hairs grew in, making his upper lip look like a comb missing a few teeth. The girls had teased him about it so much that he shaved it off after a couple of weeks.

Roberts went to bed that night thinking about Greg and the newsreel he had watched at Jeff's house. Throughout the night, he dreamed about the war. He was driving one of the trucks along Cu Chi, Highway 13 as they often referred to it, going to Tay Ninh in the war zone. Along the way, they often passed Vietnamese civilians walking along the highway. Some of them waved at the American soldiers; others spat at them or gave them the finger. They were both loved and hated in Vietnam. Never knowing who the enemy was, they trusted no one, that's how they made it through each day.

THE DAYS WENT by quickly with Roberts doing his job, coping with his memories and waiting patiently for Dorothy's next visit. Two days before her scheduled February visit, Roberts left work in time to drive to Bloomfield to select a tuxedo for the wedding. It was the same shop where he had been fitted for his sister's wedding, so he knew how to get there, but for some reason he wanted to visit the South Mountain Reservation again. He wanted to find the area where he'd heard the noises that caused him to panic the first time he had attempted to visit the shop. It was sort of a test for him. He was testing himself, testing his sanity.

The reservation was as deserted this time as it was last spring when he had driven through it. Roberts eased the Mustang along the road slowly, his eyes moving from left to right, his ears perked up for any unusual sounds. He frequently checked his rearview mirror, looking for police cars. The quiet was unsettling; the only sounds were the wind and the birds. Roberts kept expecting to hear loud noises like he did before, but nothing happened. He drove the car out of the reservation and headed toward the main road that would take him to the tuxedo shop. He had passed the test.

Chapter

23

"This is the first time that I've been to New York City," Dorothy said, as giddy as a high school girl. Looking up at all the tall buildings, she kept saying, "This is just amazing." She couldn't stop smiling.

It was Saturday morning. Dorothy had gotten into Newark the night before and after a restful night's sleep, they'd ventured into New York to select their wedding rings. She had on her red coat with the matching scarf and gloves; she looked radiant.

Coming out of the PATH train station located beneath the newly erected World Trade Center, Roberts held Dorothy's arm and steered her toward Broadway. The jeweler that had been recommended to him had a shop near Battery Park. Dorothy let him lead her while she took in all the sights. Roberts felt proud that he knew his way around Manhattan, and he could tell that Dorothy was impressed.

As high school freshmen, Roberts and Greg would often venture into Manhattan, sometimes playing hooky from school to learn their way around the Big Apple. They would take the number 118 bus that left from in front of Public Service Electric and Gas Company, across the street from Military Park. Fifty cents was all that it cost. By the time they were sophomores, they had found their way up to Harlem.

"After we've taken care of the business with the rings, I'll take you on the Staten Island Ferry, and you'll get to see the Statue of Liberty. You'll like that."

"Okay." Dorothy held his arm tighter. "Is it always this crowded over here?" she asked as a man bumped into them and kept walking without even looking at them.

"Yes."

"Are all the people so rude? He didn't even say excuse me." Dorothy looked at the man's back as he hurried down the street.

"This is New York; everyone's in a hurry." Roberts stopped to buy some roasted chestnuts off a street vender. "Do you like chestnuts?"

"I don't know if I've ever had any." She watched as he peeled one and held it out for her to take a bite.

"Hmm, this is good. Peel some more."

The jeweler was an African-American. His shop, located on the second floor of an older building on lower Broadway, was quaint and warm. The décor was African. He had a chart on one wall that was full of African symbols with the meaning of each symbol written below it.

"A-din-kra," Roberts said, trying to pronounce the word that was written above the chart.

"They're Adinkra symbols," the jeweler said.

"What does that mean?" Dorothy asked.

"The Adinkra symbols come to us from West Africa, mostly Ghana, but some are from the Ivory Coast. I use them a lot in my jewelry. What are you looking for?"

"We're getting married in June," Roberts said. "We're looking for wedding rings."

"Bands or do you want an engagement ring for the lady as well?"

"Just bands," Dorothy said. "I'm not interested in an engagement ring. We're putting all of our money on a house."

"Are you sure, Dorothy?" Roberts asked. She'd told him on several occasions that she didn't want him to spend money on an engagement ring.

"Yes, I'm sure. You can buy me a diamond on our 25th wedding anniversary. Right now, I want a house. That's more important. Don't you think so?"

"Yes, I agree."

They looked at wedding bands that were custom made with various Adinkra symbols embedded in the design. "I want a symbol that stands for undying love. That's what we have, right?" Dorothy looked at Roberts for him to agree.

"That's what we have all right, baby." He smiled at her and gave her a quick kiss on the forehead.

"The Akoma is a very popular symbol that I use on wedding bands. It is a strong love symbol." The jeweler said.

"I like it," Dorothy said. "It looks like a heart."

After Roberts placed an order for the rings and left a deposit, he and Dorothy walked over to catch the Staten Island Ferry. Even though the temperature had to be in the mid-twenties, they stood outside on the deck and looked out over the water. Dorothy got excited as they approached the Statue of Liberty.

"It's so beautiful," she said. "Immigrants coming into America must have been awed by this sight." Dorothy stared at the statue as though she, too, were in awe.

"None of our ancestors got to see it," Roberts said. "Our ancestors didn't come by this route. The Statue of Liberty was a gift to America presented by the French as a symbol of the end of slavery and the newfound freedom for slaves. I read somewhere that the original design had lady liberty's feet in a broken chain. They later changed it and put a torch in her hand instead."

"Why?" Dorothy asked.

"Some Americans were offended, especially Whites in the South."

They got off the ferry and strolled around Staten Island for a while. They went into a library to get warm. Dorothy checked out the collection of books in the fiction section and Roberts headed to the history section; he had become a real history buff. A half-hour later they met up again at the main entrance.

"Anything interesting?" Roberts asked her.

"No. They didn't have one book by an African-American author, not even James Baldwin." Dorothy looked frustrated.

"They probably don't have much demand for books by African-American authors in Staten Island. This is a lily white town, you know, and White people don't generally read books by Black authors."

They left the library and walked a little further into town looking for a place to eat. Before they actually spotted the restaurant, they detected a wonderful aroma emanating from it, enticing them to go in. It was a little past noon and the restaurant was already starting to fill up. They waited about five minutes to be seated. When no one came to seat them, they seated themselves at a nearby table. They waited for a waitress. They watched as other people came in and got seated, but still no one came to their table.

"Let's go," Dorothy finally said. "They have no intention of serving us here." She could see that Roberts was getting really agitated. She didn't want him to make a scene.

"Not until I talk to the manager," he said, anger evident in his voice.

"Please, let's just go. I don't want a scene. I don't want to stay where we're not welcome."

"I can't believe that now in the 1970's, after we've just come back from serving our country in wartime, we can't get served in a restaurant in New York," Roberts said, loud enough for the whole restaurant to hear him. He stood up, and Dorothy stood up next to him. She grabbed his arm and practically dragged him out of the restaurant.

They were silent on the ferry ride back to Manhattan. Roberts was still angry at the treatment they had received at the restaurant, but he didn't want to spoil Dorothy's first trip to New York. He led her to the subway and they took the A-train up to Harlem. They got off the train at 135th Street. The first thing Dorothy noticed was Harlem Hospital.

"I've heard good things about this hospital," she said.

"This hospital has been serving the needs of Harlem residents for a long time," Roberts said, glad that he was finally coming out of his angry mode.

"What else is there in Harlem that's interesting?" Dorothy asked.

"Let's go across the street. I'll take you into the Liberation Bookstore; all of their books are by Black authors. If you can't find the African-American author you're looking for in there, he doesn't exist."

After Dorothy purchased a couple of books in the Liberation Bookstore, Roberts took her to the Schomberg Research Center and Library. She was disappointed that they couldn't browse the bookshelves, but she was impressed with the art gallery.

"I'd like to hang some of these pieces up in our new home," she said. "Do you think they have prints of this Romare Bearden piece? I love his work."

"I don't know, but we can ask. If they don't have it, maybe they know where we can purchase a print." Roberts looked around for an attendant.

They left the library with the name and address of an art dealer who would help them get prints of the paintings they wanted, then walked to Sylvia's Restaurant to have lunch. Dorothy couldn't help but notice that a good number of the patrons in Sylvia's were White people.

"How come they can come into Black communities and are made to feel so welcome, and we have just the opposite experience in their communities?" Dorothy said, noticing how friendly the waitress was to a table of Whites sitting across the room from them.

"Makes you wonder who the better people are, doesn't it?" Roberts said, and then studied his menu. "I'm starving, what are you going to have?"

"I'll have whatever you have," she said, not wanting to make a choice, everything looked so good. "Speaking of food, we've been invited to have dinner at the restaurant where our reception will be held. We'll get a chance to sample their menu free of charge."

"Sounds good to me. When are you planning for us to do this?"

"After our next session with Pastor Washington."

They ate fried catfish sandwiches with side orders of coleslaw and sweet potatoes. Roberts ordered peach cobbler for dessert and an extra helping to take home. He was feeling wonderful again; the woman he was about to marry always made him feel that way.

"I'm sorry if I upset you on Staten Island," he said after they finished eating.

"No need to apologize. I understand how you feel."

"It's just that I get so angry when I think about how much I sacrificed over in Vietnam for this country only to come home and have to deal with racism. I probably will never be the same man that I was before I enlisted. I have been changed forever, yet nothing has changed here." Roberts' expression showed his frustration with the situation.

"Don't worry, you're still the good person you've always been."

"I wish I could believe that."

Roberts took Dorothy to the art dealer's shop on 125th Street. They purchased the print that she liked and left it for framing. Harlem street vendors were busy selling everything from leather purses to silk scarves. Artists were sketching portraits for $25. Roberts begged Dorothy to pose for one. He wanted her portrait to hang in his bedroom. She balked about the cold, but gave in to his pleading. When it was finished, she was glad that she had.

"It's absolutely beautiful," she said, smiling. "Do you think it looks like me."

"It's a good likeness, but you're prettier," Roberts said, causing her to blush.

They shopped for a frame for the sketch, and Roberts purchased a frame for Greg's photograph as well. Then they took the train back downtown and walked to the PATH train station.

Not unusual, lower Manhattan was swarming with people of all sorts. Many were tourists coming to get a glimpse of the brand new World Trade Center. The buildings were awesome in their magnitude though only Tower I was open to the public. It had opened only a short time ago, and Roberts had anticipated visiting it. Tower II was not scheduled to open until next year. It was obvious that Dorothy was ecstatic being in the midst of all the excitement of the opening of Tower I.

"Do you want to go in?" Roberts asked, already anticipating her response.

"I thought you would never ask," she said. "How can I tell people back in Ohio that I was in New York and didn't visit the World Trade Center?"

"We were in the building when we got off the train," Roberts corrected her.

"But I want to go to the top." Her eyes were wide with excitement.

They took the elevator to the top of Tower I and made their way to the observation deck. Roberts was surprised to see that most of the observers were servicemen in uniform. He learned by listening to their conversations that they were on their way to Vietnam. They were leaving in four hours from JFK Airport and had been invited on a special tour of the World Trade Center by the mayor of New York City. Roberts listened to them laughing and joking as though they didn't have a care in the world.

"If I'd known we'd get perks like this once we got in Uncle Sam's Army, I would have enlisted instead of waiting to be drafted," one of the soldiers said. Roberts detected the accent of an Iowan. He'd met many of them while he was an enlisted man.

"This is probably the only way I ever would have gotten to New York," another soldier said. "Uncle Sam had to foot the bill." He laughed with his buddies.

"The next time I come to New York, I want to be with my girl and not a bunch of knuckle-headed guys," the Iowan said. "This is a sight to share with a pretty woman on your arm."

Dorothy smiled when she heard the remark and held Roberts' arm a little tighter. He smiled at her thinking; *These poor jerks don't know what's facing them. They may never get another chance to visit the World Trade Center or any place else for that matter.* He stood at the railing looking out at New York City and remembered the day he had left to go to Vietnam.

He and Greg had been home on a two-week leave before they were sent to Vietnam. Mr. Roberts had driven them to JFK Airport at 7AM where they met up with two hundred other GI's heading for combat. Roberts remembered he hadn't been scared at that time. Most of soldiers were meeting each other for the first time. No one knew anyone, but he and Greg had each other. This made a big difference. He remembered their conversation at the airport.

"Whatever happens, man, remember I'll always have your back," he had said to Greg. He had clasped Greg's shoulder for emphasis.

"And I will have yours," Greg had said.

"Suppose they don't put us together." Roberts' confidence had been diminished at the mere thought.

"I'll know that you are the closest person I have in Vietnam, and I'll feel better just knowing that you're there." Greg had a look on his face that reminded Roberts of the time when they were twelve and had become blood brothers. They had used a small penknife to cut their fingers and held their bleeding fingers together, mixing their blood. "You're my blood brother, remember?" Greg had said as though reading his mind.

Four hours later, they had boarded a 747 commercial jet airliner that took off for California, where they would meet other soldiers and then board another flight that would take them to Vietnam. Roberts remembered the silence on the plane. At first he had thought that everyone had gone to sleep but as he looked up and down the aisle, he knew that they weren't sleeping. Each man was into his own private thoughts. They were anticipating what would happen next. Roberts remembered thinking, Hell; *I'm only twenty years old. I don't want to die.*

Dorothy held his arm a little tighter, jogging him out of his thoughts. The wind was picking up and he shivered from the cold. He turned Dorothy to face him and tightened her scarf snugly around her neck.

"Is it getting too cold up here for you?" He adjusted her hat on her pretty head.

"Not really. You're mighty quiet. Are you okay?"

"Yeah, I'm okay." He noticed that the soldiers were leaving the observation deck. In less than twenty-four hours, they would be arriving in Vietnam. He remembered his arrival in the Republic of South Vietnam. Tan Son Nhut Air Base was where they had landed. It seemed like it was only a matter of hours after their arrival before they were put to work. Roberts and Greg had both been assigned to the 25th infantry division. They spent their first three months as infantrymen, doing what they had spent weeks training for. They had been trained for war.

Roberts watched as the last of the soldiers left the observation deck. This could be their last outing on American soil. *I hope they enjoyed the visit,* Roberts thought. He wished Greg had gotten a chance to see the World Trade Center completed. He remembered how Greg had looked forward to it. They'd talked about it before the plane had left JFK Airport and headed to California.

"Next time you fly over this area, you'll be able to see the World Trade Center in all of its glory," the captain had said as they flew out of New York City.

"I can't wait to see that," Greg had said. "Can you imagine a building one-hundred and ten stories high. Man, I love high places. I wish I could have been a pilot."

"I feel like I'm on top of the world," Dorothy said.

"Let's go," Roberts said, taking her arm and leading her to the elevator.

THE FIRST THING they did when they got back to Roberts' apartment was to hang the picture of Dorothy above his chest of drawers, directly across from his bed.

"There, I'll be able to see your pretty face first thing in the morning, even when you're in Ohio." Roberts straightened the picture on the wall.

"We should have gotten a sketch of you, too. I'd like to see your handsome face when I wake up in the mornings." Dorothy smiled at him.

"In three more months, we won't need pictures." Roberts hugged her, still staring at the picture. "I'll be waking up every morning with you beside me." He smiled, too.

"I'll put the picture of Greg in the frame for you," Dorothy said, going into the sitting room. "Where do you want to put it?"

"I think I want to keep it right here on the end table. When we move into our new house, I'll put it on the mantle above the fireplace like Jeff has it in his house. He will always be an important member of our family and will have a place of distinction in our home."

"That's just fine with me." Dorothy framed the picture and placed it on the end table before she came and sat on the sofa next to him. He lay down, pulling her down with him. He kissed her gently and looked deeply in her eyes.

"I love you, Dorothy Campbell." They stretched out the full length of the sofa and just lay there relaxing, holding each other, tired from the day in New York City. Finally, they got up and went into the bedroom where they undressed and then cuddled on the bed, eventually stroking each other, and finally making passionate love. Roberts went to sleep feeling like he was one of the luckiest men in the world for having found Dorothy. And then the dreams came.

Throughout the night, Roberts dreamed about the time he spent in Vietnam in the 25th infantry. In his dream, he and Greg were trudging across the hot, humid jungles of Vietnam, carrying heavy equipment for days at a time. They were tired from being without sleep, sometimes without sufficient food, and always hunting the enemy. They were scared, knowing that, when they encountered the enemy, they had to kill or be killed.

CHAPTER

24

Preparations for the wedding were under way by the middle of March. Dorothy had the first fitting for her wedding gown and was delighted with the design. The bridesmaids' dresses had been selected, and the seamstress had promised that the whole package would be complete by the end of May, two weeks before the wedding. The church had been booked, as well as the Diamond Room at Oxford's most prestigious banquet hall, The Five-Carat Club, owned by a contingent of Black businessmen living in the area.

Walking around the grounds of Oxford's only public park one Sunday afternoon following church services, Dorothy couldn't help but smile when she saw a red breasted robin, the first harbinger of spring that she'd seen so far, perching on a tree limb. Public parks were a rarity in Ohio's farm country where people had so much open space to picnic, play and do just about anything else that they wanted.

Isis Park had been built to bring the citizens of Oxford together for socializing beyond their own property limits. Dorothy remembered playing on the swings at Isis Park as a child. Her mother often took her and Sandra there after church on Sundays. Dorothy always enjoyed the time they spent there. More than anything, she loved visiting Isis, the Egyptian goddess associated with love.

The Isis statue was actually a fountain that sat in the middle of the park. There were lovely gardens surrounding the statue with stone benches for lovers to sit and gaze at the statue. As an adolescent Dorothy had been obsessed with the notion of love, and the Isis statue had become her symbol of love.

When she was old enough to venture into the park on her own, she would head to the fountain and find a place to sit on the grass far enough away not to be noticed, but close enough to see all that went on. She would watch young lovers kissing on the benches and holding hands while staring at the fountain. She thought about doing the same thing one day with her boyfriend. Only she'd never had a chance to find out what it would be like. She'd had a couple of boyfriends in high school, but they weren't the types to visit fountains in the park and gaze at the Isis statue. They had had too much work to do on the farms and, once the school bus dropped them off at their stops she would not see them again until the next school day.

Dorothy decided that after the wedding she wanted the whole bridal party to be driven by limousine to Isis Park to take pictures before heading to the Diamond Room for the reception. She'd decided that the cocktail hour, where hors-d'oeuvres would also be served, could take place in the interim between the ceremony and the reception. While her guests were waiting for the bridal party to arrive, they could be socializing with each other in the Ruby Lounge at the club.

When Dorothy called Roberts later that evening to discuss the wedding plans, he seemed a little agitated. He'd been that way a lot lately; since their visit to New York, he had become sullen and distant. Sometimes he appeared evasive, not wanting to tell her what was bothering him. He'd even asked to postpone his March visit to Ohio until later in the month. Dorothy wondered if he was getting pre-marital jitters. *Maybe he's having second thoughts,* she thought.

"Is something wrong?" she asked after he told her in so many words that he wasn't really interested in the minute details of the wedding.

"Nothing's wrong," Roberts said, realizing that his tone had reflected his state of mind. He had been remembering a lot of his dreams lately, and they were really disturbing. He didn't want to alarm her. "I'm just tired. The thought of getting up early and going back to work tomorrow is making me more tired."

"Haven't you been sleeping well?" She remembered the last time she'd slept with him, the night they had come home from selecting the rings in New York. He had been so restless. She'd awaked during the night to find him tossing and turning in his sleep again. He had even mumbled something unintelligible. She had massaged his back and his shoulders, and he had appeared to become more relaxed.

"Go on and tell me about the wedding plans," Robert said, not answering her question.

"It's just that I want you to be a part of the planning, so you won't be surprised later on. I don't want to make all the decisions by myself."

"Honey, I wouldn't care if we got married at city hall without a reception or pictures or anything. I just want you to be my wife. I want you here with me." Roberts hoped he didn't sound too indifferent. He quickly added, "I want whatever makes you happy."

"But I want you to be happy, too."

"Being with you makes me happy. Tell me about the wedding plans; I'll listen."

After updating Roberts on the wedding plans, Dorothy hung up the telephone, feeling a little uneasy. Roberts had avoided her question about how he was sleeping. She'd been hearing a lot of stories about Vietnam veterans and the difficulty they were having readjusting to society. *Should I be worried?* she wondered.

The following weekend when Roberts drove to Ohio, Dorothy's first thought was that she had worried needlessly. Roberts appeared to be his charming self again. He agreed to spend the weekend at her parents' farm so they could have an early dinner at the Five-Carat Club after church on Sunday before driving back to Newark. Dorothy did, however, take advantage of their pre-marital counseling session on Saturday evening to explore his feelings a little more in the presence of Pastor Washington.

When Pastor Washington asked them again if they had any reservations about entering into marriage, it was Dorothy who suggested that Roberts' war experiences could create a problem. Surprised, both Pastor Washington and Roberts looked at her for an explanation.

Avoiding eye contact with her fiancée, but speaking directly to him she said, "It's just that I've noticed that the more you remember about the war, the more distant you become. Lately you've been avoiding any conversation about your dreams." She fiddled with the fringes of her scarf. "I don't know how this may affect our marriage."

Breaking the silence that followed Dorothy's comments, Pastor Washington said, "Honesty is a policy that I can't stress too much for young people entering into marriage. Withholding information from your partner is the same as being dishonest," he said, looking at Roberts now.

"I just didn't want to worry you," Roberts said quietly.

"But I do worry when you don't tell me." Dorothy continued to fiddle with the scarf. "I'd feel better if you would talk to me about what's going on. I'd like to help you deal with this."

Pastor Washington looked from Dorothy to Roberts, waiting for him to open up, not saying anything.

"I don't want to tell you all the ugly things I did in the war. I don't want you to think badly of me. I'd rather just deal with them by myself." Roberts kept his head down.

Breaking the silence again, Pastor Washington said, "Maybe he's right in wanting to keep those things from you. I've been talking to other veterans coming back from Vietnam. They don't want to talk to about their war experiences with their spouses, but they are opening up with other veterans and with their pastors. Is there someone that you can talk to about what you saw and what you did in the war?" He looked at Roberts even though Roberts kept his head down and avoided making eye contact.

"Sometimes I talk to my father, he was a veteran of World War II, but there really isn't anyone else. I see the doctors at the VA Hospital, but they aren't really interested in my war experiences beyond treating the symptoms of post-traumatic stress syndrome with medication. The best medicine so far has been having Dorothy at my side. She's been the best thing for me." Roberts finally held his head up and looked into the kind eyes of Pastor Washington.

"Do you feel you're getting better?" Pastor Washington asked.

"Yes," Roberts said quickly. "My memory is almost fully restored. I remember most of what happened, and I'm dealing with it. I know that sometimes I appear to be withdrawn, but I'm dealing with the after effects of what happened. I'm not hallucinating or acting out my dreams–I'm coping. I think in time I'll be able to function normally again. I just need to know that Dorothy will be with me." He looked at Dorothy, hoping to hear her say that she would be.

"I'm marrying you, aren't I?" she said. "I'm making a commitment to be with you until death do us part."

As he walked them to the door, Pastor Washington said, "Perhaps you should ask about group therapy for Vietnam veterans in your area. It sounds to me as though you need to discuss your experiences with others who have had similar experiences."

"I've made inquiries," Roberts said. "They keep telling me that there is nothing available yet." He took Dorothy's arm and escorted her out the door.

They slept in the barn that night even though it was initially a little cold. Dorothy had brought enough blankets to keep them warm even when they were both naked. The kerosene lantern hanging from a post in the loft glowed, giving off warmth of its own. They lay snug and warm under the blankets, cuddled up together looking at the stars and the moon. Dorothy's hair smelled like coconut, and her body smelled like lavender. Roberts sniffed loudly as though he were trying to inhale her very essence, causing her to laugh.

"What are you doing, silly?" She pressed herself deeper into the curve his body had created for her.

"I can't get enough of you. I love it when I penetrate you. Now I want your smell to penetrate me." He stroked her smooth, soft skin. It felt silky like flower petals and smelled just as wonderful.

They lay there enjoying the quiet, the warm glow, the touching of their bodies, and the heavenly bodies just outside the window.

"I never want to do anything that will make you stop loving me, Dorothy. If I'm doing something to upset you, just tell me, and I will change it, okay?" He pulled her a little closer and then rubbed her breasts and stomach.

"Okay," she said. "I know that there are some things that happened in Vietnam that you don't want to tell me, but promise me that if you remember something that is too big for you to handle by yourself, you will tell me. I may be able to help you deal with it. Promise?"

"Okay, I promise," he said, turning her over and covering her with his body, hoping it would never come to that.

The next morning, they got up early and went back to the farmhouse, where they went to their respective rooms, showered and dressed for church. When they got downstairs, Mr. and Mrs. Campbell were both at the kitchen table although they had finished eating their breakfast. Mr. Campbell was reading the Sunday paper.

"I didn't know if you two were going to get up in time for church today," Mrs. Campbell said. "Breakfast is ready, sit down and have something to eat. We've got a little more than an hour before the service begins." She put fresh hotcakes on the table.

Mr. Campbell kept reading the paper, barely acknowledging the interruption. "You two must have come in mighty late last night," he finally said, not taking his eyes off the paper. "I was up until after midnight, and you hadn't come in when I went upstairs to bed." He looked over his reading glasses that were sitting low on his nose.

"It was after midnight when we came in, Daddy," Dorothy said, giving Roberts a wink. "We took our shoes off at the door; we didn't want to wake anybody."

Roberts dug into a plate of hotcakes and then took a sip of his orange juice. He didn't say anything; he was taking his cues from Dorothy. They ate quickly; Dorothy barely ate a thing. She helped her mom clean up the dishes, and then she motioned for Roberts to get up from the table.

"We've got to go; I have something to show you before church. You should get your things. We won't be coming back here after church since we'll be eating dinner at the restaurant. You'll probably want to drive home from there." She watched Roberts drain the last of his juice before he headed upstairs to get his bag.

"You're not having dinner here tonight?" Mrs. Campbell asked.

"No, Mom. I told you we were invited to have dinner at the club tonight. I'll be driving back to Dayton after dinner."

"I guess we'll see you in church," Mrs. Campbell said, and then sighed when Roberts came back into the kitchen. He gave her a quick hug and brushed his lips across her cheek before he and Dorothy headed out toward the door.

"See you in church," he said to Mr. Campbell.

Dorothy and Roberts drove their respective cars, Dorothy leading the way. She drove directly to Isis Park. Walking around the park, she showed Roberts all the places where she thought they should take wedding pictures. First they stopped at the garden.

"By June this garden will be full of roses," she said. "Don't you think this will make a wonderful picture?"

"This is a beautiful park," Roberts said. "I can just imagine my lovely bride in her gorgeous gown standing right there." He pointed to a spot where two sculptured lions were sitting on either side of a marble bench, as though guarding the occupants. "Let's sit down for a minute." They sat on the bench for a few minutes just looking at the surroundings. Then they went to the fountain and sat on one of the benches overlooking the beautiful Isis fountain.

"The water will be flowing in June," Dorothy said. "The fountain is just magnificent when water is cascading down into the pool."

They sat looking at the statue of Isis, holding hands just like Dorothy had imagined when she was a girl. She looked out into the field where she used to sit watching lovers, searching for onlookers, them, but no one was there. Roberts cupped her face in his hands and kissed her deeply. "You're the best thing that's ever happened to me," he said.

CHURCH SERVICES had barely begun when they slipped into the family pew at the front of the church. The choir was singing, and Pastor Washington was at the pulpit looking through his notes, getting ready to deliver his sermon. Dorothy smiled at her nephews and slipped out of her jacket. She was going to miss them when she moved to Newark, but she knew she would be seeing them often enough. The choir stopped singing, and Pastor Washington began his sermon.

"In case there is anyone else in the congregation thinking about getting married in June, I want you all to know that the church is booked. Four of our members have scheduled a wedding in this church for the month of June. My sermon today, appropriately, will be focused on love."

Roberts felt Dorothy move a little closer to him. She squeezed his hand and then smiled a radiant smile that lit up her face. Pastor Washington apparently saw the glow, too. He smiled directly at them before his eyes wandered off in search of the other three couples getting married in June.

"The Bible talks about love, you know. There are several love stories in the good book, including the stories of Abraham and Sarah, Jacob and Rebecca, and let's not forget Mary and Joseph. All of these couples were devoted to each other and were married for life."

Dorothy and Roberts left the service more secure in their love than ever. It was after two o'clock, so they drove hurriedly to The Five-Carat Club. Dorothy took Roberts on the same tour of the facility that she had been taken on. They went into the Emerald Room, the largest banquet hall with a capacity for 500 guests. The emerald green wallpaper and huge chandeliers shimmering with green glass that looked like the ocean was breathtaking.

"This is the room where Sandra and Brad had their reception," Dorothy said.

"This is a big room," Roberts said, looking around at the décor.

"Well, they're both from Oxford, you know. Just about everybody in Oxford knew one of the families, if not both, so practically the whole town was invited to the wedding. Only a few people came from out of town."

The Sapphire Room had a capacity for 300 guests and was just as beautiful as the Emerald Room only the décor was a beautiful cobalt blue. The Diamond Room where they would have their reception was perfect for their needs. It had a capacity for 200 guests. It had beautiful crystal chandeliers and glittering accents that reflected off the walls, giving the appearance of sparkling diamonds throughout the room.

"How do you like this room?" Dorothy asked, looking at the amazement on Roberts' face. "Isn't it beautiful?"

"I knew I could trust you to make our wedding perfect. You didn't need my input at all; everything is wonderful."

She took him into the Ruby Lounge, where their guests would be served cocktails before the reception. Everything in the lounge was, of course, ruby red. Finally she ushered him into The Pearl Restaurant, the only room in the facility that was open to the general public. They feasted on oysters, caviar, standing rib roast, roasted potatoes, green beans with slivered almonds and a large assortment of other delicacies that they would be serving their guests.

When they left The Pearl Room, Roberts was stuffed. The food had been absolutely delicious. He couldn't resist eating a little bit of everything that was put in front of him. There was no way that he could drive back to Newark feeling like this. They left Dorothy's car at the farm, and her dad agreed to drive it to Dayton the next day. She drove the Mustang back to her apartment. For the first time in over a year on the job, Roberts was going to use a sick day.

CHAPTER

25

*E*ven before spring's official entry in late March, Weequahic Park had been splendid with early blooming yellow forsythia, crocus in various shades of pink and purple, and daffodils sprouting all over the place. By mid-April, flower bearing trees were in full bloom, mixing their scent with the fragrance of fresh new grass and filling the air throughout the whole South Ward with a delicious aroma that couldn't help but entice people outdoors.

Winter was over, and the streets of Newark were filled with people glad to get out of stuffy apartments in the projects, dank basements, and homeless shelters scattered throughout the city to accommodate a growing clientele. Some of the homeless were Vietnam veterans unable to readjust to civilian life.

Homeowners were opening their windows to let warm breezes flow through open windows protected with heavy security bars designed to keep them safe in their own homes. Children were skipping home from school with their jackets swinging from their arms or tied around their waists. The elderly were also enjoying the good weather and getting in a little exercise walking around their blocks, taking advantage of the longer daylight hours.

Roberts swung his legs over the side of his bed and looked at the alarm clock on the night table to his right. It was only 5:30AM, and already it was getting light outside. He sat on the bed, thinking about the dream that he'd experienced throughout the night. He'd been covered in mud that he couldn't seem to wash off no matter how many showers he took. The mud covered his shoes, his clothes, and even his hair. In his dream, he'd frantically tried to wash the mud off. Dorothy had been in the dream with him. She was quite disturbed about the mud. He remembered her telling him that he couldn't get in bed with her with all that mud on him.

He tried to associate the dream with something that had happened in Vietnam, something that he had repressed. With elbows resting on his knees, he pressed his head further into his open hands as though he could force himself to remember. The first picture that came to his mind took him back to the time he'd been an infantryman in Cu Chi. There were muddy rice paddies that he'd trudged through looking for Viet Cong, flushing out the enemy. The picture got bigger in his mind.

He remembered people running; he and his comrades began to run after them thinking they were the enemy. The people wouldn't stop running so he and his comrades stopped and fired at their backs. He saw three bodies fall. When they approached, the enemies were laying face down in the mud. He and his comrades turned the bodies over. An old man, an old woman, probably his wife, and a teenage girl, all covered in mud stared up at them. "Damn! They're civilians," one of his comrades had said. "Why were they running from us?"

Roberts remembered being so distraught that he had sat right down in the muddy rice paddy and cried. He knew why they ran. They all knew why they ran. They'd spotted American soldiers with guns, and that's what their instincts told them to do at such a sight.

Roberts finally got off his bed and went to shower, thinking, *Another memory that I will have to learn to live with*. Learning to live with the memories meant acknowledging what had happened and trying not to dwell on those things that caused so much anguish. Roberts was learning to do just that. Every time a memory came to his mind, he'd acknowledge that it happened, pray for forgiveness and try not to think about it again. Sometimes a memory would resurface at the most inopportune time, causing him even more anguish and sometimes compelling him to act out.

One Wednesday night while he was out with "the boys," just such an incident occurred. Roberts, Jeff, and Big Man were leaving JFK recreation center in the Central Ward of the city where they had just finished shooting a few hoops of basketball. As they passed through the courtyard heading to their cars, they came upon a teenage girl being harassed by a young man of about the same age as she.

"Leave me alone," they heard the girl say. At first she sounded agitated.

"Not until I get what I want," the young man had said.

"Don't touch me." The girl's voice sounded frightened and panicky this time.

It wasn't so much what the girl had said, but how she had said it that triggered the memory. Roberts remembered an incident where he and four of his comrades were searching an abandoned village, looking for enemies, when they came upon two village girls who had somehow gotten left behind. The girls were teenagers and very frightened. They huddled together in a deserted hooch, watching the American soldiers but saying nothing.

Two of the soldiers began to touch the girls inappropriately, laughing the whole time. Roberts and the other soldiers stayed back but watched from the doorway.

"Don't worry, pretty girls, we're not going to hurt you." one of soldiers said as he stroked the girls face, attempting to kiss her.

"I just want to touch your tits," the other soldier said, groping the second girl's breast.

That's when Roberts heard the frightened sound in the girl's voice. It was in a different language, one he couldn't understand, but it had the same sound of fear and panic. In Vietnam, outside that hooch, Roberts had walked away. He didn't go back even when he heard the girls screaming. He just kept searching the other hooch's, looking for the enemy, doing his job.

Two years later, when he heard the same panicky voice coming from a teenage girl in Newark he acted. He grabbed the young boy and threw him against the wall. He punched him, hard, in the face.

Blood splattered from his nose. Roberts was about to hit him again, when Big Man and Jeff pulled him off the boy. The boy fell to the ground crying loudly. Roberts looked at him and then walked off to his car. *Why didn't I do that in Vietnam?*

Showering with cold water helped to clear his head. The time he spent in the shower each morning enabled him to replace the dreams from the previous night and the early morning memories with thoughts of the future, the future he and Dorothy were preparing for. Roberts scrubbed his body hard as though he were trying to scrub away all the mud from Vietnam. He thought about Dorothy. She had left two days ago heading back to Ohio completing her April visit to Newark. The thought of the time they had spent together put a smile on his face. He began to whistle the tune *Oh, What a Beautiful Morning.*

Dressing in his work uniform, Roberts remained upbeat. He spotted the unopened mail from the previous day. Scanning through it, he noticed an envelope from City National Bank. He ripped it open and quickly read the first line. "Congratulations, we are happy to inform you that City National Bank has approved your mortgage application." He reached for the telephone and called Dorothy.

"Guess what?" he said when she picked up the telephone.

"What are you so happy about at six o'clock in the morning?" She was getting ready for work, too. She loved it when he called her in the mornings, especially when he was in a good mood.

"How do you know I'm in a good mood?" *This woman reads me like a book,* Roberts thought.

255

"I can feel it. Tell me what's making you so happy?"

"Guess." Roberts said again.

"Oh, I don't know, the mortgage was approved," Dorothy said quickly.

"How did you guess? Are you clairvoyant as well as beautiful and smart?"

"We got it? We got it?" Dorothy was ecstatic. "When do we close?"

Roberts read the entire contents of the letter, which informed them that they had a closing date of May 5.

"The first week in May is your turn to come to Ohio." Dorothy sounded a little disappointed.

"You want me to postpone the closing until later in the month?"

"No! I was hoping that we could move it up a little bit. I want to get in the house as soon as possible to find out what needs to be done before we move in."

"Done?" Roberts was incredulous. "What do you mean what needs to be done? I thought we could just move in."

"We both agreed that we were going to change the color of paint in the bedroom and living room and paper the kitchen. I thought we could do the painting and wallpapering before we move in. As a matter of fact, I was thinking that after we closed on the house you could move in and get started with the work."

"Oh! Is that what you were thinking?"

"Yes. You think about it, too. I've got to get out of here before I'm late for work. I'll call you tonight."

Roberts loved the way Dorothy planted ideas in his head. He

hadn't given thought to painting or wallpapering or anything like that. All he thought about was getting married and moving into their new home. But as he walked out the door heading to the depot to pick up his truck, he was wondering what color he was going to paint the living room and how receptive Jeff and Big Man would be to helping him with this chore. *She has me twisted around her little finger already,* he thought, and then smiled.

Although Roberts was making progress in learning to deal with his memories and put them in perspective, sometimes even a seemingly good day could turn itself around in just a little while. His very first delivery of the day sent him back to a place that he didn't want to go.

The good weather was indeed bringing people outdoors again after a severe winter. However, not only were people coming out to enjoy the weather, but some people were coming out to compensate for their loses over the cold months. The thieves, drug dealers, and other undesirable types were also taking advantage of the good weather. On his way into the housing project, Roberts was almost knocked over by three young men running out the building. One of them had a gun. They ran right past him, never stopping.

Roberts proceeded cautiously into the lobby, hoping that the fleeing young men were finished with their business in the building. He walked slowly up the stairs, not knowing what to expect. He spotted blood running down the steps from the landing above him. He continued climbing the stairs and there, at the top of the landing, was a body lying on the floor.

Almost immediately, Roberts was transported back to Vietnam. How many fallen comrades had he seen lying in the jungles, sometimes in the mud, sometimes writhing in pain, sometimes lifeless and still? Instinctively, he yelled out "Medic, medic." He bent over the body trying to detect a pulse, a heartbeat. He screamed out again, "Medic, medic." He was still there when the police arrived. "Where's the medi-vac?" he asked them. "He's still alive, where's the medi-vac?"

When the ambulance finally arrived to pick up the shooting victim, the police officers insisted that Roberts go with them for observation and treatment. Roberts couldn't understand why they were treating him as though he had been injured. He heard them mumbling to each other behind his back; they were talking about him. "Vietnam vet, shell shocked," were some of the words that he could distinguish.

It took a while to convince the officers that he was all right. How could they know what he had been through? How could they understand what seeing a body lying in a pool of blood meant to him? How many of his comrades had he seen die like that? His reaction may have appeared strange to the police officers, but another combat soldier would have understood.

Civilian life had been difficult for Roberts to resume, but, he appeared to be adjusting. He wondered if other Vietnam veterans were experiencing the same thing. He felt as though he were moving in and out of reality, back and forth from Vietnam to Newark. *When will I get back to normal? Am I always going to be like this?* Roberts thought as he made his way back to his truck.

He was behind schedule now. He had to work faster to make up for the time he had lost. He hoped he wouldn't have any more incidents. He had to focus and stay in reality. He couldn't afford any more trips back to Vietnam during the course of the workday. He needed this job; he was getting married in less than two months and moving into his own home with his new bride.

KILL . . . OR BE KILLED

CHAPTER

26

May arrived, bringing with it warm breezes, colorful tulips, and azaleas, but best of all Dorothy came for her last visit to Newark. She was going to become a permanent resident of the city after their marriage in June, one month away. On this visit, Dorothy drove herself to Newark. She had an interview for a position at Beth Israel Hospital on Monday morning. Trying to get as much done as she could on this last visit, she had carefully packed several fragile items that she wanted to put in their new home after the closing.

Roberts couldn't help but laugh when she pulled up in front of his parents' home with the back seat loaded with crates and boxes. "We haven't even had the closing yet and you're ready to move in already. Couldn't you wait and let the moving company bring this stuff?" He helped her out of the car and held her close to him for a few seconds.

"I wasn't going to trust my grandmother's crystal with a moving company. There are some things that I wanted to personally make sure got here safely." She lifted one of the boxes out of the car.

Roberts helped her carry the boxes into the house, leaving them downstairs in the foyer. "No need to carry all of this stuff upstairs only to bring it back down tomorrow after the closing."

It was Thursday evening and the closing was scheduled for the next afternoon. "I'm so excited just thinking that this time tomorrow we'll be homeowners." They arranged the boxes in the foyer so that they would not obstruct the entrance.

"Do you think we can spend tomorrow night in our new home?" Dorothy was just as excited.

"I don't think so. We won't have any utilities, and we'll need water at least. I'll have all of that taken care of early next week." Roberts said just as the front door opened and his father walked in.

"Are you starting to move out all ready?" Mr. Roberts asked, looking at the pile of boxes.

"I guess so," Roberts said. "Dorothy brought a few of her things from Ohio that will go into our new home. Is it all right if we leave them here in the foyer until after the closing tomorrow?"

"Of course, you can," Mrs. Roberts said, coming into the room from the kitchen. "All of you just come on in the kitchen and eat up all of this fish I fried for you. Besides Daddy and I have a surprise for you." She looked at her husband for a signal. Smiling, he put his arm around her waist and steered her toward the kitchen.

Roberts and Dorothy followed, even more excited than they already had been. The table was set for dinner; a platter of fried fish served as the centerpiece. Mr. Roberts went to the sink to wash his hands, and Dorothy and Roberts went to the powder room to do the same thing. When they returned to the kitchen, Mrs. Roberts had placed a bowl of salad and several ears of steaming corn on the table along with a smaller platter of cornbread.

"Sit down and eat now before my dinner gets cold," she playfully ordered.

Two minutes after they were seated, Roberts asked, "What's the surprise?" He reached for a piece of porgy.

Smiling from ear to ear, Mrs. Roberts said, "Give them the tickets."

"Tickets?" Dorothy echoed.

"Yes, tickets," Mr. Roberts said. "I just picked these tickets up, and Mom and I want to give them to you as an early wedding present." He, too, was grinning from ear to ear now.

"Tickets to what?" Roberts asked.

Mr. Roberts reached inside his jacket and pulled out an envelope and handed it to his son. "Your mother and I want only the best for you and Dorothy. We hope this gift will start you out on a journey of happiness."

Both Roberts and Dorothy huddled over the envelope as Roberts pulled out the contents. "A cruise," they both said in unison.

"You're giving us a cruise?" Roberts looked at his parents in disbelief.

Tearfully, Dorothy said, "A honeymoon?"

"Yes, a honeymoon," Mrs. Roberts said. "I don't know any two kids more deserving than the two of you. You have both worked so hard to do something positive with your lives, this is the least we could do."

Dorothy and Roberts both jumped out of their seats and hugged his parents. They were going on a seven-day Caribbean cruise following their wedding.

THE CLOSING WENT well the next day. When Dorothy and Roberts left the attorney's office with the keys to the house, it was six o'clock in the evening. Both their cars were packed with things they wanted to take to the house. Dorothy followed Roberts in her car as he drove up Lyons Avenue before turning onto their street and then pulling their cars into their own driveway for the very first time. She jumped out of her car, carrying a small duffel bag.

They both rushed up to the front door and stood on their front porch as Roberts fumbled with the keys until he got the right one before opening the door to their new home. He looked at Dorothy and, before she could say anything, he scooped her up and carried her over the threshold.

"Silly, you're not supposed to do this until after we're married."

"As far as I'm concerned, we are married. I couldn't love you anymore than I do right now. I couldn't be any happier than I am now. The wedding will only be a formality for our friends and family to witness," Roberts kissed her before putting her down on the floor of their new home.

"Come on, let's check out the kitchen," Dorothy grabbed his hand and pulled him into the kitchen.

The kitchen wallpaper was hideous; it had big yellow flowers and brown stems with big green leaves. The appliances were harvest gold, the latest color for kitchen appliances.

"I love the harvest gold color of the appliances," Dorothy said. "I've only seen white appliances in my mother's kitchen, but I hate the wall paper. Let's go shopping Saturday for wallpaper and paint." She reached in her handbag and pulled out a pencil, pad, and tape measure. "Can you figure out how much wallpaper we'll need?" She handed him the tape measure.

"I don't know anything about wallpapering." Roberts took the tape measure.

"Then find someone who can do it for us. We'll just have to pay for it."

"I'm pretty much broke. All of my money went towards the house," Roberts started to measure the kitchen walls. "Can't some of this wait until later? I can live with this wallpaper for a little while."

"I have some money, besides we'll probably get lots of money for wedding gifts. I'd like to have the house ready when we move in." She gave him a look that pleaded for him to let her win this little battle.

"Okay." Roberts gave in. "I hope you like the floor tiles and the carpeting."

"They're fine. It's just the wall color in the living room that I hate." She walked through the dining room and into the living room, still carrying her duffel bag. "I'd like a softer color in here." She kept walking, heading towards the stairs. Roberts followed her.

Upstairs, Dorothy assessed what needed to be done in the master bedroom and bathroom, taking notes. Roberts looked around, noticing all of the doors. He counted seven doors, one for each of the four bedrooms, one bathroom door, a closet door, and the door that led to the attic. *So many doors,* he thought. Something about the doors was unsettling to him. He barely listened as Dorothy rattled on about what she wanted done.

"Come in the bedroom," she said, startling him out of his thoughts.

"We should bring in the boxes before it gets dark outside," Roberts said, following her into the bedroom. He still felt a little uneasy, but couldn't put his finger on what was causing it.

Dorothy opened the duffel bag and pulled out a tablecloth that she spread on the bedroom floor. Then she pulled out two candles, a bottle of sparkling cider, two wineglasses and a box of cheese and crackers, all of which she put on the tablecloth.

"Come, come and sit next to me." She sat on the carpet at the edge of the tablecloth. "I want us to toast our first community property." She opened the bottle of cider and poured them both a glass.

Roberts smiled at the sight of her sitting with her legs folded under her. She looked so pretty. *How I love her,* he thought as he joined her on the floor. They toasted to their first community property and nibbled on the cheese and crackers, and then Roberts took her in his arms and christened their new home with the best lovemaking he could give.

THEY SPENT SATURDAY shopping for items they needed for the house. They drove over to Channel Lumber Company in Kearny, New Jersey, a neighboring city. Channel's was the place to shop for homeowners looking to remodel their homes or just fix it up a little. They purchased paint for the master bedroom and the living room, wallpaper for the kitchen and downstairs powder room, and an assortment of gadgets Dorothy wanted for their new home, some of which Roberts had no clue as to what they were for. Standing in the checkout line, he held up a utensil that he had never seen before.

"What in the world is this?" he asked, twirling the long plastic thing around with his fingers. "It looks like a letter opener, but I know it isn't."

"It's for removing veins from shrimp," Dorothy took the item and demonstrated its proper use. "You know how much you love shrimp. This will make cleaning them a lot easier. My mother uses one."

"And what's this?" Roberts held up another strange-looking utensil.

"It's a garlic press," she said. "I see you don't spend much time in the kitchen."

"I don't even have a kitchen." He laughed. "I don't know a thing about cooking."

"That's going to change once we get married. I love men that know their way around the kitchen. I know that you'll want to please me by acquiring some culinary skills."

"What skills are you going to acquire to please me?"

"I think I already have all the skills you'll ever want." She gave him a seductive smile.

"You got that right." He grinned at her, squeezing her hand.

They skipped church on Sunday, instead lying in bed all morning reading the local newspaper, checking the sales, and waiting for Mr. and Mrs. Roberts to leave the house for services. Dorothy made breakfast in Mrs. Robert's kitchen. She made biscuits from scratch and home fries with lots of onions and green peppers. They had fresh-squeezed orange juice and coffee.

After breakfast, they went back upstairs to the attic apartment and packed some of the things that Roberts would be taking to their new home. Dorothy wanted to visit the new house once more before she left to go back to Ohio. She wanted to make sure that she didn't overlook anything that she felt he needed to do before they moved in as husband and wife.

"We'll use your bedroom furniture for the guest room, and mine for the master bedroom. Is that okay with you?"

"Sounds fine to me." Roberts took some pictures off the wall and wrapped them in newspaper. "I'll be moving into the house in a couple of days in order to complete all the work you want done before the wedding. Everything will be perfect when we get back from our honeymoon," he said. When he got to the framed picture of Greg in his dress uniform, he stared at it for a long time before he started to wrap it in newspaper.

"Does looking at Greg's picture stir up memories from Vietnam?" Dorothy rubbed his arm as he wrapped the picture.

"Not really. When I look at Greg's picture, I remember the old days, hanging out, going to school, wrestling; you know, the good things." He put the picture in a box with the others.

"Good, then we'll give it a prominent spot in our new home. I don't want things around that will conjure up bad memories for you."

I don't know what might or might not conjure up memories of Vietnam anymore, Roberts thought, remembering his uneasy feeling about the doors in the house they had just purchased.

KILL . . . OR BE KILLED

CHAPTER

27

After all the utilities in the new house except the telephone were turned on, Roberts enlisted the help of Jeff and Big Man to move his bedroom furniture and the remainder of his personal belongings out of his parents' home on Saturday morning. For the first time in his life, he was going to be living alone, if only for a few weeks. Moving day turned out to be a fun day; Jeff kidded him about being all grown up now that he was finally leaving the nest.

"No more home-cooked meals courtesy of mom," Jeff teased him.

"Dorothy's a good cook; I'm sure she'll see to it that I don't starve."

"I don't care how well your wife cooks, there is no one that can replace mom, trust me," Big Man said. "Hell, I might just stay in my mother's basement forever, just to keep eating her home-cooked meals." He laughed at his comment.

"There are some things that make up for mom's cooking, though,"

Jeff said. "That's why most men move out of their mom's house. Don't you miss having Marcia to snuggle up to at night?"

"No. And who says that I don't have someone to snuggle up with? Marcia wasn't the only fish in the sea." Big Man and Jeff struggled to move the dresser through the bedroom door."

"There's nothing like having that special one, though, right, Roberts?" Jeff looked back at Roberts for confirmation as Roberts held the door open for them.

"Having that special one makes all the difference in the world," Roberts said, squeezing past them to get to the bottom of the stairwell in order to open the outside door.

They were using Jeff's van, the one he used for work. They'd cleaned the van out, taking out all the equipment he used for his carpet cleaning business and storing it in the garage.

They drove the few short blocks to the newly purchased house and pulled into the driveway. Once the bedroom furniture was set up in the guestroom, and Roberts' clothing was hung in the closet in the master bedroom, the three men moved to the living room where they set up drop cloths and ladders to begin the task of painting the living room. Roberts had packed the refrigerator with beer and soft drinks for his friends and had used the telephone at his parents' house to place an order for pizza to be delivered in a couple of hours.

Everything seemed to be falling into place. In a few weeks, he would be married and Dorothy would be there with him. How he wished that would resolve his Vietnam conflicts. Roberts hooked up his stereo equipment while his friends mixed the paint. He put in a Marvin Gaye tape and the sultry sound of Marvin singing "What's Going On" filled the room.

"Do you know how fortunate you are to be moving into your own home before you even get married?" Big Man was saying. "Most Black families have to save for years before they can buy a house."

"That was one of the benefits of going into the military, I guess," Roberts said. "Dorothy and I both had an opportunity to get our mortgage guaranteed through the Veterans Administration. We were fortunate that we had some money saved for a down payment. Generally veterans don't need a down payment; they just need the closing costs. But with a ten-percent down payment, we were able to get a thirty-year mortgage fixed at 5% interest. You can't beat that." He picked up a roller, dipped it in the paint tray and started to paint a wall.

"Belinda and I had to put down twenty percent for a thirty year fixed at 8%," Jeff said. "Besides we had to borrow most of the twenty percent from our families. So we're paying a mortgage as well as repaying the loans to our families. We still feel blessed, though. We love the house, and we don't mind working hard to pay off the loans."

"Well, I never could get a house," Big Man said. "I don't have steady employment, no veterans help, and no family that would lend me any money. Maybe I should have gone into the service?" He looked a little forlorn, but only for a moment. "But on the other hand, I could have come back in a body bag like Greg. I'll just be content to live in my momma's basement until something better comes along."

"I'd trade places with you anytime, Jeff," Roberts said. "Even though I didn't come back in a body bag, I'm still so scarred from Vietnam that I don't know if I'll ever really heal. War is hell, and I wouldn't wish it on my worst enemy." Roberts shook his head as though trying to shake the experience out of his system.

"You'll get better," Jeff said. "Remember, time heals all wounds."

I certainly hope you're right, Roberts thought just as the doorbell rang.

"Pizza," the three of them said in unison.

The three men spent the next half-hour eating pizza, drinking beer, except for Roberts, who stuck with soda, and cracking jokes about Big Man's decision to be single.

"I'm just not interested in taking on the responsibility that comes with marriage. I don't want a mortgage, two car notes, huge grocery bills, and nursery school tuition expenses right now. I like doing construction work because I get a lot of time off. I'm not ready to settle down with a woman who wants me to work my butt off to help her pay for a bunch of stuff. What's wrong with that?" Big Man took a bite out of his third slice of pizza.

"You should have thought about that before you said, 'I do,'" Roberts said, grabbing his third slice, too. "I just think you should have been honest with Marcia. I plan to be honest and truthful to Dorothy about everything right from the beginning."

"Belinda and I have a trusting relationship, too. I can't lie to her even If I wanted to. The woman reads me like a book. I don't even think about trying to get over on her."

"I was truthful with Marcia. When she told me she was pregnant, I said I wanted to marry her. I was telling her the truth. I did want to get married. I just didn't tell her it was because I wanted to avoid the draft."

"Did you tell her you put a hole in the condom?" Jeff asked.

"She just asked me to use a condom, she never asked about the condition of the condom. Withholding information is not lying. You have some nerve, Jeff, you did the same thing to Belinda."

"You're right, I did. Belinda wasn't sure she was ready to get married and I wanted to avoid getting drafted, too. I've confessed to her what I did. She's forgiven me, but I know she was disappointed in me. Her trust in me was damaged as a result of that single incident. I try to make up for it by being honest about everything now, and trying to be the best husband and father that I can be." He reached for his fourth slice.

"What about you, Roberts? Have you come clean with Dorothy about everything?"

"Yes, so far I have."

Big Man and Jeff didn't leave the house until close to 11PM. The living room was finished. The paint job was superb, the three of them agreed, as they stood back admiring their work.

"You want us to help you with the bedroom tomorrow?" Jeff asked as he was leaving.

"Yeah," Big Man said. "I can come back tomorrow and help you with the bedroom."

"No," Roberts said. "You guys have been very helpful. I can do the bedroom by myself. I have some guy from my dad's job coming to wallpaper the kitchen tomorrow. I'll paint while he papers. It will give me an excuse not to attend church tomorrow. I'll see you guys next Wednesday."

"Boys' night out," they said in unison.

After Roberts cleaned up the mess they had made downstairs, he climbed the stairs, thinking he would shower and go to bed. He missed having a telephone; he wanted to call Dorothy. As he climbed the last step, he automatically focused on the doors again. All seven of the doors were closed. He felt his body stiffen as fear overtook him. He was frozen at the top of the steps, unable to move any further. He contemplated going back down the steps.

This is crazy, he thought. *This is my house; there is nothing here that can harm me.* He forced himself to approach the first door. It was the linen closet. He listened at the door and then cautiously opened it. He left the closet door open and moved to the next door. This was the bathroom. Roberts did the same thing, listened first and then opened the door, leaving it open. He proceeded in the same manner with each room; the room that Dorothy decided would be her office, on to the master bedroom, then the guest bedroom, the future nursery, and finally the door leading to the attic.

Once Roberts opened the door to the attic, he turned on the lights and ventured up the steps. He checked out each nook and cranny until he was satisfied that no one was there. He finally went back downstairs and into the guestroom where he would be sleeping, making sure that all of the doors were left open.

Roberts removed his clothing, took out clean towels and underwear from the bureau drawer and headed to the bathroom to shower. He still felt a little eerie, but he tried to put the feeling aside. He sang, "Go-ing to the Chapel and we're/gonna get Ma-a-a-ried," at the top of his lungs as he scrubbed his body.

Feeling more relaxed, Roberts took his nightly medication and climbed into his bed. But sleep did not come right away. He generally fell asleep five or ten minutes after taking the medication and slept through the night. But, five minutes after getting into bed, the eerie feeling returned and Roberts felt a need to get up and check the doors again. He went so far as to creep down the stairs and double check the lock on the front door.

Once back upstairs, Roberts looked at all the open doors. He peeked into the closet, the bathroom, and all the other rooms before going into the master bedroom. He turned on the light and instinctively went to the closet where he had put his personal things. He reached for his hatbox at the top of the closet. He felt the heaviness of the box, knowing instantly that the gun was responsible for the weight.

Roberts opened the box, took out the gun, and went back into the guestroom. He climbed into bed, placing the gun under his pillow. He told himself, *This is just in case someone tries to come in while I'm sleeping.* Two minutes later he was fast asleep.

The sound of the doorbell woke Roberts up on Sunday morning. As his eyes got used to the light coming through the windows, Roberts realized that he was in his new home. He had spent his first night in the home he and Dorothy would share as man and wife. The doorbell rang again. He looked at the clock next to his bed. It was 9:10AM. He'd told the guy coming to paper the kitchen to be there by nine. He pulled on his jeans and rushed downstairs to open the door.

While the paperhanger worked in the kitchen, Roberts finished dressing upstairs. He thought about his behavior the night before. *Why am I obsessing about doors, now,* he wondered? He tried to recall his dream from the previous night. He'd gone to sleep with doors on his mind and had dreamed about doors through the night. He remembered thatch covered doors used in all the hoochs in Vietnam. *What's the significance,* he wondered?

As Roberts made the bed, he saw the gun under his pillow. He carefully placed the gun back in the hatbox and put it at the top of his closet, far to the back. *I don't want Dorothy to discover that I have a gun in the house.* Then he remembered what he had just told his friends the previous evening. *I plan to be honest and truthful with Dorothy about everything right from the beginning,* he recalled saying. Could he tell her about the gun?

Painting the walls of the master bedroom, Roberts was consumed with thoughts of how he was going to deal with his latest behavior. *How am I going to deal with the matter of the doors? I've got to get this under control before Dorothy moves in. I've got to talk to someone about it,* he decided.

TWO DAYS LATER Roberts got the opportunity to talk about the door situation. He'd gone to the VA Hospital to pick up his new prescription. After getting his regular checkup, in which he got his blood pressure read and his heart checked with a stethoscope, he asked the receptionist if he could speak to the resident psychiatrist. "You may have to wait a while," she told him. "There's a long line of men waiting to see him," she pointed to a waiting room right outside from the reception area.

"Are all of those guys waiting to see the psychiatrist?" Roberts counted the men in the waiting room. Fifteen men were in the room. All of the men were young, about his age, ranging from twenty to thirty.

"Yes, sir. They're all waiting to see him, and he has to leave at six."

Roberts checked his watch, four o'clock. He'd left work a little early to keep the appointment to get his prescription refilled. If the doctor got to see all of the men in the room, he would only be able to give each man less than ten minutes.

"You want me to put your name on the list," the receptionist asked.

"Why not?" Roberts said, going to take a seat. He had nothing better to do.

When Roberts was finally called to see the doctor it was 5:53PM.

"You understand that I have less than ten minutes to give you," the psychiatrist said as Roberts walked in the door. Roberts remembered speaking to this doctor on at least one other occasion.

"I understand, Doctor." Roberts took a seat in front of the desk.

"What's troubling you, Mr. Roberts?" The doctor had to check his chart in order to recall his name.

The Vietnam War, Roberts thought, but didn't say. "I've been experiencing a lot of anxiety related to doors," Roberts said. "I just moved into a new home and I can't seem to stop thinking about doors."

"How are these thoughts manifesting themselves?" The doctor sat down in his chair, and looked directly at Roberts.

"I open all the doors in the house as though I need to see what's behind them. Last night I got out of bed to check the doors again. I'm afraid for the doors to be closed, except for the front door. I want that one to remain closed and locked." He didn't mention sleeping with the gun under his pillow.

"It sounds as though you're obsessing about something associated with an occurrence in Vietnam. That's part of the post-traumatic stress syndrome that you're experiencing."

"But what is the occurrence? What's causing me to obsess about doors? I'm afraid that my fiancée won't understand this behavior after we're married. I'm getting married in less than a month."

"I've seen this before with Vietnam veterans. Your mind is gearing up to recall suppressed information. Let it happen; it wants to come to the surface. Once you remember it, you will learn to deal with it the same way you have learned to deal with all the other memories that your mind suppressed."

"How will I handle it with my future wife? What am I supposed to tell her when she finds all the doors open? When will I be normal again?"

"Your life experience puts you in a position where you will never be the person that you were ever again. Your wife, and other people as well, will have to accept you the way that you are now. I'm not saying that in time you won't feel better. But your experiences have changed you forever, Mr. Roberts. You can't think of going back to where you were before your Vietnam experience. You need to concentrate on going forward and putting everything into perspective," the doctor said, getting out of his chair and walking toward the door, signaling Roberts that his time was up.

KILL . . . OR BE KILLED

CHAPTER
28

The remainder of May went by quickly and, before he knew it, Roberts was making his last visit to Ohio before the wedding. It was the Friday of Memorial Day weekend and this time he wasn't driving the Mustang, and he wasn't alone. It was only two weeks before the actual wedding and Dorothy had planned a wedding rehearsal for Sunday after church, but before the rehearsal her bridesmaids had planned a bridal shower for her on Saturday night. Mr. and Mrs. Roberts, Deneen, Derek, Big Man, Jeff, and Belinda were all coming along, too. With the seats reinstalled, they were using Jeff's van for the occasion.

Roberts was happy to be a passenger for the long drive. He was in no mood for conversation, though, and hoped that the others would be content talking with one another. He sat in the front with Jeff in order to navigate the way. Belinda, Deneen, and Mrs. Roberts sat in the back with Big Man, Derek, and Mr. Roberts sitting in the middle. No one in the van had ever been on an active farm before, so they were pretty excited about the trip.

"I can't believe that I'm going to be staying on a farm with cows, pigs, and hogs," Big Man kept saying. "This is certainly going to be a highlight of my life."

"I thought you said Dorothy's family got rid of all their animals," Mrs. Roberts said to her son. When he didn't answer, she said, "Are you all right, David? You've hardly said a word since we left."

"David, don't you hear mom talking to you?" Deneen asked from the back seat.

"I'm sorry, I guess I'm just tired. I've been working hard trying to get things in order before the wedding. You know, painting and stuff."

"Don't complain, Roberts. Jeff and I volunteered to help you, remember." Big Man reached up to tug at Robert's shoulder.

"Yeah, you did. Anyway, it's all done and I'm just tired. What was the question?"

"Are there any cows and pigs and animals on Dorothy's parents' farm?" Mrs. Roberts asked again.

"Only a few, but her sister's farm is loaded with animals. Dorothy said that the arrangements are for mom, an dad, Deneen, and Derek to stay with her parents. Jeff, Belinda, and Big Man will stay with her sister."

"I hope her sister doesn't put me in the barn with the animals," Big Man said, and then laughed.

"You mean with the other animals," Deneen said.

"Don't think you can pick on me now that you're pregnant and have your husband to defend you." Big Man turned around and gave her a mean look.

"You two have been picking on each other for as long as I can remember. When are you going to grow up?" Mrs. Roberts said, giving them a maternal reprimand.

"She started it," Big Man said, defensively, sounding like a little boy.

Roberts ignored the playful bantering, retreating into his own thoughts. *Why am I obsessing about the doors? Why can't I figure it out?* For the past few nights, he had been plagued with dreams about doors. He was still getting the eerie feeling about the doors in his house. Every night since he had moved into the house, he would check more than once to make sure that the front door was locked before he went to sleep. He was also still sleeping with the gun under his pillow.

He'd finished painting the master bedroom and had decided to paint the guestroom as well. The kitchen was papered, and he'd raked up the yard and prepared it for the garden that Dorothy was anxious to plant when they returned from their honeymoon. She'd told him about her gardening ideas the last time they had spoken on the telephone. "It will be the middle of June," she had said. "That's a little late for planting a garden, but I'm going to do it anyway."

I can't wait to see Dorothy puttering around in our backyard, Roberts thought. As a surprise, he'd bought her a set of gardening tools with a pair of little flowered gloves and a wide-brim straw hat to shade her from the sun. *She's going to look so cute in this hat,* he remembered thinking when he had purchased it. He truly believed that Dorothy's presence would make everything better for him.

"Hey, Roberts, are you asleep?" Jeff said, jolting him out of his thoughts. "This is the exit for Oxford. Do we make a left or a right when we exit?

"Make a right," Roberts said, looking out the window to get his bearings.

DOROTHY AND HER entire family were there to greet them when they pulled up in front of the farmhouse. After all the introductions and hugs were given, Mrs. Campbell ushered them into the house, where she had fresh lemonade and her famous tollhouse cookies on hand. After a half-hour of socializing, Mrs. Campbell took Mr. and Mrs. Roberts up to the guestroom, and Deneen and Derek to Dorothy's bedroom, in order to rest and let the women freshen up before the bridal shower. Dorothy's sister took Big Man, Jeff, and Belinda to her farm to do the same thing. Dorothy and Roberts headed to the barn.

In the loft of the barn with Dorothy, Roberts felt relaxed and free of anxiety for the first time since he'd moved into their new home. He lay down on the comforter Dorothy had spread out and watched her as she spread extra blankets and placed pillows all about to make the place comfortable for them. He looked around the loft. There were no doors anywhere in sight, just the one window and plenty of hay.

"I wish we could live here," he said, reaching for her hand and gently pulling her down beside him.

"Why? Don't you like our new home?" She had a puzzled look on her face.

"Oh, I like it. It's just that this is the first place that we were really alone and the first place that we made love. I just like being here with you." He positioned her on top of him and held her close. "I just wish we could stay like this forever, shutting out the rest of the world." Roberts closed his eyes and squeezed Dorothy a little tighter.

"Are you all right?" She sat up, straddling him and looking him right in the eye.

"What do you think?" he asked, avoiding looking into her eyes. "I'm about to marry the most wonderful woman in the world." He pulled her down and kissed her passionately. He didn't have the heart to tell her how troubled he was.

"We don't have time for this right now," Dorothy said, pulling her legs from around his body. "I've got to take our moms and Deneen to the shower."

"Come on," Roberts tried to persuade her. "We have time for a quickie, don't we?"

"Not really, the shower is being held at the home of one of my bridesmaids, which is about ten miles from here. Besides, I have some things that I want to talk to you about, and I have a lot to get done in a short period of time." She sat cross-legged on the comforter.

"I thought we were just about finished with everything. What else needs to be done?"

"Well, after the shower, I have to take Belinda for a final fitting of her dress. She wants to take it home with her on Monday. Tomorrow, we have the dress rehearsal and the rehearsal dinner, besides that Pastor Washington wants to have a final word with us before the wedding. Oh, and did you notice the U-Haul truck parked near the house?"

"Yeah, I saw it, what's it for?" He stroked her back, hoping she would lie down again.

"I moved out of my apartment, and I quit my job. The lease was up and I had to renew or go. The U-Haul is full of my things from the apartment. I thought you could drive it back to Newark when you leave on Monday. You can turn the truck in at the U-Haul place in Orange, NJ. Is that all right with you? We can save a lot of money by not hiring professional movers."

"I like the idea of saving money, too. I guess we can do that. What else do you need to tell me?"

"Oh, yeah, I got the job at Beth Israel Hospital. I'm so excited. They want me to start the day after we get back from our honeymoon. There's only one drawback."

"What's that?" Roberts sat up; she had his full attention now.

"I have to work the 3PM to 11PM shift." She held her breath waiting for his response.

"No, no, I don't want you working the night shift. I won't have any time with you." Roberts became so agitated that he jumped to his feet. "I want to have dinner with you every evening, and I want to go to bed with you every night. I've been looking forward to this for so long."

"It'll only be for a short time," Dorothy said softly, standing up herself. She moved closer to him and stroked his arm, trying to soothe him. "The head nurse told me it will be a maximum of six months. They had to reschedule, and this was the only way they could do it and fit me in right away. It'll be all right. I'll make it all right, I promise you." She kissed him softly on his neck.

Relaxing at her touch, Roberts pulled her closer and held her to his body, thinking, *Maybe I can cut down on my sleep. Maybe I can wait up for her to get home every night.* His regular routine was to take his medication at 11PM in order to fall asleep by 11:15 so that he could get up at 5:30AM. Dorothy's routine had been similar; she had to be at work by 7AM, the same as he. One of the things that they had grown accustomed to since their courtship began was speaking to each other on the telephone until they both fell asleep at approximately the same time each night, and sometimes calling each other in the AM just to say good morning.

He was still holding her in his arms when they heard the door to the barn open and the voice of Mr. Roberts.

"Would you believe this is the first time I've ever been in a barn," he was telling Dorothy's father.

"Me, too," Derek said. "I've always wanted to visit one, though."

"Come on, I'll show you around," Mr. Campbell said, just as Roberts and Dorothy started climbing down the ladder from the loft.

"There you are, Dorothy. Your mother and guests are waiting for you to take them to the shower."

"I'm on my way," Dorothy said, giving Roberts a peck on the cheek before running out the barn door, leaving him with the other three men.

WHILE THE WOMEN attended the shower, Mr. Campbell drove Roberts his dad and Derek to his son-in-law's farm, where they joined the other men and Dorothy's two nephews for some man talk. When they pulled up, Roberts saw that Big Man had made himself comfortable on the porch swing while Jeff cooked hamburgers on the grill. Brad, their host, was setting a nearby picnic table with buns and condiments.

"This is the life," Big Man said as soon as Roberts joined him on the porch swing. "I love this farm. I think I could be a farmer."

"I like visiting the farm, too, but I have no interest in being a farmer. There's a lot you have to learn in order to run a farm of this size."

"I think I would like that. I've never been motivated enough to learn anything that would keep me gainfully employed before. This may just be my calling." Big Man looked serious.

"Being a farmer is a lot of hard work, disappointments sometimes, but mostly pleasure," Mr. Campbell said, overhearing the conversation as he joined them on the porch. "I don't know any other life, and never wanted to."

"This farm is my life," Brad said, beckoning them to the picnic table to eat. "Not only has it kept me gainfully employed, but it's something that I can pass down to my two sons, just like my father passed it down to me."

"That's something very rare among African-Americans," Mr. Roberts said. "Being able to pass down the means to gainfully employ the next generation is a luxury that has escaped the majority of African-Americans and doesn't appear to be within our reach. That's why so many of our young people join the military." He looked sad.

"You think that's not by design?" Jeff asked. "This country needs a reserve group of troops because that's how they stay in power. I remember a Christmas card that you sent me from Vietnam a couple of years ago, Roberts. It had a picture of a dove carrying an olive branch in its mouth on the cover and the caption said 'Peace on Earth.' When I opened the card, it read, 'Through Superior Weaponry.' To me that says it all. We all know that Blacks are disproportionately drafted to fight America's wars. That's because we have few options to do anything else that's both productive and lucrative." He passed the platter of burgers to Big Man, who put two of them on his plate.

"While I was in Vietnam, I remember most of the Whites saying that the only reason they got drafted was because they couldn't get into college," Roberts said before biting into a burger. "They had options like going to college or moving to Canada. The brothers couldn't afford college and couldn't move to Canada without finances. The other guys had finances provided by their parents."

"The Whites also got the better jobs that kept them off the streets and gainfully employed. Those recruiters stalked brothers for months, checking every week to see if they'd found a job yet. They knew there weren't any jobs for us. We didn't have many choices." Jeff said.

"I know what you mean," Derek said. "They hounded me from my senior year until Deneen and I got married. Even though I had a job, they kept after me until I gave them proof that my wife was with child. They were unrelenting." He shook his head in disbelief.

"You're right about that, man. The only option to avoid getting drafted was to get married like I did," Big Man chimed in. "Even if my marriage didn't work out, it kept me out of Vietnam and maybe from coming home in a body bag like our friend, Greg."

The men were still sitting on the front porch talking when Sandra and Belinda returned from the bridal shower. Roberts was surprised when he glanced at his watch and saw that it was almost ten o'clock. *Where had the time gone?* he asked himself. He was anxious to get back to the barn and be alone with Dorothy. He listened to the two women talk about the fun things they had done at the shower for a few minutes before he stood up, signaling his future father-in-law that it was time to return to the Campbell farm.

ROBERTS AND DOROTHY missed breakfast with their parents the next morning, but got to the house early enough to see them leaving for church services. Deneen and Derek were still upstairs sleeping.

Seeing that they were not dressed for church, Mrs. Campbell said, "You two know that Pastor Washington wanted an opportunity to talk to you again before the wedding," as they came in the front door. She was obviously disappointed that they were missing Sunday services.

"Pastor Washington will understand," Dorothy said. "We'll be coming to the church right after services. We'll get a chance to speak to him before the rehearsal begins."

"We'll see you at the rehearsal then," Mrs. Roberts said, shaking her head in disapproval.

The meeting with Pastor Washington was brief. There was little left to say that hadn't been said in the previous five sessions. "I just want you to be happy and to continue to be faithful servants of the Lord," Pastor said to the beaming couple in his office, while the other members of the wedding party gathered in the sanctuary.

"Oh, we intend to be just that," Dorothy said. "We are so grateful to you for all the guidance that you have given us." She looked at Roberts, urging him to acknowledge their appreciation.

"Yes, Pastor, we are truly thankful for your words of wisdom and the time that you extended to us," Roberts said.

"Well, that being said let's get on with the rehearsal. The next time I see you, I'll be pronouncing you man and wife." He stood up, signaling that the session was over.

Roberts stood and reached across the desk to shake the pastor's hand. Pastor ignored the extended hand and came around his desk and embraced the couple, extending his arms and bringing them both to his chest.

"I missed you two in church today, but I understand that you have a lot to do before the wedding," he said. "We said a special prayer for you and asked that you receive your blessings in abundance." He smiled at them and walked them into the sanctuary.

The entire wedding party had arrived and was sitting patiently in the first two pews of the church. Roberts could not help but notice that Big Man was chatting away with one of the bridesmaids. Roberts hadn't met the bridesmaids yet, but he'd seen pictures from Dorothy's yearbook. He knew that although they were both single only one of them was unattached. Big Man evidently had found the unattached one.

Dorothy introduced Roberts to the two bridesmaids, Rita and Marilyn. Rita was tall, close to six feet. Standing, she was able to look right into Big Man's eyes. She was quite pretty, golden brown with a short, natural hair style, much like Belinda's. The other bridesmaid was of medium height, with a light complexion and long brown hair. They both appeared friendly.

The rehearsal took about an hour before everything had been fine-tuned to Dorothy's expectations. She wanted each groomsmen to walk into the sanctuary at the signal of a drumbeat. Each groomsmen would then walk to meet a bridesmaid, who would enter from the opposite side of the aisle, and escort her down the aisle. Right before the bride entered, escorted by her father, the best man would meet the maid of honor halfway down the aisle and escort her to the altar where they would wait with the groom for the bride to reach the altar. It was perfect.

After the rehearsal, the wedding party had a scrumptious dinner at the Pearl Restaurant, compliments of the groom's parents. Throughout the dinner, Big Man kept his eyes on Rita, and she appeared to genuinely return his attention. Roberts could not remember a time when he had been happier. Everyone he had ever loved was together in one room. The only one missing was Greg. He wished Greg were there.

EARLY THE NEXT MORNING the van was at the house to pick up Mr. and Mrs. Roberts and Deneen and Derek. Roberts and Big Man were riding in the U-Haul. Roberts didn't have a minute to retreat into his own thoughts. Big Man talked continuously.

"Man, did you see how pretty Rita is? I could fall in love with a girl like that. She's everything I want in a woman. She lives on a farm, too. She still lives with her parents. She's a nurse, like Dorothy." He sighed, looking out the window at grazing cows in the beautiful green pastures.

"It sounds like you really like this woman," Roberts said, focusing on the road.

"Like her? Man, did you hear what I said. I could fall in love with her. I'm going to call her as soon as I get home. She wants to know that we got home safely. I can't wait for the wedding so that I can see her again. I think I'll stay in Ohio for the whole weekend after your wedding. I wouldn't mind having a wedding in Ohio."

"You just met her, aren't you jumping the gun a little?" Roberts asked.

"This is no coincidence man, I fell in love with Ohio and farm life before I even met Rita. After meeting her, I know that this is the place for me. Roberts don't you believe in divine intervention and destiny? This is divine. I just met her yesterday, and I feel like I'm in love. I know this is right. I just know it."

Roberts looked at his friend and smiled. "It would be nice for Dorothy to have a friend in Newark. Oh, I know she has Belinda and Deneen, but I mean someone that she grew up with. Maybe it will work out with you two."

"If it works out, she won't be moving to Newark; I'll be moving to Ohio. I want to be a farmer. That's the life for me. I can't wait to get out of Newark." Big Man laid his head back on the headrest, closed his eyes and was silent. Suddenly he blurted out, "Man, you and your family will be coming to Ohio to visit me and my family. Do you believe this?" He had a happy smile on his face as he slipped back into his silent mode.

Roberts thought about how content he had been in the barn with Dorothy. Now he was going home alone. He thought about the doors. *What is it about the doors that are bothering me? Maybe I should have considered moving to Ohio, too.*

CHAPTER

29

Big Man was truly a loyal and helpful friend Roberts determined once again, after they arrived at the newly purchased house. It was after 8PM, and he stayed until the entire contents of the U-Haul had been moved into the house. He helped Roberts set up Dorothy's bedroom furniture in the master bedroom. Then they arranged the living room furniture. Roberts couldn't thank him enough and offered to pay him for his time.

"Man, what kind of friend would I be if I took money from my best friend for helping him out? It's the least that I can do for you and Dorothy." Big Man gave Roberts a look that he couldn't tell whether it was disgust or disappointment.

"Well, I just want to thank you for all your help and let you know that you're a good friend. I didn't know that I was your best friend, though."

"Well, you are and you have been for a long time. I loved Greg, and I love Jeff, but you've always been special. You've always been there for me, so even though I'm not your best friend, you're mine." Big Man grabbed his jacket and prepared to leave.

"Why don't you stay over tonight?" Roberts asked. "I've been sleeping in the guest room, but now that the master bedroom is ready, I think I'll sleep in there tonight. You can have the guest room." Roberts hoped that Big Man would take him up on his offer. He really didn't want to be alone in the house.

"No, thanks." Big Man started towards the front door. "I have a new construction job tomorrow, and I want to get there on time. I need to make some money if I'm going to move to Ohio and begin a courtship with Rita," he smiled. "I'm really serious about this, Roberts."

"I can tell that you are. I wish you the best." The two men hugged at the door, and then Big Man was gone.

Alone in the house again, Roberts tried to get into bed and fall asleep as quickly as possible. He made up the queen-size bed, took his medication, showered and then climbed between the sheets, hoping that sleep would come quickly. It was after midnight and he, too, had to get up in a few hours for work. As soon as he lay down, the eerie feeling began to creep over him again. He tossed and turned, hoping that the medication would kick in immediately and put him to sleep.

Five minutes after getting into bed, Roberts was out of the bed again. He walked in the hallway, noticing that Big Man had shut all of the doors. He reopened them, looking in each room and closet to make sure that they were empty. *Of what?* he asked himself, *Viet Cong?*

After assuring himself that all was well, he started back towards the master bedroom, then stopped. He turned around and went downstairs and checked the front door. When he came back upstairs, he went to the closet, got the gun and put it under his pillow. His last thought before falling asleep was, *Once Dorothy is sharing this bed with me I won't need to do this every night.*

The next morning, Roberts awoke to the sound of the telephone ringing. He checked the alarm clock, 5:30AM. It could only be Dorothy. Still a little groggy from a restless night in bed, Roberts answered the telephone.

"Wake up, sleepy head." Dorothy's voice sounded so cheery for such an early hour.

"Hi." Roberts managed to get out, rubbing his eyes and shaking his head as if to clear it. "What're you doing so cheery so early in the morning?"

"I'm getting married in less than two weeks to the most wonderful man in the world. Wouldn't you say that's something to be cheery about?" She laughed softly.

"Yes, I'd say that's something to be real cheery about." He still sounded sleepy.

"Did you sleep all right?" Dorothy was concerned.

"It was a little late before I got into bed, and I guess I just need a couple of more hours of sleep."

"Well, it's time for you to get ready for work. I just wanted to say good morning to you. Oh, did you get everything out of the U-Haul?"

"Everything is out of the truck, set up, and ready for you to move in." Roberts swung his legs out of the bed.

"Good. Don't forget to take the truck back this morning so we won't have to pay for an extra day. I'll talk to you tonight." She hung up the telephone.

Sitting on the edge of the bed, Roberts put his elbows on his knees, his head in his hands and tried to recall the previous night's dream. He had had a disturbing dream, causing him to move about restlessly in his sleep all night. He had heard someone talking to him. He thought he recognized the voice. The voice was saying to him, "Keep your eyes on the door." He'd heard that over and over in his dream. "Keep your eyes on the door."

Roberts left the house a few minutes earlier to take the U-Haul back, and then he had to wait for a bus to take him back to the depot. He was fine, though, except when he had to sit still for any length of time. Sitting on the bus, he thought about the dream and the voice. Suddenly it dawned on him that it was Greg's voice. "Watch that door, Roberts. Keep your eye on the door." *What does it mean? What was Greg trying to warn me about?*

The day was pretty much uneventful, but Roberts kept thinking about the dream every chance he got. When he entered the house that evening, he went into the kitchen washed his hands and brought the bag containing takeout from a local Chinese restaurant into the living room. He was starving; he'd skipped lunch to make up for the time he'd taken to return the truck. He almost didn't buy the Chinese food; he'd gotten so upset when the cashier asked him to pay before she would start to fill his order.

"Pay first," she had demanded in an unpleasant tone.

"This is some way to treat your customers. You behave as though you don't want my business," he had said angrily, pulling the money out of his pocket.

"Pay first," she had said again.

Roberts had shaken his head in disgust. Since the rebellion, all of the Chinese restaurants had become take-out only, and there were bulletproof barriers separating the customers from the workers. In order to get your order, you had to first slip the money under a bulletproof window, get your change, and then wait in a dreary waiting area for the order to be slipped under the barrier for you to take out. He tried to ignore the humiliation of it all because he was too hungry to go somewhere else. Besides, he was using public transportation to get home tonight.

Sitting in his living room with the television tuned to channel eleven, Roberts laughed at the antics of Gilligan on Gilligan's Island while he ate his Chinese food. He looked around the room and contemplated whether Dorothy would be satisfied with the arrangement of the furniture. He liked it, but Dorothy might want the sofa facing the fireplace rather than in front of the windows.

When he finished eating, Roberts rearranged the furniture with the sofa facing the fireplace. He sat on the sofa and decided that it looked better this way. Noticing the empty mantle, he went upstairs to get the framed pictures Dorothy had neatly packed in a cardboard box. He also took out Greg's framed picture. He placed the pictures of Greg, Dorothy's grandparents, and two other framed photographs on the mantel. They looked fine to him.

Sitting on the couch, watching television, Roberts would periodically look at Greg's picture. *What are you trying to tell me, buddy?* he would ask himself. He tried to remember when and where Greg had told him to "Watch that door." For the life of him, he couldn't recall the events that had caused Greg to issue such a warning. Finally, he decided to turn in.

At eleven o'clock, Roberts took his medication. Dorothy hadn't called him, and he decided not to call her either. She was probably tired from getting everything perfect for the wedding. Besides he was anxious to get into bed and resume the dream. He wanted to remember the incident that Greg had warned him about. He checked the doors making sure the front door was locked, and then he put the gun under his pillow. By 11:15PM, he was sound asleep. He was dreaming about Vietnam, when he heard the phone ring. He couldn't wake up though; it was as if his body were frozen. He couldn't move. The phone rang and rang.

When the phone started ringing again at 5:30AM, Roberts answered it this time. "Hello," he said groggily into the receiver.

"Where were you last night? I called you, and you didn't answer the phone." Dorothy sounded worried.

"I fell asleep early and just didn't hear it, I guess," Roberts said.

"Is everything all right?" He was now concerned. Her voice had sounded a little panicky.

"Everything is fine. I was just worried when I didn't get you."

"There's nothing to worry about." Roberts looked at the clock. "I'd better get ready for work. How many days left?"

"Eleven more days before our wedding day."

"I can hardly wait," he said. "But I've got to get ready for work right now." Roberts pulled the covers back and sat on the side of the bed. "I'll call you tonight, okay?"

"Okay."

Before heading to the shower Roberts sat, head in his hands, and tried to recall his dream. *Yes, it was definitely Greg warning me to 'watch the door.'* Roberts recalled more of the incident. He had dreamed that he and Greg were in the jungle running, he remembered gunfire, and he remembered pain. He stayed on the side of the bed for a full ten minutes trying to remember more. Finally he got up and headed to the shower. He had to get to work.

Throughout the day, Robert's thoughts would drift to the dream. He moved about robotically, making all of his deliveries and greeting people with a smile, but inside he was haunted by the dream. This was the dream he was anticipating, the one that would reveal how he had gotten injured and how Greg had been killed. He hoped he was ready for it; he hoped he could deal with it.

He and Greg had spent three months with the 25th infantry. They were the worst three months of his life, so when they were over, he and Greg were delighted. They had hugged each other and laughed, congratulating themselves on staying alive. They thought they would be safe then. *So, what the hell happened?* Roberts wondered.

Roberts got assigned to a base camp in Cu Chi as a truck driver. It wasn't the job that he had wanted, the job that he was trained for, but anything was better than being an infantryman. He still had an opportunity to use his auto mechanic skills whenever the truck broke down.

Greg got assigned to a surgical unit near Tay Ninh as a medic. He was ecstatic about it. Roberts was happy for him and especially happy that the two bases were not that far apart. Cu Chi was about twenty miles northwest of Saigon. The drive from Cu Chi to Tay Ninh could take about two hours considering the bad roads.

Roberts remembered that Greg had flown by helicopter to Cu Chi to pick up a number of injured soldiers after a mysterious blast occurred at one of the barracks. By the time he had arrived with the pilot and another medic, the number of seriously injured soldiers had grown. In order to fit the injured comfortably into the helicopter with at least one medic, Greg had been obliged to stay behind. Roberts was going to drive him back to Tay Ninh along with some medical supplies. Roberts was familiar with the route; he'd driven up and down highway 13, in and out of convoy many times.

Greg and Roberts had been sitting in the cab of the truck, and there were three of his comrades riding in the back. All five of them were armed. Roberts finally remembered that there had been an ambush.

The truck was disabled, and they abandoned it, running on foot into the jungle. The gunfire had been intense, but they couldn't see the enemy, and they were looking for cover. Roberts was hit twice, once in the thigh and again in the shoulder. He felt a burning sensation first, then pain. He fell in the mud. He couldn't remember anything after that. *Is that where Greg died?* he asked himself.

The dreams and memories continued to haunt him for the next few days. He paced the house at night trying to remember more. *How does this tie in with the doors?* he wondered. He was anxious to start his new life as a married man, and he was becoming weary from trying to force his memory to put the pieces together so they would make sense to him.

BOY'S NIGHT OUT provided Roberts with the distraction that he needed. He had agreed to meet Big Man and Jeff at the Bridge Club for dinner after work. It was only three days before his wedding. When he walked into the Club from the back door, which faced the parking lot, he was surprised to find the place practically empty. Only the bartender and one or two patrons who sat at the bar were there. He didn't see Big Man or Jeff or any of the regular Wednesday night crowd. Music and loud voices were coming from upstairs, though. He swore he heard Big Man's laughter. He walked through the bar and climbed the stairs to the second level.

When Roberts entered the room, everyone yelled "Surprise!" He couldn't help but laugh; his friends were throwing a bachelor party for him. Roberts looked around the room into the smiling faces of Jeff, Big Man, Derek, and even his father. There were old friends from high school and some from the gym. He couldn't believe it. How blessed he felt having friends that would go to all this trouble for him. *Yes, things are certainly going to get better,* he thought again.

CHAPTER

30

The weather predicted for the weekend of June 11th couldn't have been more perfect for a wedding. The temperature was in the mid-seventies when Roberts climbed into the driver's seat of the Mustang. His sister, brother-in-law, and Big Man were coming along as passengers. It was the day before the wedding and a caravan of cars, including Jeff's van loaded with his and Belinda's family members, and Mr. Roberts' five-year-old-sedan with Mrs. Roberts, Aunt Louise, and her daughter, were following the Mustang to Ohio. It was a little after 6AM, when they started the journey.

Roberts was high on love despite the recurring dream that had plagued his sleep for the last couple of weeks. The dream came every night shortly after he took the medication that put him to sleep and kept him in his bed. Each morning when he awoke, he could remember running through the jungle, the burning sensation where the bullets had pierced his leg and his shoulder, and then falling into the mud, but nothing thereafter. He had rehashed the dream over and over again trying to remember more, trying to fit the doors into the dream, but each time he had given up trying to force the memory.

They anticipated arriving at 4PM in Oxford where they would check into the local Holiday Inn. Dorothy had family and friends flying in from as far away as California; some of them would be staying at the farm, but most of them would be checking into the Holiday Inn as well. Roberts could hardly believe that in a little more than twenty-four hours, he would be a married man, and he and his bride would be off on their honeymoon.

"This is your last chance to get out of it," Big Man said, watching Roberts maneuver the car out of the driveway. "Once we get on the highway, there's no turning back."

"Can't you tell by that big grin on his face that he's not thinking about turning back?" Deneen said. "I can't remember when I've seen my brother so happy. Just because you blew your marriage doesn't mean that David doesn't recognize a good thing." She gave Big Man a playful poke on the shoulder from the back seat.

"Ouch," Big Man cried out, exaggerating the pain. He turned around to stick his tongue out at Deneen. "I sure hope your baby is not as mean as you are."

"Leave my baby out of this mess," Derek said. "I sure hope we won't have to listen to you two carrying on like kids all the way to Oxford."

It was a beautiful drive, and they all marveled at the colorful wild flowers springing up along the highway and the wonderful smelling country air. Off and on throughout the trip, Roberts was able to conjure up a vision of his bride coming down the aisle on her father's arm and into his waiting arms. The vision caused him to keep that big grin on his face for the whole ten hours. He was so happy, everyone could see it.

Once they checked into the motel, the New Jersey guests mingled with other out-of town guests in the hospitality room that the Campbell's had reserved. Roberts managed to slip away in order to be alone in the room he and Big Man were sharing to call Dorothy. Sandra answered the phone and said that her sister was too busy to talk to him.

"Just for one minute," Roberts coaxed her. "I won't keep her, I promise."

"Okay," Sandra finally said, relenting to the pleading in his voice. "I don't think you're supposed to talk to the bride before the wedding, though."

"That's 'see' the bride right before the wedding," Roberts said. "I just want to talk to her for a minute, and this is the night before the wedding."

Roberts could hear Dorothy being called to the phone. After waiting for about three minutes, he finally heard her voice.

"Hi," Dorothy said cheerily in the telephone.

"I just wanted you to know that I'm in Oxford at the Holiday Inn in case you want to slip out and meet me in the barn for a quickie." He laughed, knowing that she probably had a scowl on her face.

"How did you get such a one-track mind? Don't make me laugh. I don't want to crack the mud pack on my face."

"Why do you have mud on your beautiful face?" Roberts relaxed on the bed, happy to hear her voice.

"I'm having a facial and a pedicure. I still have to get a manicure and finish wrapping the favors for the guests."

"What about slipping away and meeting me in the barn at midnight." He was only kidding, but secretly hoped she would say yes.

"No. I want to be sound asleep by midnight, resting up for my big day tomorrow. You'll have to wait until after the ceremony. The next time we make love, we'll be on the ocean, can you imagine?"

"I'm going to love making love to you on a ship. We'll be able to feel the motion of the ocean as we float off toward paradise." Roberts felt himself getting aroused at the thought.

"I have to go now," Dorothy said. "They're ready to take the mud pack off. By the way, has Big Man agreed to drive my car back to Newark?"

"Yes, Big Man will drive your car back, and Derek and Deneen will drive my car back to Newark. Big Man is anticipating remaining in Oxford for a day or so after the ceremony."

"Good, I'll see you at the church at 11AM."

STANDING AT THE ALTAR, Roberts counted his blessings. Despite the atrocities he had experienced in the Vietnam War, he had gotten on with his life. He was about to marry the most wonderful woman in the world. He looked around the church and saw his family and friends laughing and talking with each other, waiting for the bride to make her appearance. Jeff stood next to him, both of them handsome in their black tuxedos with the kente cloth cummerbunds and matching bow ties. The cummerbunds were Belinda's idea; she'd made them herself and sent pictures of them to Dorothy who loved them.

The sound of the drums signaling that the ceremony was about to begin resonated in the church, causing a hush to fall over the sanctuary. Everyone's eyes went to the back of the church. The second sound signaled Big Man to begin his trek down the aisle, escorting the beautiful bridesmaid, Rita. The colors in Big Man's cummerbund matched the color of Rita's gown perfectly. They made an attractive couple; Roberts couldn't remember a time when Big Man looked more handsome.

Derek was just as handsome and couldn't help but glance over to share a smile with his very pregnant wife as he escorted a beautiful Belinda down the aisle. Belinda kept her eyes on Jeff as she held onto the arm of her escort. Finally, Brad escorted the last bridesmaid, and they took their place in the front of the church. Everything was going according to plan; the wedding had begun at exactly 11AM. After the bridesmaids and groomsmen were in place, Jeff followed his cue and met the very lovely maid of honor, Sandra, and escorted her to her place of honor.

The drums stopped, and the pianist started playing "Our Love," the tune that Roberts and Dorothy had chosen to be their wedding song, as her father escorted her down the aisle. Necks strained to see the bride as she made her entrance. Roberts had the best view in the house. He stood at the opposite end of the aisle where he had an unobstructed view of his bride walking toward him to recite the vows that would make her his wife.

Dorothy had never looked more beautiful. The gown she wore was dazzling white with tiny pearls sewn into the silky fabric creating jeweled swirls that reflected the light and gave the impression that the gown was floating as she walked. Her shiny auburn curls were visible from the top of the veil that she wore, but her face was partially shielded from him. He couldn't see her eyes, but her smile was radiant. Roberts looked at her from head to toe. The sexy white sandals that she wore were made of a silken fabric that also reflected the light; he could see the pale pink polish on her toenails.

Clinging to her father's arm, Dorothy walked slowly, moving with the rhythm of the music. Despite the veil, Roberts could tell that her eyes were on him. Mr. Campbell deposited his daughter at the altar with her groom and stepped back to take his place with the rest of the wedding party. The ceremony began. Roberts took a deep breath and felt as though he didn't exhale until Reverend Washington pronounced them man and wife. He lifted the veil that shielded his bride's eyes from him, looked her in the eye and mouthed the words, *I love you.* Then he took her into his arms and kissed her passionately to the cheers of the guests.

After the ceremony, the bride and groom along with the wedding party were ushered into a limousine where the driver whisked them to

Isis Park for picture taking. The park was magnificent with roses, and the Isis fountain was splendid. Roberts was delirious with happiness.

"How did you manage to get all of these roses to bloom just for our wedding?" he asked Dorothy.

"I told you this park is known for its rose garden, although Sandra and I planted a few more in late April just to make sure there would be enough. Do you like?" She gave him a dazzling smile.

"Yes, Mrs. Roberts." He kissed her passionately, causing the photographer and Big Man to say, "Whoa."

"Save some for the honeymoon," Big Man said with an arm around Rita.

"The honeymoon can't get here fast enough for me," Roberts said. "Let's get this picture taking over so we can get to the reception."

The guests were crowded in the Ruby Lounge, drinking cocktails and eating hors d'oeuvres, when the bridal party entered the club. It was exactly 12:30PM, and everything was going according to schedule. The bridal party proceeded to the Diamond Room and was seated at the bridal table when the guests were ushered in. Roberts and Dorothy beamed as the guests lined up to congratulate them. After congratulations, everyone was seated for the toast to be followed by feasting and dancing.

"Roberts and Dorothy are the best looking couple that I've seen since my own wedding three years ago," Jeff said as he started the toast. "I want to toast to their happiness and wish them the best that life has to offer. They both served their country well in the military and now that they have found each other, let's toast to their remaining together until, like the preacher said, 'death do them part.'"

Glasses clicked for the toast and the drummers did a special drum roll. Not to be outdone by Jeff, Big Man offered a toast to the happy couple.

"Roberts," he said. "You've been my main man since we were kids and, now that you've taken the plunge, I want to wish you happiness. Know that not only will Dorothy be there for you for better and for worse, I'll be there for you, too, through thick and thin. Best wishes to you." He raised his glass and laughed at his toast.

The Five-Carat Club lived up to its reputation and served some of the best food that Roberts had ever tasted. Some of it he had never tasted before. Dorothy fed him wild quail and raw oysters, and then he ate oven-fried potatoes that were delicious. He felt like a king and almost wished that the day would last forever. He was more anxious, though, to get on with the honeymoon.

At two-thirty, after the cake had been cut, the bride's bouquet thrown, and the garter tossed, Roberts and Dorothy were finally able to slip out from the reception, change clothes and head to the limousine that would drive them to the local airport. Dorothy's rich uncle's gift to them had been their own pilot who was taking them in a private, chartered plane to Miami, where they would board the ship for their honeymoon cruise. They had a 6PM deadline for boarding the ship.

Buckled in one of the passenger seats of the twin engine Cessna plane, Roberts pulled his wife into his arms and held her close.

"You're finally my wife, and I have no intention of ever putting another 600 miles between us." He kissed her forehead.

"You mean no separate vacations?" She teased him, watching for his response.

"No separate vacations, no separate beds, no separations period. Since I fell in love with you over a year ago, I've never been with you for more than four or five days a month. I want to make up for all that lost time." He kissed her nose and then her chin.

They settled back in the leather seats and cuddled up for the beginning of the journey that would keep them together for the rest of their lives.

Kill . . . or be Killed

Chapter

31

Magnificence of the Sea was a spectacular ship. Roberts and Dorothy were spellbound from the moment they boarded. They walked about the main deck, marveling at the opulence of the decor. There was plush carpeting on the floors and the stairwells, mirrors on the ceiling and walls, beautiful chandeliers and furniture, and a general look of luxury. They rushed to their cabin on deck seven, where a bottle of champagne and a bouquet of roses were waiting for them, compliments of the travel agency. There was also a basket of fruit and a box of Godiva chocolates, compliments of the captain.

Their cabin which provided them with a window that looked out over the sea, was more than adequate. There was a bathroom with a shower that could easily accommodate two, and a well-lit vanity. The king-size bed took up most of the room in the cabin, but there was enough space for a sitting area with a sofa and coffee table. The closet was well organized for space, and there was even room for a dressing table and a television.

Before they could even unpack, Roberts pulled his bride down on the bed and began to undress her.

"It's a good thing we signed up for the late dinner seating," Dorothy said. "We would never have made the early seating." She lay back and let her husband remove her clothing.

"I don't care if we skip dinner all together," Roberts said, unfastening her bra. "Food is the last thing on my mind right now."

It was after midnight when they ventured out of the cabin to check out the nightlife aboard the ship. The brochure they had been provided had boasted three nightclubs, a piano bar, a casino, and a midnight buffet. They made their way to the buffet, hoping they weren't too late for a snack. They were in luck. There was still plenty of food remaining and they ate until they were content. Then they made their way to a disco where they danced late into the night.

When they returned to their cabin they were both exhausted. They were surprised to find that the covers on the bed had been turned back for them. There was a chocolate mint on top of each pillow, and sitting on top of the bed was a cute little elephant fashioned out of a towel. They quickly undressed and climbed into the bed.

"Don't forget to take your medication," Dorothy reminded Roberts.

He got out of bed, went into the bathroom and took his medication. *This is one of the advantages of being married to a nurse,* he thought. *She will be looking out for my health.*

When they woke up the next morning, the ship was in Barbados. They showered and dressed, ate a quick breakfast on the Lido deck and made their way ashore. They grabbed a cab from the dock and went into town where Roberts tagged along with his bride as she shopped. At 1PM, they ate a delicious lunch of grilled flying fish at a seaside café. Roberts looked out at the beautiful Caribbean Sea and thanked God for the blessings that had been bestowed on him. The last twenty-four hours had been the best in his life, and he hadn't once thought about Vietnam.

The following morning, they woke up in Martinique. Wearing bathing suits under their shorts and T-shirts, and carrying beach bags, they made their way ashore. They hadn't gone very far when a young man approached them offering to take them on a private adventure aboard his sailboat.

"I don't want to spend a whole day fishing," Dorothy said.

"I'll take you snorkeling on a special reef and to a private island where you can swim and sunbathe in the nude. I'll provide you with lunch and drinks all for a very small fee."

"Sounds like something I'd like to do," Roberts said when he heard about the swimming and sunbathing in the nude. "What's your name?"

"I'm Sam," he held out his hand for Roberts to take.

"Where's your boat?" Dorothy asked.

"Come, I'll take you," Sam said.

They followed him to a jeep, jumped in with him and were on their way to who knows where. "We must be crazy," Dorothy said. "Going off with a complete stranger." She looked at Roberts for his reaction.

"He looks trustworthy to me," Roberts said and smiled at her. "Nothing bad is going to happen on our honeymoon. Relax and enjoy the trip."

The Ninja was a thirty-foot sailboat docked at a reputable looking marina. As they approached, they could see that the boat was well maintained and looked quite comfortable. They climbed aboard. Sam untied the Ninja and set sail with Roberts and Dorothy settled in for an adventure of a lifetime.

"I have to make one stop, and then we'll be on our way." Sam stopped in town, pulled up to the dock, tied the boat up and went ashore. He returned about twenty minutes later with his arms loaded with packages.

"What you got there?" Roberts asked, relieving Sam of some of the packages.

"Just a few provisions to make the trip enjoyable," Sam said, climbing aboard. He went below. When he came back on board, he untied the boat and set sail again.

The first stop was at the reef where Roberts and Dorothy stripped to their bathing suits, put on their snorkeling equipment and jumped off the boat. The water was perfect, warm and clear. They swam together marveling at the fish, beautiful blue and yellow fish, stripped fish, and big and little fish. It was absolutely wonderful. They stayed in the water for almost two hours before they climbed aboard the boat for a rest. While they were toweling off Sam came from below carrying a tray with sandwiches, punch, crackers, cheese, fruit, and other delicious tidbits.

While Roberts and Dorothy lay on deck eating, talking and smooching, Sam pulled anchor and set sail again. This time the trip was a little longer, about forty minutes.

"Look ahead," Sam called out to the dozing couple all shiny and bronzed from the sun. "That's the island where we will stop."

He dropped anchor. Roberts and Dorothy swam ashore with Sam behind them, carrying their beach bag. Once Sam saw that the couple was safely ashore, he started back to the boat.

"Where are you going?" Roberts asked.

"Back to the boat so you can have some privacy. You can explore the island and do whatever you want. When you are ready to leave, just call me and I'll swim back for your things. He jumped in the water and left them alone on their own secluded island. As Roberts removed his bathing suit for a little skinny-dipping, he couldn't help but think that the best was yet to come.

Later, while they were docked in Jamaica, they hired a driver to take them on a tour of the Jamaican hills, where they hoped to get a feel for the local country life. The driver asked if they wanted to see a Jamaican farm. Dorothy jumped at a chance to do this; she was anxious to see how farm life in Jamaica compared to that in Ohio. She marveled at the lush green countryside and smiled when she saw local women washing clothes in a stream, but it was the farm itself that shocked both her and Roberts. As they were touring the grounds, they suddenly realized that they were on a marijuana farm. Marijuana plants, many as tall as trees, hundreds of them, grew everywhere. Roberts was amazed and couldn't help but remember his teenage years when he, Greg, Big Man, and Jeff would get high off a five-dollar bag and talk a lot of shit. The thought of those days put a smile on his face.

"What are you grinning about?" Dorothy asked.

"Have you ever smoked marijuana?" he answered her question with one of his own.

"No, we didn't do things like that in Ohio. Have you?"

"Haven't you ever been curious?" he asked.

"Maybe, just a little."

Roberts smiled, thinking, *I'm going to make tonight a little more interesting for her.* He pulled the driver over to the side and whispered in his ear, turning their backs to Dorothy. When they returned to the ship, Roberts had a little surprise for her. *Oh, life is wonderful,* he thought before he went to sleep that night.

The last day of their honeymoon cruise was spent at sea. They lounged in the pool and the Jacuzzi, ate lunch aboard with another honeymooning couple they had met at the dinner table and played the slot machines in the casino. When they turned in that night, Roberts went to sleep thinking that marriage was just the thing he needed to take his mind off the dreams and the war. Since their marriage, he had not remembered one bad dream, and the obsession with the doors had ceased as well. *My father was right; all I needed was to take on some responsibility and focus my attention on something else.*

SUNDAY AFTERNOON AT 2PM, Roberts and Dorothy were leaving the airport and heading to the taxi stand. They were back in Newark. The honeymoon was over and no sooner had they entered the green cab than an eerie feeling came over Roberts. For some reason, he was dreading going home. The driver exited at Frelinghuysen Avenue and proceeded up Meeker Avenue. The closer they got to home, the more solemn Roberts became.

"You all right?" Dorothy asked, noticing how he had tensed up and was staring straight ahead.

"Yeah. I'm just sorry that our honeymoon is over." Roberts hoped he sounded convincing.

"Our honeymoon is not over, sweetheart. Just the trip is over. We'll be honeymooning for a long time." Dorothy squeezed his arm.

I certainly hope so, Roberts thought as the cab driver pulled up in front of the house.

"Well, both our cars made it safely back to New Jersey," Dorothy said, observing the cars in the driveway. She jumped out of the cab, grabbed a bag and practically ran up the driveway. "We're home." She looked so happy.

Roberts carried the remaining luggage up to the front door, fumbled for his key, and then opened the door. He had picked up the luggage and started to enter, when he felt Dorothy tugging at his arm.

"Aren't you forgetting something?"

"What?" he gave her a puzzled look.

"You have to carry me over the threshold," she reminded him.

"Didn't we do this already?"

"That was before we were married. We have to do it again now and make it official."

Roberts dropped the luggage and carried her over the threshold again. He kissed her on the lips and deposited her on the floor in the foyer. No sooner had her feet hit the floor than she started moving through the house, inspecting everything.

"The living room looks marvelous." She kept moving, heading toward the dining room. She paused to look at the dinette that had been perfect for her old apartment in Dayton. "We need a real dining room set."

"This will do just fine for a while," Roberts said. "We'll probably be eating most of our meals in the kitchen anyway." They walked into the kitchen together.

"I love the wallpaper. He really did a good job in here." She looked happy. "Let's go upstairs." She practically ran towards the stairs.

Roberts grabbed a couple of bags and followed her up the stairway. Before he reached the top of the stairs, he heard her shutting the linen closet door.

"Why are all these doors open?" she asked, looking around. She closed the door leading up to the attic and then went into the master bedroom. "I love it," she said, flopping on the bed. "You did a wonderful job," she grabbed his hand, pulled him down beside her, and gave him a kiss. "Everything looks wonderful."

Their first evening together as husband and wife in their new home was quiet and peaceful. They were like any other newly wed couple adjusting to married life. Roberts went through the mail that had piled up while they were away, and Dorothy unpacked their suitcases and started a pile of laundry to be done. While the clothes were washing, they both went to the supermarket to get groceries for dinner. Then, while Dorothy prepared dinner, Roberts put the clothes in the dryer and swept off the walkway in front of their house. They were falling into a routine of marital responsibility.

After dinner, they both lay down on the sofa, cuddled up together watching television. The telephone rang and startled them. It was Deneen.

"So, you're back," she said when Roberts answered the telephone.

"Yes, we are. You're our first caller." He sat up on the couch with Dorothy's feet on his lap. He massaged her toes.

"How was the honeymoon? Or should I ask." Deneen laughed.

"It was wonderful." Roberts continued stroking Dorothy's feet. "Everything all right with you?" He stopped rubbing Dorothy's feet when he heard a whimpering sound in the background coming through the phone. "What was that?" he asked Deneen.

"That was your new nephew," Deneen said. "He was born three days ago, and this is our first day home from the hospital."

Roberts stood up. The news that his little sister was a mother and that he was an uncle overwhelmed him for a minute. "I'm an uncle?" he asked.

"Yes, you're an uncle."

"What's his name?"

"His name is David, and we're going to call him David, no nicknames, no last names, just David."

"I like that," Roberts said as Dorothy stroked his arm.

At eleven o'clock, they climbed the stairs to spend their first night sleeping together in the master bedroom. Once Roberts took his medication and climbed into bed next to his beautiful wife, who was wearing another one of her sexy gowns he felt completely relaxed. Dorothy laid her head on his shoulder, and he tightened his arms around her waist.

"Our life is off to a great start," she said. "Wouldn't you agree?"

"Yes," Roberts said. He drifted off to sleep, thinking about the sounds he'd heard in the rain forest in Dominica, one of the Caribbean islands they had visited. The sounds were of crickets, frogs, and running water. He didn't hear any bombs exploding or gunfire or strange, foreign voices. *Yes, marriage is going to be great for me.*

When Roberts woke up the next morning, he smiled when he saw Dorothy curled up in a tight little ball on her side of the bed. They had gone to sleep wrapped up in each other's arms, but they had found their sleeping positions sometime during the night. She looked so peaceful, like a little girl. He kissed the top of her head and got out of the bed. He had to get ready for work. She was starting her new job that afternoon, and he wanted her to be fully rested. He quietly went into the bathroom, closed the door and stepped into the shower.

When he came out of the bathroom, Dorothy was not in the bed. He looked out in the hall and listened for her. He heard her downstairs in the kitchen. He finished dressing and went downstairs where she was making him coffee, eggs and toast for breakfast. She had on a pink housecoat to match the gown she had worn to bed.

"Good morning, beautiful," Roberts said, putting his arms around her waist and kissing her neck.

"Good morning." She twisted her head to smile up at him.

"You don't have to get up and fix breakfast for me in the mornings," he said. "I generally pick up coffee and a doughnut on my way to the depot."

"Not anymore. You have a wife now." She buttered toast for him. "This is what wives do. Besides it will give us a few minutes to be together in the mornings before you go running off to work. I won't be here when you get home, and I'm hoping that the morning time we spend together will sort of make up for it."

"It will, sweetheart, it will." He kissed her again before he sat down to eat. "What time will you be getting home tonight?"

"No later than eleven-thirty." Dorothy put a plate of food in front of him. "Take a nap before I get home so you won't be too tired. I'll want to tell you all about my first day on the job." She poured coffee into a mug for him.

The day went well for Roberts; all of his deliveries were

completed shortly after three o'clock. He delivered the truck back to the depot by four. He had plenty of time to visit his sister and meet his new nephew before heading home. It was almost 7PM when he entered the house. The eerie feeling came over him again almost immediately; he dismissed it, though, and went into the kitchen. Dorothy had prepared dinner, and a plate of food was waiting for him in the refrigerator with instructions for warming. Roberts smiled; having a wife was going to be wonderful.

He took the heated dinner into the living room and ate his meal while watching television. Later he called his parents to let them know that he was home. Then he called Big Man. "So how did you make out with Rita?" was the first thing that he asked.

"Man, she's the one." Big Man sounded ecstatic.

"I've heard that before," Roberts reminded him.

"This is it, Roberts. I'll bet the two nights I spent in Ohio could compete with any two nights you had on your honeymoon. I'm in love, man. For the very first time, I'm in love."

"Well, I guess you'll be the one commuting to Ohio every week now. Good luck." Roberts yawned and stretched.

"You sound tired, man. Did Dorothy wear you out on your honeymoon?" Big Man laughed.

"None of your business. But I think I will take a little nap before my wife gets home from her job. I want to be able to stay up with her for awhile." Roberts yawned again. After hanging up the telephone, he checked his watch, nine o'clock. He stretched out on the sofa and fell asleep. Almost immediately, he began to dream.

He was back in Vietnam running through the jungle. He was limping, and his shoulder was burning something fierce. His leg was bleeding. Greg was with him, urging him on. "Come on Roberts, we can't stop now." Roberts remembered falling, but Greg helped him up and they kept going. He remembered that his comrades had been killed; it was just him and Greg running in the jungle. They couldn't see the enemy, but they could hear voices speaking in Vietnamese.

Uninhibited by the medication, the dream was so real. Roberts actually felt the pain in his leg; he felt Greg's strong arm supporting him as they ran. They came upon a burned-out village and wandered through it. There was a hooch still standing, the only one that wasn't burned to the ground. They took refuge in it, and Greg applied a tourniquet to his leg and managed to stop the bleeding in his shoulder.

"I'm going to find help," Greg had said, propping Roberts up in a corner of the hooch. "Watch the door, Roberts. Keep your eyes on the door. Anyone that comes through that door, shoot them. Remember, kill or be killed." He'd checked Roberts' gun to make sure that it was fully loaded.

Roberts sat there in that hooch, forever it seemed, watching the door. He held the gun so tight that his knuckles had paled. He held his head stiff, although he wanted to drop it down and nod off. He was so tired, but he knew that if he nodded off he would die. He kept his eyes on the door, and then he heard voices. Vietnamese voices were just outside the door. He lifted the gun and aimed at the door.

He heard gunfire, and he heard screams. He kept his eyes on the door, waiting.

The handle on the door started to move, and the door started to open. Roberts saw a figure begin to enter the hooch; he opened fire. A body fell into the doorway. He got up from the floor and made his way to the door.

"Oh, no! Oh, my God!" It was Greg's body that had fallen in the doorway. Roberts picked up his friend's body and ran into the jungle.

"Help! Help me!" he screamed. He ran and ran and then he collapsed. When he woke up again he was in the field hospital.

Roberts got up from the sofa as if in a trance. He roared like a wounded lion. Then he screamed. He walked over to the mantel where Greg's framed picture sat. He cried. He had killed his best friend. He swiped his arm across the mantel knocking everything to the floor. He screamed again. He made his way to the stairwell and crept up the steps. He went directly to his closet and got the gun out of the hatbox. He was in such anguish. He was so distraught. *How can I live in the world with myself, knowing that I killed my best friend?* He walked back to the stairwell.

Roberts sat on the steps staring at the door. He put the gun to his temple. It was all so clear to him now. Greg had come back to save him and had encountered Viet Cong coming into the hooch to kill him. Greg must have been the one to fire the gun; those were the gunshots that he had heard. The screams were from the Viet Cong as they fell, mortally wounded by Greg. Greg had saved his life.

Now that the truth had been revealed to him the world wasn't big enough for him to live in knowing what he had done. He wasn't a hero. Roberts hadn't tried to save his best friend; he had killed him. He tightened his grip on the gun and just as he was about to pull the trigger, at 11:30PM exactly, he heard a noise at the front door. A voice went off in his head. "Watch the door, Roberts."

The door started to open. Roberts turned the gun and aimed at the door. He pulled the trigger.

"MR. ROBERTS, MR. Roberts, do you understand what it is that I'm trying to tell you?" the young man in the dark jacket, blue shirt and burgundy tie was saying. "Mr. Roberts, I'm an attorney, and your parents have engaged my services to help get you out of this prison facility and into a hospital. They know that you need treatment, and they want to see that you get it."

Roberts just stared at the stranger. He'd heard every word, but he just didn't care. When he finally spoke, he raised his head and looked directly into the man's eyes.

"Dorothy, is she..?"

"Dorothy is dead," he said. "Do you remember what happened? Can you tell me about it?" The attorney looked at Roberts sympathetically.

Roberts hung his head again. Of course, he remembered; he had killed his wife. *All of these months when I couldn't remember anything and so desperately wanted my memory to come back, why is it that I can't forget for one minute that I killed my wife.*

331

"Mr. Roberts, the emergency staff at Beth Israel Hospital said that you ran all the way to the hospital carrying your wife's body in your arms. They said you were limping as though you were hurt. What was going on in your mind, Mr. Roberts? Did you believe that you were back in Vietnam? If that's true, then that's the defense we'll use."

Roberts said nothing. He sat there silently until they returned him to his cell and left him alone. He sat on the side of the cot, staring at the ceiling. If he had thought he couldn't continue to live in the world with himself knowing that he had killed Greg, how could he be expected to live with himself in this little cell, knowing that he had killed his beloved Dorothy? His eyes darted around the cell, scanning the tiny eight-foot by eight-foot room. The only contents were a commode and the cot. The cot was without a sheet, but there was a sturdy looking ticking covering the mattress.

Ripping the mattress ticking with his teeth, Roberts tore it into long strips. He fashioned the strips into a rope and then a noose. Looking around the cell, he found the perfect place, a place that would hold his 185-pound frame. He placed the noose around his neck and then climbed up the bars of his cell. Throwing the loose end of the rope over the top bar he secured it tightly. His last thought before he pulled his feet off the ledge of the cell bars was *war is hell.*

ANASA MAAT

Marquis Book Printing Inc.

Québec, Canada
2008